NICOLE CRONIN ASHONG

Love's a Beach

To my father, who taught me to write and to persevere

Contents

Chapter 1: Thalia - Now

Thalia picked her way across the rocks, the salty waves lapping at her feet. For once, no camera was trained on her. The knots in her stomach, which had kept her awake all night, slowly dissipated. As she looked out over the crystal clear water, she experienced a sense of calm emanating from her core, like the sunrise glowing across the ocean. She held a moment of gratitude for the sea's calming effect on her.

Since arriving at the Paraiso Maya resort a month ago, she had made a commitment to take this time each morning to reflect and ground herself. She knew it was the only way to maintain her mental well-being as a cast member on *Love's a Beach* during the grueling filming process. She'd been surrounded by four fellow female contestants and five men they were supposed to fall in love with, all under the constant eye of fifty-some crew members.

The last month had been a whirlwind of emotion, culminating in the last twenty-four hours. While she had second-guessed her decisions a million times since last night, she knew now she had done what she needed to do. She was at peace and ready to take on what came next.

You've got this. Thalia repeated the mantra to herself as she started to rise up from the rocks. The temptation of a cup of the resort's specialty coffee beckoned her away from the beach. As she turned back toward the grounds, a distant scream shattered the serenity of the morning. She had witnessed arguments between the cast members during the last few weeks of filming, but this was different. The voice didn't sound angry—it sounded panicked. Her stomach jolting, Thalia picked up her pace, and in the process, lost her balance on the algae-covered stones, her bare foot flying out behind her and her knee crashing through the shallow water to meet a jagged edge. She gasped at the searing pain, but gritted her teeth with resolve to press on.

Wobbling for a moment as she stood up, Thalia blinked back sharp tears. She began limping toward the villa where the male cast members were staying, which seemed to be the source of the increasingly intense yelling. She tried to take deep, calming breaths like she'd practiced during years of yoga sessions, but struggled to fight the creeping sense of dread that had begun to bubble in her stomach last night, and now threatened to boil over.

She broke into a run, numb to the pain, as white sand flew behind her. Shouted phrases flew toward her like mosquitoes buzzing past her ears.

"Dude, what's going on?"

"I just found him like that!"

"Why isn't he moving?!"

Finally, she reached the front porch of the villa, catching her reflection in the huge glass windows. A small trickle of blood trailed down her throbbing knee. She patted down her curls, askew from the fall and her sprint from the beach, and wiped the sweat creeping its way from her hairline down to her eyes.

As she attempted to slow her breathing, Nick burst onto the porch, throwing open the whitewashed wooden door and nearly tripping over one of the large cactuses framing the entrance. At first, she was relieved to see the fellow cast member, since they'd built an easy friendship, but his usual good-natured expression was replaced by one of terror.

His eyes wide and unfocused in his round face, he bellowed, "Somebody call the paramedic! And get Blake in here!"

"Nick, what's wrong?" Thalia grabbed him by the shoulders and tried to catch his gaze. His shaggy brown hair fell over his eyes as he shook his head frantically, seemingly in shock.

Thalia startled at the sound of footsteps behind her, spinning around as a clear, confident voice cut through the frantic shouts streaming out of the villa windows. "Camera one, take the wide angle of the villa. Camera three, I need you tight on Nick and Thalia. Camera two, where the hell are you? Forget your breakfast, get yourself to the boys' villa stat," the producer Christina barked into her radio. She lowered her walkie-talkie and turned calmly to Nick and Thalia. "What's going on?"

Nick remained dumbfounded, unable to speak even as Thalia jerked his shoulders back and forth with increasing desperation.

Another male contestant rushed through the open door, finally answering Christina's question. "Yo, he's unresponsive," Marcus exclaimed as he reached the threshold, his jaunty yellow superhero T-shirt at jarring odds with the moment of crisis.

Thalia caught a momentary flash where Christina's composure faltered before her face returned to its usual impassive state. "Who is?" the producer asked slowly, and then, without waiting for a response, brought her radio to her lips. "We need the paramedic at the boys' villa now. Call the Mexican EMTs on your way." Her eyes flicked between Marcus's shocked face and Nick, who appeared to be on the verge of tears. "And, Blake, I think you'd better get down here, too," she muttered into the walkie-talkie. After weeks of admiring Christina's confident command of the set, Thalia knew something must really be wrong for the producer to call in her boss.

Turning to Marcus, who had beads of sweat glistening on his ebony forehead, Thalia repeated the question Christina had asked him, though in her gut she already knew the answer. "Who is unresponsive?"

Marcus looked away, his eyes not quite meeting Thalia's. "It's Andrew."

The fear rumbling in Thalia's stomach suddenly erupted. *Not again,* her brain screamed. Without thinking, she pushed past Marcus, rushing upstairs to Andrew and Nick's shared bedroom.

She rounded the corner, stopping as suddenly as if she'd slammed into a glass door. Scanning past the clothes and empty beer cans strewn across Nick's side of the room, her vision focused on Andrew's tidy bedside table, lined with deodorant, his straight-edge razor, and an amber bottle of the aftershave he loved so much. Thalia slowly forced her eyes to move toward Andrew's bed, feeling like she was dragging her gaze through wet sand.

Another cast member, Tae-Hyun, sat on the floor next to the bed in a posture of defeat, his lanky legs curled up with his knees to his chest, and his head of straight dark hair resting on his crossed elbows. He looked up at Thalia, who stood paralyzed in the doorway. "I'm sorry, Thalia. I tried giving him CPR, but nothing is happening. He…" Tae-Hyun hesitated.

No, stop. Stop speaking, Thalia willed him silently, not wanting to hear what he would say next. If he said it, it would be real.

Tae-Hyun's glistening eyes met hers. "He doesn't have a pulse. And he's cold. I'm so sorry. He's gone."

His words cutting through her like a knife, Thalia held her breath for a moment, wishing time would stop before she had to see him with her own eyes. Her eyes finally landed on the beige crochet bedspread, and Andrew's eerily still body on top of it—his arms spread at an awkward angle, at odds with the way he had normally moved with such grace and athleticism. Her knees buckled beneath her and her heart was a wild tangle of emotions as the reality washed over her: her newfound, complicated, swept-her-off-her-feet love was gone.

Chapter 2: Blake - 4 Months Ago

"Fuck," Blake said as he stormed into his office. "FUUUCKKK!!" he repeated, anger coursing through his veins. Who did the CBC board think they were, passing him up for executive vice president of Reality Segments? He'd brought so much to the table, running their most popular show for over five years, after being the face of it as host for almost ten years before that. He was a rising star. Not like that grunting Neanderthal who was the showrunner for *Call of the Wild,* or that homely woman who had ironically landed a spot running *Mommy Makeover.*

The CEO, Robert Corbin, had just broken the news to him from his expansive corner office. "You've done a terrific job with *Love's a Beach.* And I know we've been through a lot together. Had a lot of fun times, too," he said, his sly chuckle faltering at Blake's icy expression, "but right now the focus is on fresh perspectives. And the general sentiment is that you're too ingrained in the show to bring that."

Ingrained because I've dedicated my life to this show since I was twenty-four years old, Blake stewed.

Robert continued, "This woman we're hiring as the VP of Reality, Ava Taylor-Washington—she's a real firecracker. Lots of energy. Very seasoned. I actually think you're going to like her a lot. And hey, if she helps *Love's a Beach* ratings climb back up past the peak from three years ago, then you also reap the rewards come bonus time, right?"

Fresh perspectives, my ass, Blake thought now as he fumed behind his large cherry wood desk. He knew what that meant: not a white guy. Going into the hiring process, he knew the company was paying a lot of lip service around diversity. But he didn't actually expect them to do much about it, and especially not something that would impact him, after he'd spent years working his tail off.

He needed to get out of this office and blow off some steam tonight. Where was Sharon? She wasn't sitting at her desk outside his door, where her long nails normally tapped away at the keyboard, the Gucci bangle he'd bought for her as a Christmas gift last year clanking against the desk. Picking up his phone, he called her on speed dial.

"Sharon?" he said after her nasally voice answered. "Get my yacht crew lined up for tonight."

"Tonight? But you have those reservations for dinner with Robert. I already told them to line up that 1953 bottle of Bordeaux for the special—"

"Cancel the dinner reservations," he growled, cutting her off.

He heard a barely audible gasp at the end of the line, followed by a brief silence, and took this to mean she understood what was going on. "Sure, Blake, will do. And I'll get the yacht lined up, no worries."

The showrunner slammed down the phone, running his fingers through his thick, wavy blond hair. Gazing out the window at the shining waters of Marina del Rey, he suddenly felt a guttural urge to get out of this place. He desperately needed to get his mind off of this rejection, this failure, this usurpation of what was rightly his. He stood up quickly, bouncing on the balls of his feet to dispel the furious energy coursing through his body. He pulled out his phone and began texting a slew of friends. *Party on the yacht tonight at 8. Get ready to get fucked up. Invite those hot chicks we met at Terrace65 last week.*

As the enthusiastic confirmations poured back in, Blake started to relax the tiniest bit. In a few hours he'd be well on his way to forgetting about this nightmare of a day. Then, tomorrow, he could start fresh and begin figuring out how to manage the situation. He needed to get some intel on his new boss. Fortunately, his buddy Tom, who worked at Ava's previous network Paracon, confirmed he'd be joining the party tonight. Blake knew he'd be able to get some good dirt out of Tom once he started drinking.

His phone buzzed with another friend's response. *Terrace65 chicks are in -*

they wanna know if it's gonna be a party party? Blake grinned. He knew how to throw a party.

Hell yeah, he replied, then quickly shot off a text to his dealer, José. *Need the hookup for tonight, got 20 people coming to party.*

Setting down his phone, he glanced at his laptop. He had a few emails from this afternoon, but nothing urgent and nothing officially announcing the VP hire yet. He was dreading the conversations with the rest of the crew once they found out. Slamming the laptop shut, he committed to going radio silent for the rest of the day. He didn't owe this network anything after the move they just pulled.

As he was packing up to head home, the reply came from José. *Got you bro. See you at 6 at your place?*

Blake sighed, happy that something at least was right with the world. *Thanks, man - see you then.*

* * *

Despite his anger, or perhaps because of it, Blake spent extra care getting ready that evening. His tailored button-down lay perfectly against his broad chest, the Cornwall blue stripes matching the exact shade of his eyes. Fastening his Audemars Piguet watch, he took a moment to admire himself in his full-length mirror. *They're making a big mistake,* he thought to himself. *Their freaking loss.*

A ring of the doorbell interrupted his self-pep talk, and he bounded down the stairs to answer it, rubbing his hands together with anticipation. He opened the door and greeted José with a fist bump. The guy had been his dealer for almost ten years. While Blake didn't ask for details, it was apparent from the increasingly nicer cars José drove that he'd done well for himself. Blake got the impression he ran a team now and didn't do much of his own work directly, but the dealer always made time for one of his biggest and most loyal customers.

"What's up, man?" José greeted him.

"It's been a day. Got passed up on a big promotion for work."

"Aww shit, I'm sorry, man. At least you still gonna be partying down in México this summer for your show, right?" he said playfully, his shoulders swaying back and forth. "You good?"

"Yeah, I'll be fine," Blake shrugged. "I'm trying to get my mind off of things tonight."

José grinned. "Well, you know I got you for that. You said twenty people, right? So should forty Gs be good?"

"Yeah, that's good. Thanks, José." Blake passed him a wad of cash as the dealer reached into his back pocket and withdrew a bag.

The pair bumped fists again and José saluted as he headed toward the door. "Go live it up tonight, man. Keep your chin up and don't worry about those suits. Fuck 'em."

Blake shot him a smile of gratitude as he closed the door.

* * *

"One more, one more!" someone yelled, clapping Blake on the back as he passed another round of shot glasses to the crowd gathered in the boat's cabin. Through the thump of the sound system, Blake heard the high tinkle of laughter from the women out on the deck, probably giggling at something Tom said. At only five foot seven inches, with a head of already thinning hair, Tom wasn't blessed with quite the looks Blake was, but he always compensated with personality and did fine with the ladies.

Blake threw back the shot of tequila, chasing it with a lime, its bright green peel swimming a bit before his eyes. "Who's up for another hit?" he asked, pulling another baggie of cocaine from his pocket. In response to the enthusiastic cheers from the group, he set up a few lines on the sleek marble table and did the first one, sinking back onto the cream leather couch.

His head cleared immediately, a pleasant thrill coursing through him as he looked around, admiring his yacht and his friends, and feeling pleased with himself for always throwing the best ragers. *They're idiots for not putting me in that job,* Blake thought to himself. *I'm a fucking winner.*

As if reading his mind, a tall, thin blonde in a tiny black bikini turned to him, holding up a glass. "Cheers to our host, Blake!" she yelled, starting to sway her hips as a nineties R&B throwback blasted through the stereo. Her toast was met with whoops of enthusiasm, though whether they were for Blake or the song, it was hard to tell. Rising from the sofa, Blake made his way toward the door, tapping the blonde's exposed ass as he shimmied past her.

Climbing up the stairs to the top deck, he spotted Tom, who, as he suspected, was surrounded by a throng of women, including the two girls they'd met last week at their favorite club, Terrace65. "My brother from another mother," his friend shouted, pumping his cup over his head and sloshing some kind of very expensive liquor onto his shirt. "Don't we look like brothers?" he asked the ladies as Blake approached with his own glass raised. "Except, of course, I'm the handsome one," he added with a wink, eliciting drunken giggles.

"Can I steal you for a second?" Blake asked his friend, motioning his head to the lower deck, which was empty at the moment.

"You got it," Tom said. "Excuse me, ladies, you know what they say: bros before...respectable young women," he finished with a mock bow. The girls' laughter trailed after them.

As Blake followed his buddy down the stairs to the lower deck, the reflection of the magnificent Pacific sunset bounced across the gentle waves, and Tom's shiny head. Plopping onto a smooth bench, Tom looked up at Blake, the levity fading from his eyes. "Hey, man, I'm really sorry about the job. You would have rocked it."

"Thanks, I appreciate it." He paused, downing another swig of whiskey. "So, what do you know about Ava Taylor-Washington?"

"I still can't believe she's the one who snagged this job. But I gotta hand it to her. I know she's been good at playing politics internally at Paracon, but I had no idea she was so well-known at other networks. Okay, so you're going to be working for this woman. What do you need to know about her?" He paused, thinking for a minute. "Well, she's super smart. Like she's pulled some genius stuff both for the content and promo of the two series she's worked on at Paracon. She did some amazing casting and editing for the show about online relationships, and helped pull it out of a pretty big ratings slump. And then, when she helped launch the *Famous Bakers* celebrity baking spinoff from our top cooking show, she actually got a lot of credit for the idea."

Blake made a sour face. The last thing he wanted was to spend his night listening to a list of this woman's accomplishments and why she had gotten the job over him.

"Anyways," Tom said quickly, noting Blake's expression, "so, yeah, she's smart, but she's also pretty ruthless. I've heard lots of rumors about her cutting people out. There was another guy working on the *Famous Bakers* launch with her, but she apparently maneuvered her way to the showrunner role, and he got moved onto some dumpy daytime show. Then there was talk about how pushy she was with the cast of the dating show. I mean, footage turned out great, don't get me wrong, but I guess she had some… questionable tactics. Apparently, she'll do pretty much anything for the ratings," he concluded with a shrug.

Blake took another drink, absorbing all Tom's intel. "This is really helpful, thank you. Gotta know how to look out for myself, you know?"

"Absolutely," Tom said. "My advice? Get on her good side. Like I said, she's tough but she knows what she's doing. Do what she says without questioning it, and she'll bring you along for the ride."

Blake bobbed his head in agreement, as the cocaine high began to wear off and the warm buzz of the alcohol replaced it. "I don't like it. But I'll do what I have to in order to survive. I've invested too many years at this damn place to give it up now because of some chick."

"Amen to that," Tom replied, clinking his glass against Blake's. "Now let's get back to the party. You deserve it tonight, big guy."

* * *

Later that night Blake drove home, his head and heart still thumping with the echoes of music and laughter. He was feeling much better, knowing that whatever happened with CBC, he still had his friends, his boat, this Ferrari, and plenty of female company.

He could even coast a little bit this season and let his junior producer, Christina Park, take more of the reins. She was young and a little too eager, and he usually limited her control mainly because she annoyed him, but she was decently competent. God, she would be salivating over the chance to impress someone like Ava. She'd been pestering him about diversity and changing things up for years now. Fine, let her do all the work this season and he'd just treat it as a vacation. That wouldn't be such a bad thing, right? The network didn't deserve his full effort anyways. He thought about the bright Mexican sun and soft white sand, the delicious tamales and the strong margaritas the kitchen whipped up, and that sexy waitress he'd had his eye on last summer—what was her name again? Yes, he'd have one last hoorah this season, then start networking for a new role in the fall. He was sure Tom would introduce him to some people at Paracon.

Blake was suddenly yanked out of his tropical fantasy by the loud whooping of a police siren behind him. The flashing red lights cast an ominous glow over his handsome features in the rearview mirror. "Shit," he muttered under his breath, smoothly guiding the Ferrari to the side of the road.

He parked and waited patiently for what felt like an eternity until the cop meandered up to the car. *What is taking this guy so long?* Blake just wanted to get home and pass out. The social media team had set a meeting for early the next morning and he preferred not to show up totally hungover. As the policeman finally reached the car, the producer rolled down his window. "Good evening, officer," Blake greeted him with what he hoped was a winning smile.

"License and registration please," the cop said, peering into the car with his flashlight.

"Can I ask why you've pulled me over?" Blake asked, his tone bordering on condescending.

"You ran a stop sign back there. And you cut that last turn pretty close to the guard rail." He paused, studying Blake's face. "What have you been up to tonight? Have you been drinking?"

Blake's heart sank. *Seriously, today of all days?* he thought to himself. *You've got to be fucking kidding me.* Silently chiding himself to get it together, he decided that partial honesty was the best approach here. "Yes, officer," he said, dropping any attitude that had peeked through earlier. "I had a drink or two with a couple of friends. But I'm fine to drive, I promise. I was thinking about work back there, that must be why I missed the stop sign. I'm sure you know the feeling, being in such an important and demanding job yourself." He grinned in apology at the officer, who did not return the expression.

"No. I focus on the road when I'm driving," he said stoically, clearly unconvinced by Blake's excuse. "Can you step out of the car, please?"

Containing a groan, Blake nodded and grabbed the door handle as the cop stepped back a few paces. He got out of the car, gripping the doorframe to ensure he didn't wobble as he stood, then eased the door closed.

"Walk along the line," the officer said, pointing lazily to the bright white line on the edge of the road. He seemed bored with the exercise, as if he pulled over fancy cars with impaired drivers all the time. In Marina del Rey, he probably did.

Channeling all of his focus, Blake fixed his eyes on the line and precariously placed one designer loafer in front of the other. He had made it several feet along when his head began swimming again, and he felt himself sway. Blake willed his foot back onto the line, but it refused to obey, darting instead a few inches to the left, his body tipping to follow it.

The officer sighed, as if disappointed that yet another of his entitled citizenry had decided to drink and drive. "I'm gonna need to take you to the station. Hands on the car, please, so I can do a search. Do you have any weapons on you?"

Blake's foggy brain struggled to process everything happening so quickly. "What?" he said to the officer, his voice thick and dumb with disbelief.

"Hands on the hood," the cop repeated, a little more forcefully this time.

Drifting back toward his car, Blake obeyed the order, placing his hands on the shiny black finish of his Ferrari. The cool metal jolted him into focus, and he spun his head around suddenly. "Listen Officer..." he glanced at the cop's name badge, "...Miller. This is a misunderstanding. I'm perfectly fine."

Officer Miller didn't respond as he patted the sides of Blake's boat shorts. With a frown, he instructed him to empty his pockets. Blake's mind clawed frantically back through his hazy memories, trying to recall if they'd finished the coke. "Last call, everyone's done?" he recalled himself saying, his voice booming inside the boat cabin as he'd looked around at people shaking their heads, ready to call it a night. "Guess we'll have to save this little guy for next time," he'd said, tucking the last baggie safely into his pocket.

You fucking idiot, Blake swore at himself now.

"Pockets," Officer Miller insisted.

His heart racing, Blake reached into the side of his tan chino shorts, knowing what he would find. He was cornered—there was no way out of this. As his fingers wrapped around the smooth plastic, extracting it from his pocket, he turned around toward the cop. "Please," he said, hating the desperate tone creeping around the edges of his voice, hating the feeling of not being in control of this situation. "I'm sure we can figure something out."

"The only thing you need to figure out," Officer Miller retorted as he pulled on a plastic glove and carefully took the little bag from Blake's sweaty palms, "is your lawyer's phone number. Let's go, big guy." He guided Blake toward the back of the squad car, admonishing him, "Look, I'm not gonna cuff you, but take it easy."

Sitting on the cheap plastic seat liner, a faint odor of old burritos permeating the cop car, Blake rubbed his eyes. *This is absolutely the worst fucking day of my life*, he thought to himself. He silently stewed in his misfortune during the short ride to the station. Once they arrived, processing was completed in a blur of instructions and camera shutters.

Thankfully, his close friend was an excellent defense attorney, and he arrived less than an hour after Blake called, waking him from a deep sleep. A fraternity brother from Dartmouth, Alexander Clifton, affectionately known as Cliff within the frat, had settled down quickly, unlike Blake. After graduating from law school, Cliff married the girlfriend he met in their freshman dorm, and now spent a lot more time with their three kids than he did partying with Blake.

"Oh, buddy," Cliff exclaimed as he entered, looking presentable despite the hour, "you kind of fucked up."

"I know." Blake grimaced. "I should have Ubered, right?" he joked half-heartedly.

"Would have been much cheaper than my hourly rate," Cliff shot back, clapping him on the shoulder. "It's alright, I'm going to get you out of this with barely a scratch." He paused, rubbing his jaw absently as he gathered his thoughts. "So, the bad news is that they're really cracking down on drugs right now. The new mayor is pretty gung ho about it, you know she ran on all the family values, tough on crime stuff, blah blah. The even worse news is that if they find out that you gave coke to everybody on the boat, they can technically bring distribution charges against you, which can carry a sentence of a few years. But," he continued, with a pause for dramatic effect, "the *good* news is that they're being smart about it and trying to get to the source. So they've been pretty willing to make deals in order to get a bite higher up the food chain."

Blake had been studying his hands dejectedly while Cliff spoke, but now perked up. "What does that mean?"

"It means if you give them your dealer's name, I'm pretty confident they will drop the drug charges. I'll push for the DUI to be dropped, too, though I can't make any promises on that one."

Blake's stomach contracted. "Give up my dealer? But José has been my boy for ten years." Studying his friend's furrowed brow, he prodded, "What are my other options?"

With a shake of his head, Cliff ran his hands through his thick dark hair then shrugged in frustration. "There are none. I don't know what to tell you, Blake. This is the game. And honestly, what's more important: your life, your career, you staying out of jail—or some low-life drug dealer?"

Sitting in silence, Blake considered this advice. He trusted Cliff's legal experience, and believed that if his friend said there were no other options, then there were none. The alternative was to risk jail time, and watch the career he was trying so desperately to salvage go up in smoke.

José is a drug dealer, he thought. *He knows the risk of what he's doing. It's not my fault it's catching up to him. Plus, I have a lot more to lose. My show is watched by millions of people, and I can never get a job at another studio if this charge goes forward.*

He weighed these points against the twinge of guilt he felt when he thought of José's easy smile, the way he could always tell when Blake seemed stressed, and the goofy antics he used to pull him out of a funk. *Fine, so he's a good guy. But Cliff is right. It's me or him.*

Pushing down the shouts of protest from his conscience, Blake lifted his eyes to meet Cliff's. "Alright, bring the officers in here. Let's do what we have to do."

Chapter 3: Blake - Now

Blake sipped his gin and tonic, his handsome face absorbing the sun's caress as the waves gently lapped against the side of his yacht, beckoning him to drift back into his afternoon nap. The waves grew in volume and in urgency, and he sat upright, yanked out of his pleasant dream as he realized the sound wasn't gentle ocean waves, but rather someone pounding on the door to his suite at the resort. He groaned, the wrath of last night's partying at the local bar bearing down on him as he struggled to rise out of bed. He wondered if he had time to do a quick bump of coke to clear his head before he answered the door.

"BLAKE!" a voice called angrily behind the door. "Wake up!"

He groaned again as he recognized Christina's snarl, and glanced at the clock. It was only 8:15. He really couldn't deal with her this early in the morning. She better have a good reason to be waking him at this hour.

Pulling a soft gray V-neck shirt over his ruffled hair, Blake shuffled to the door and threw it open, ready to tell Christina off. However, the look on her face stopped him cold. After years working in production, Blake had honed his natural ability to read people. Especially in reality TV, he often saw people pretending to be a certain way or to want a certain thing in front of the cameras. Part of what had made Blake so successful was he could look beyond the facade and see who people truly were and what they most deeply desired. This knowledge allowed him to orchestrate situations and elicit genuine reactions from his cast members, while his natural charm kept people from ever suspecting they'd been manipulated.

As Christina stood before him, a less experienced man might have seen her lips set into a thin line and her high cheekbones flushed, and assumed she was simply frustrated with him for not responding to the radio. Blake, however, peered past her indignant expression and saw the fear dancing in her eyes. Even though they butted heads often, he knew that his junior producer usually kept the set running as smoothly as his Ferrari engine. Seeing her rattled alerted him that something was seriously amiss.

"Sorry," he apologized. "I was uhh…sleeping. Must have missed your calls. What's up?"

"Andrew is dead," Christina said curtly. She didn't even wait for Blake to react before she began running down the list of steps she'd already taken, obviously eager to demonstrate how utterly useless she found him to be. "Mexican EMTs are here. We're holding them on site, and our best production assistant, Sol, is monitoring their phone usage to make sure they don't post anything on social media. She's been helping to translate for them too. Security has locked down the perimeter of the resort, no hotel staff or crew in or out without clearing it by me or you. Cast is gathered in the main gazebo, with the counselor on hand."

"Shit," the showrunner exhaled, his mind spinning as he sunk into a chair on the front patio of his suite. A wave of remorse washed over him. Blake had seen a little bit of his younger self in Andrew, and had been pleasantly surprised when Christina suggested casting him. She hadn't been shy in letting Blake know how tediously boring she had found similar starring men in the past. "Even my blind grandma will be able to see this Ken doll fuckboy doesn't want to get married," she'd moaned about a contestant last year.

While Blake had to admit that not all of his previous picks had been winners, Andrew proved to be different. Blake had seen plenty of cast members play the hero in big moments, looking for a "nice guy" edit. But Andrew's genuine kindness played out more subtly during the day-to-day of filming—the way he made an effort to thank the waitstaff in Spanish, and how he made everyone on the cast feel included.

Christina's nagging voice interrupted Blake's reminiscing. "Unfortunately, the EMTs insisted that because of the cartel violence, there is a state-wide policy that every drug-related death needs to be investigated by the police. So, I'll be meeting some officers shortly."

Blake jerked his head up. "What do you mean, 'drug-related'?"

"It seems like he overdosed. Won't be confirmed until they run a tox screen, of course, but that's what the EMTs said."

Blake knew from her narrowed eyes and pursed lips that she was holding back, and given their history of disagreements, combined with her knowledge of his own habits, she was likely ready to throw daggers of blame at his head. *Shit,* he thought. *Police coming to the resort? Not good. Not good at all.*

"Last but not least," the junior producer continued, "I'll leave it to you to call Ava. But you better do it fast, because there's no way we can stop this from leaking for much longer."

Blake groaned inwardly, picturing his boss's furious face and cursing Christina for assigning him this task, even though he knew it was the right call. Ava was going to absolutely lose her shit. Eventually he'd need to have a talk with Christina about what version of this morning's events would make its way up to Ava, because he did not need the VP to hear that he'd been hungover and slept through the entire incident. Not to mention his recreational activities on and off set. However, Christina was also right in saying they didn't have much time before the press got wind of this, so it was urgent that he call Ava. His chat with the junior producer could wait until later today.

"All right." Blake nodded, standing and bouncing on the balls of his feet. "Let me break the news to Ava. Thank you for handling everything else, Christina," he said sincerely, eliciting a slight arch of her thin black eyebrow.

"Of course," she replied with a faux casual shrug.

As Blake headed into his suite, he turned back to Christina, and somberly asked, "Can you also get me his parents' phone number? Should be in his emergency contact info."

She nodded slowly, letting her dark hair fall over her eyes as she looked toward the ground. He suspected she was hiding a rush of emotions, which she was only allowing herself to process now that she'd gotten the situation under control.

"Thanks," Blake said gently. "Appreciate it."

He walked inside, dreading the call to his boss. Glancing around, he spotted his phone lying face down on the ground next to his loafers. As he strode across the room and picked it up, he saw that not only was it dead, but a crack sprawled across the screen like a spider trying to escape from a cage. Blake cursed under his breath as he tossed it on the nightstand and shoved the charger into it, praying it would turn back on. He must have dropped it last night, though when he tried to recall it happening, hazy memories gathered in the corners of his mind like clouds over the horizon.

"Damn tequila," he muttered. He'd deal with the phone later.

Before he called Ava, he really needed to clear his mind. He dug into the pocket of his jeans from last night, pulling out a little baggie of cocaine. There was barely enough left to do a quick line.

Fuck, I went through a lot last night, he thought to himself. After carefully dumping the last remnants of the powdery substance out on the desk, he cut it into a neat line and rolled up a 500-peso bill. With a sharp inhale, he felt a quick, tiny rush to his head—enough to keep his headache at bay while he dealt with the VP.

Taking a deep breath, he picked up his laptop and, without giving his nerves a chance to take over, immediately FaceTimed Ava. LA was an hour behind Puerto Engaño, so it was only 7:30 a.m. there, but he knew she was an early riser.

"Morning, Blake," she crowed, her vibrant eyes and deep brown skin glowing in the sun. He'd expected her to be driving into the office right now, but it looked like she was sitting outside, probably on her balcony. He enviously recalled her home's spectacular view of the Malibu coastline from the party she and her wife had hosted for the entire *Love's a Beach* crew. It had been a nice way for Ava to introduce herself to the staff but, frankly, his end-of-season party on his yacht last year had been much more fun.

Good, Blake thought to himself. *Better that she's not in the office, and has some time to digest this alone.*

He had a fleeting hope that perhaps she was home sick and wouldn't have the energy to be up his ass about this. But that quickly deflated when she jumped into the show updates. "So how are things? How's the storyline with Nick and Ashley coming? I'm really loving the footage of him winning her over with his humor. It feels very natural. Oh, and how about Thalia and Andrew? I'm still so thrilled he skipped right past the busty blondes and slinky cocktail dresses to talk to our biracial beauty the first night. And their on-screen chemistry! Unbelievable."

As usual, Ava's mind was going a mile a minute. Steeling himself for her reaction, Blake interrupted her, surprised at the evenness of his voice despite his nerves. "Actually, Ava, speaking of Andrew, we have an…issue."

Perhaps his voice wasn't as smooth as he'd imagined, or perhaps the lack of his usual joviality gave him away. In any case, he saw Ava's face shift as she recognized he did not come bearing good news.

"Blake," she said firmly, "tell me what's up."

"We've had an incident on set," he began.

Ava's perfectly made-up eyes narrowed with suspicion. "What kind of… *incident*, Blake?"

"Well, Andrew. He umm," Blake shifted in the plush chair, his elbow squeaking awkwardly against the leather. "Well, he passed away."

"Oh, my God," Ava whispered quietly, eyes wide as she leaned back away from the screen. "What happened? Was he ill?"

Blake squirmed. "No, he apparently overdosed last night. His roommate found him dead this morning."

"Excuse me?" Ava's voice jumped through his speaker. "I tell you that you're on probation this season, and you turn around and let something like this happen on my set!?" She brought her hand up to cover her mouth, as if forcefully preventing herself from saying something she'd regret. Her eyes closed tightly like she was praying for self-control.

Blake froze, waiting for what felt like an eternity. When Ava's eyes reopened, her voice was controlled, but a thread of danger ran through it, like a shark fin slicing through calm waters. "I need two hours to get in front of the CBC board on this, probably three hours until we can get a formal statement out. If I see so much as a mention of *Love's a Beach* on

Twitter before that press release, your illustrious career at this network—or any network—will come to a very sudden end. Is that clear?"

He gave her a tight-lipped nod, realizing that anything else he said, any explanation or excuse, would only enrage her further.

"Good," Ava said, the sharp edge lingering in her voice. "And one more thing. Did you know Andrew was using drugs?"

Even though he'd known the question would come at some point, it still hit him like a punch in his gut. His instincts told him that a flat-out denial would only give her reason to suspect that he was hiding something. She was smart, and wouldn't believe that he'd been surrounded by cast members partying and remained clueless. Considering this, he quickly decided to be forthcoming.

"Some people on set were," he admitted carefully. "But I honestly didn't know Andrew was."

Ava studied him through the screen, clearly trying to determine whether he was lying. Finally, she nodded. "Fine. I'm sure the local police will ask more about it. That's all for now."

She hung up abruptly, leaving Blake alone with his thoughts. He was glad he'd decided to tell her the truth. Or at least part of it.

Chapter 4: Christina - 3.5 Months Ago

Christina honked her horn as a driver cut in front of her. Groaning at the traffic sprawled for miles ahead, she checked the time again, cursing herself and her perpetual tardiness. She absolutely could not be late today. Not only was it casting day, when they flew in all the applicants who had made it to the final round of interviews, but it was also the first time their new VP of Reality Segments, Ava Taylor-Washington, was going to introduce herself to the entire *Love's a Beach* crew.

For the last few seasons, Christina had dreaded casting day. Her boss, Blake, constantly steered the selection criteria away from cast members with interesting backgrounds, opting instead for another season full of aspiring models and influencers too young and naive to recognize love if it slapped them across their perfectly contoured faces. Some days she felt like she'd wasted so much time and money getting a bachelor's from UCLA just so she could babysit these kids on set.

However, she was hopeful that Ava's arrival would change things. Christina had admired her from afar, following Ava's work ever since she heard her speak at an industry panel a few years ago. According to the industry chatter, not only was Ava a big proponent of inclusion, but she also was known for empowering young female producers and giving them opportunities to advance.

Christina's mood was buoyed by the thought of meeting Ava in less than an hour, and she happily switched on her favorite podcast, *Love's a Pod*, which recapped *Love's a Beach* episodes and divulged gossip about the show and its alumni. Despite her friends' insistence that it was weird to spend her free time hearing more about her job, she enjoyed the co-hosts' witty banter, and being reminded that her work was enjoyed by so many people.

"What's up y'all! Monique here," the first host began the episode. "Welcome to *Love's a Pod.*"

"And this is Connor," Monique's co-host chimed in. "We've got some exciting news this week. There's a new head honcho of reality shows at CBC, and there's a lot of talk about how she's going to shake up things in production." Christina turned up the volume, eager to hear how Ava's hiring was being covered in the media. "We'll have one of your fave former *Love's a Beach* stars on later to get her thoughts, but first—Monique, what do you think?"

"I am *so* excited," she replied, and Christina sighed with relief at the host's positive reaction. "So, for those of you who have been loyal fans of the show, you know it's been a lot of the same-old for a loooong time now. The current showrunner, Blake Jennings, started out with the franchise *fifteen years ago.* Some of y'all might have watched him as a charismatic young contestant searching for love. But when his romantic interest declined his proposal during the season finale, his popularity skyrocketed with female viewers, who were quick to express how eager they would be to 'comfort' him."

Christina gagged a little bit at that, knowing more than she wanted to about Blake's reputation with women.

"Mmm, girl, not only female viewers. I would comfort that man any day!" Connor piped up, eliciting a chuckle from Christina. Her mood continued to buoy as the traffic finally began moving ahead of her.

"Okay, keep it in your pants," Monique retorted. "Anyways, the tabloids at the time speculated that his rejection had been staged to earn him some sympathy points, but those rumors didn't seem to deter his enthusiastic fanbase. The network sensed an opportunity to make some booya money off of him, and they asked him to become the new host of the show. Blake is apparently a real charmer, and that helped him to climb through the CBC ranks, eventually being named as showrunner and becoming a well-known favorite among the network executives."

That's definitely true, Christina thought to herself, annoyed. Given the initially high ratings when he'd become showrunner five years ago, she had to admit Blake wasn't bad at his job. He simply had what she viewed as an outdated vision for the show.

Connor interrupted Monique's monologue. "Okay, so if he's such a big deal, what's the scoop about this promotion?"

"Well," the co-host replied, "everyone knew the old head of reality was retiring soon, and apparently the entire *Love's a Beach* crew was waiting for the announcement that Blake got the gig. Get this—according to my source, the crew even bought him a Rolex as a congratulations gift!"

Christina gasped as Connor burst out laughing. Monique definitely had a solid source, because that story was pretty accurate. The day the announcement was expected, Christina had received a frantic call from Sharon, Blake's executive assistant.

"He didn't get the job! I'm at the freaking Rolex store right now and can you believe he didn't get it? Glad I didn't buy this damned watch already!" Sharon's Long Island accent dripped through the phone, practically oozing into Christina's mouth, which had fallen wide open.

As Connor insisted that Monique must be joking, Christina was relieved to see the modern glass office building towering in the distance. She listened absently for a few more minutes, then switched off the podcast as she pulled into the CBC parking lot. She took a deep breath of excitement as she hurried inside, eager to meet Ava.

She was one of the last crew members to arrive at the large conference room where the all-staff meeting was being held. She spotted her favorite production assistant, Sol—*not Marisol, only my abuela calls me that*, she'd corrected Christina with a side-eye during her interview—who was sporting a hot pink streak through her dark hair. Grabbing a seat next to her, Christina whispered, "Love the new hair. Did you listen to *Love's a Pod* this morning?"

"Yasss. So juicy," Sol nodded, her eyes mirroring the shock Christina had felt at the episode. "Did you hear the part where they were speculating about a change in filming location?"

"Nooo," Christina groaned. "I didn't get that far!"

Over the last several months, there had been escalating drug cartel violence in Puerto Engaño, where their normal filming site, the Paraiso Maya resort, was located. She and the head of security had been doing a ton of research on the local cartels, tracking the violence and diving into local news stories about beef between the factions. After a few days, the tabs in her search history were full of violent images and conspiracy theories about the elusive head of the Rodriguez cartel. She'd started to hear whispers that the CBC executives were getting nervous and considering changing locations.

Looking at Sol now, she chewed her lip. "Let's hope Ava wasn't listening! We don't need any surprises thrown at her for her first season here!"

As if on cue, the woman of the hour strode into the room, a perfectly tailored navy pantsuit swaying with her as she walked. "Good morning, everyone! I'm Ava Taylor-Washington, and I'm so thrilled to be your new vice president of Reality Segments."

A surge of excitement rose in Christina's stomach at seeing her idol. *What a badass! I'll do whatever it takes to impress her this season.* She sat rapt, eagerly awaiting Ava's words of wisdom.

Over the next few minutes, Ava shared more about her background, then dove into her expectations for the upcoming season. "I want at least half of the cast to be BIPOC—that's Black, indigenous, and people of color. Representation is not just having a token Black woman or a token Asian guy on screen, but showing that people of all shapes and colors are desirable, and that they too have magical love stories waiting to be told."

Christina cheered inwardly. This was exactly what she'd been pushing Blake on for years. And now she would get to execute this vision under a brilliant executive.

The VP continued, "But this goes way beyond how our contestants look. I am looking for *original* storylines, and after casting concludes on Friday, I expect the production team to identify five to ten plotlines that you can tease out. None of this same old 'is he ready for commitment?' stuff. Or 'she feels unlovable even though she's gorgeous and has guys lined around the block' crap. I want to see real, meaningful connections between the contestants. Let's bring in some of their real-life passions. I want to see what makes them tick, what makes them different, and why I should care about who they are and who they love. Is that clear?"

Ava surveyed the room, and Christina followed suit, noting the mix of some hesitant and some enthusiastic nods. A few people snuck surreptitious glances at Blake, as if trying to read his reaction to this new direction for the show, but his handsome face remained impassive as he nodded.

"All right then," Ava concluded. "I'm really looking forward to working with you all. Now, let's go kill this season!"

* * *

Christina had been full of energy following Ava's pep talk, but a few hours later, she already found herself struggling to meet the new executive's goals for the show. The pre-screening casting work had all been done before Ava was named as VP, so it had followed Blake's past standards. After a long day of talking to a ton of hopefuls who could have passed for Carrie Underwood or Ryan Gosling, Christina was left scrambling.

Her next candidate was biracial, according to the 'Black' and 'White, non-Hispanic' boxes ticked on her application, so Christina prayed that the interview would go well. Pulling her long, straight dark hair back into a messy bun, she mentally prepared herself for the conversation.

She looked up at the pretty young woman who entered the room, noting her strong, lean figure and big, eager brown eyes. *She'll look great on camera in a bikini,* Christina thought to herself. The woman's golden brown skin and gentle curls were like a flash of light enlivening the otherwise dull parade of blondes she had been interviewing all day.

"Hi, there," Christina glanced down at her iPad, "Thalia! How are you today?"

Thalia smiled, displaying a row of gleaming, straight white teeth. "I'm great, thanks!"

"Glad to hear it," Christina replied. "Why don't you tell me a little bit about yourself? Where you're from, what you do, that kind of thing."

"Sure!" Thalia nodded enthusiastically, sweeping a loose curl off of her smooth cheek. "So, I'm originally from New Jersey, and I live in Brooklyn now. I'm the oldest child, and I'm super close with my younger sister. My parents are my inspiration and my everything, and that's why I really want to do this—to find a love like theirs." She paused, looking up at Christina earnestly.

Ugh, Christina thought. *We've heard this a million times before. So much for novel storylines.* Despite her waning enthusiasm regarding Thalia's ability to bring anything interesting to the show, Christina heard Ava's voice echoing in her head.

It's essential that we create an opportunity to tell these diverse stories, the industry titan had said. *They may take more patience and perseverance to bring to life, but they're there, underneath the soil, waiting to be harvested.*

Forcing a smile, Christina focused back on Thalia and decided to try a different tack. "Tell me," she said chummily, "what are you passionate about? What gets you excited in life?"

Christina sensed the briefest hesitation from the potential cast member, but it was replaced so quickly by another enthusiastic grin that she wondered if she had imagined it.

Thalia began cheerily, "Well, I'm the social media director at an amazing nonprofit that focuses on environmental and climate change issues. And I'm really passionate about yoga. I recently finished my teacher training, and on the weekends I teach yoga to underprivileged kids in the city."

Christina nodded with feigned interest, as if yoga were a fascinating hobby and not part of the workout regimen of every thin, fit woman she'd interviewed today. She did a mental tally of the lookbook to figure out how many BIPOC cast members she'd already interviewed, and how many more opportunities she would have to round out the cast in terms of diversity.

There was Raina, the stunning Indian-American girl from this morning; Marcus, the Black comic book author; and Tae-Hyun the tall Korean-American doctor. She'd had a good laugh with him about having Korean parents, and how he'd pleased his father with his career choice, whereas her job in television had left something to be desired for her own mom and dad.

As she ticked her way through the other conversations she'd had this morning, she resigned herself to the fact that she really needed Thalia as part of her cast if she wanted to please Ava—which she desperately did.

Mustering up enthusiasm to match Thalia's, Christina responded, "That's super to hear! Well, I need to get on to the next interview, but it was *so* great meeting you, Thalia. We'll be in touch very soon. I think you're going to like what you hear when we speak next," she added with a conspiratorial wink.

Thalia's face lit up again, her big brown eyes and thick lashes fluttering with excitement. "Thank you so much, Christina! I'm looking forward to it." She stood up with a cheerful expression, smoothing her trendy bohemian dress, and walked out the door.

Flipping through the lookbook on her iPad, Christina finalized her decision and added a note next to Thalia's picture: "Sweet girl! Total wife material. She's in."

She glanced at the time on her tablet and realized that even though it was almost two, she hadn't eaten lunch yet. Grabbing her phone, she texted Sol, asking the PA to bring up a sandwich from the production room.

As she put her phone down, her next interview subject walked in, his broad shoulders and tall frame filling the doorway.

"Hey, there," he said with an easy smile, "I'm Andrew."

Christina lifted her gaze from the screen and studied him, taking in his piercing green eyes, stylishly cut blond hair, and just enough stubble to look rugged without hiding his sharp jawline. Most candidates submitted application pictures that were way more flattering than how they appeared in person, but this guy was just as attractive as his photo…maybe even more so. He looked like he would be cast to play the quarterback in a movie about a high school football team overcoming all odds to win the national championship.

"Hi, Andrew," she responded as he lowered himself into the chair. "It's nice to meet you. Why don't you tell me a little bit about yourself?"

"I'd love to," he answered confidently. "I grew up in New York, and then I went to UVA to play lacrosse. But unfortunately, I got injured during my freshman season, so I transferred out here to California. Better weather," he added, flashing her another grin. "I ended up loving it, so I've been here ever since."

Oh no, Christina thought. *He may have the all-American football player looks, but he's definitely got the lax bro vibe.* Barely able to contain a sigh, she hurried on to the next question, eager to get through the interview and on to another, more interesting applicant.

"So, what made you want to come on the show?" she asked Andrew, waiting for what would surely be an earth-shattering answer.

"Honestly? My mom signed me up." He grinned sheepishly. "She loves the show, and she wants grandkids and all that. Plus, she has two boys, so I think the idea of a daughter-in-law sounds pretty nice to her. Someone she can enjoy a glass of chardonnay with while my dad and brother and I are watching football," he laughed. "And also," he continued, his expression softening, "she really wants me to be happy. She's an amazing mom that way. And I've had some…rough patches in the last few years."

Surprised by his gentle, genuine affection toward his mom, Christina found herself reconsidering for a moment. *But no,* she thought. *This is exactly the kind of dude Blake would love and Ava would hate.*

She began reaching for her iPad so she could jot down a NO under Andrew's name. "Okay, great, I think that's it. We'll be in touch."

"Wow, that was fast," he chirped. "Guess I'll have time to grab a drink before dinner! Well, Christina," he continued as he stood, "it was a real pleasure meeting you." He extended his hand, leaning across the table to shake hers.

As she leaned forward and felt his smooth grip, a subtle fragrance tickled her nose. Christina froze, her brain processing the warm, woody scent with a hint of citrus bursting through, and she felt a little bubble of panic explode in her stomach as the recognition burst into consciousness.

"Are you okay?" Andrew asked as he released her hand. "You look a little…off." Tiny lines framed his striking eyes as his face crinkled up with concern.

"Yeah, totally fine," Christina replied quickly, her voice strained. "Just uhh…haven't had lunch yet." She shifted behind the table, unconsciously shuffling her feet backwards.

She exhaled in relief as Sol poked her head through the doorway, her cheery "Knock knock!" interrupting the tense moment with Andrew.

Turning back to her interview subject, Christina nodded curtly. "Anyways, thanks again for coming in."

"Sure thing." Andrew gave a half-hearted smile, clearly confused by the shift of energy in the room. He walked toward the door and waved as he left, calling, "Take care!" as he rounded the corner.

"You okay?" Sol looked at Christina, concern etched across her round face.

"Yes," Christina snapped. "Just give me the sandwich please." She took it from the PA's outstretched hand, and turned back toward her iPad, struggling to process this last interview. The gears slowly turning in her mind, she stopped Sol as she was about to leave the room.

"Hey, Sol," she asked suddenly, "what are our total numbers for today?"

The PA paused, counting on her fingers. "We've got four guys confirmed, and two you put on the maybe list. And three girls confirmed, but I think Blake *really* likes the one he's interviewing right now," she said, giving Christina a knowing glance.

An idea was beginning to ebb and flow in her mind, like waves gently rolling in and out from the shoreline. With each new consideration, the tide grew stronger, until the idea was crashing insistently in tandem with her heartbeat pounding in her chest. Ignoring the lurch in her stomach as she made her decision, she told Sol, "Let's give Andrew the last male spot."

"Really?" Sol asked dubiously, pointing down the hallway where the last applicant had exited. "That guy?"

"Yes," Christina answered firmly. "He seems…sweet."

"Okay." Sol shrugged, jotting down a note on her tablet. "Blake will be pleased. He looks like a little Blake 2.0." She chortled, rolling her eyes as she left the room.

Left alone with her thoughts in the suffocating silence that followed, a little voice in Christina's head screamed, *What the hell did I just do?*

Chapter 5: Christina - Now

By now, the sun had climbed higher in the sky, its white-hot glare reflecting off the pristine beach. Christina felt exhausted from the effort of holding her shit together throughout the roller coaster of emotions over the last few hours. She couldn't stop recalling how Thalia had collapsed against the doorframe when she'd seen Andrew's body. Christina had gently lowered the cast member to the ground, rubbing her back as she sobbed. Regardless of Christina's feelings toward Andrew, Thalia had grown on her over the last month, and the producer had nearly lost control of her own emotions seeing the grief of Andrew's girlfriend.

Now Blake was off doing damage control with Ava and the higher ups, so it fell on her to manage the discussion with local law enforcement. Christina shielded her eyes as she watched two police cars glide down the resort's private driveway. "Hey," she called to the cameraman sitting in the lounge chair next to her, "at least get some B-roll of the police cars! And keep rolling when they arrive. I'm sure they'll ask you to turn it off, but we'll take what we can get."

The vehicles pulled up to the main lobby, the red lights reflecting off of the spotless glass panels looking out over the Pacific. On each car door, the word "Policía" was emblazoned next to the Oaxaca state emblem.

Christina watched in surprise as a pointy heel emerged from the passenger door of the first car, followed by a long leg in chic, wide-legged trousers. A tall, striking woman emerged, striding across the driveway and pulling her badge from her hip with one hand, while she extended the other to Christina, a set of delicate gold bangles chiming on her slim wrist as they shook hands.

"*Hola.* You must be Christina. I'm Chief Daniela Martinez, from the Oaxaca State Police," she said in a commanding voice, her accent barely detectable.

The producer faltered, completely intimidated by this badass policewoman who also happened to look like a Miss Universe contestant. "Oh, yes," Christina stammered, "Thanks so much for coming. This is such an awful thing to happen."

"Yes, it's a tragedy. But my colleagues and I are here to help. Please meet Officer Ruiz," she said, motioning to the younger cop who had been driving the first car, "as well as Officers Garcia and Torres." She pointed to the two beefy middle-aged men who had emerged from the second vehicle, as each gave a courteous nod. Spotting the cameraman behind Christina, Chief Martinez waved her hand in dismissal. "Please, no cameras. This is official police business."

"Yes, of course," Christina apologized, motioning to the crew member to stop filming.

Seemingly satisfied as he lowered the camera, Chief Martinez pressed on, "So, Christina, are you in charge on the set? Or is there anyone else we need to run decisions by?"

Bristling slightly at the question, Christina responded, "My boss, Blake, is the showrunner. But he's given me full authority to work with you on this, and I can get you whatever you need in terms of interviews with cast and crew, or anything else around the resort."

Daniela nodded, sweeping her long, golden brown hair back behind her shoulder. "That's great. Now has anyone touched the body?"

"Yes, one of our cast members, Tae-Hyun, is a doctor and tried to give Andrew CPR when they found him unresponsive in the villa this morning. I'm not sure what the EMTs did when they were here. Only two other cast members were in there—his roommate and his girlfriend—but neither touched the body. We've been holding all the cast and crew in a large gazebo after the paramedics left."

"Well done," Chief Martinez said, and Christina felt a little surge of pride, finding herself wanting to impress the woman. "Now can you take us to the villa, please?"

"Of course," she replied. "Right this way."

As the group slowly made their way down the winding sidewalk to the boys' villa, they passed the restaurant.

"Can I have anything brought to you? A coffee or snack?" Christina asked.

Daniela nodded. "Coffee would be great. I've heard it's excellent here."

"Yes, it is," Christina agreed, grabbing her radio. "Sol, can you have Maria bring four coffees to the boys' villa? Thanks." Her favorite waitress, Maria, was not only the friendliest, but also the most efficient, and she knew she'd quickly bring the refreshments for the officers.

Next, they passed the gazebo, where the cast and some of the crew were sitting. While most of the cast grouped together, with the couples cuddled on the rattan couches, Thalia sat off on her own, curled into a small armchair. A blanket was draped over her shoulders, despite the heat of the day, and her gaze drifted out over the water.

She must be taking this so hard, Christina thought, her heart aching for Thalia. *I need to check in on her after I get the detectives situated.*

Chief Martinez was speaking rapidly in Spanish to the other three officers as they walked. With her limited grasp of the language, Christina could only pick up a few words: *fotos, drogas, muerto.* She assumed Daniela was instructing her team to take photos of the body before moving it, and perhaps search the room for drugs.

Wanting to be helpful, Christina cleared her throat and interjected, "I'm not sure how much the paramedics told you, but from what they told me this morning, they think Andrew was dead for several hours before they found him. They also said it looked like a drug overdose."

"Thank you, Christina," Chief Martinez replied. "Yes, they shared that with me. My team investigates all drug-related deaths in the state of Oaxaca, and loops in the Policía Federal Ministerial—the Mexican national police—if we need additional support. I don't expect that will be necessary in this case, and we'll try to close this out quickly. Right now, my team will help transport the body to the medical examiner's office so they can perform an autopsy and toxicology screen to confirm it was an overdose."

Christina recalled an incident a few seasons ago when a contestant had gotten blackout drunk and broken their arm. The local police had done a blood test, and CBC's legal and medical team had to review it. "Yes, that makes sense. Our network will likely have an independent auditor confirm the findings as well."

She thought she saw a flash of annoyance across Chief Martinez's pretty features, and rushed to explain, "We just have to go through our formalities, too. You know how it is."

"Yes, of course," the chief replied graciously, the warmth returning to her expression. "Now, I need to ask you—did you know of anyone using illegal substances on set?"

Christina hesitated. "Though we do our best to prevent it, there is a possibility that some individuals on set may have had access to drugs," she replied carefully, knowing full well the delicacy of this question, given the ongoing cartel violence in the region.

The drug wars had escalated so much last month that it had nearly derailed the season. Following concerned emails from some executives, Ava had called Blake and Christina into her office a month before filming. "Do we have any alternate site options?" Ava asked. "I realize it might be impossible this late in this game."

Blake cleared his throat. "No, we have explored a lot of options, and it's only Paraiso Maya. That's our only shot at getting a season launched on schedule."

Christina shot a glance at him, trying to hide her frustration. The truth was she had been researching backup resorts in safer areas for months, but Blake had found a fault with each of them. "This looks like a middle school campground. No one is feeling sexy in this cabin," he'd criticized when Christina showed him photos of one. For another he'd complained, "That cost is my entire budget, Christina. What are we going to do for dates—roast marshmallows?"

Ava absorbed Blake's response, and Christina could practically see her brilliant mind churning. "Alright then," she said, patting her desk. "Give me details of the security plan, and I will pitch it to the executives and make it happen. I'm not gonna have my ratings giant out of commission the first season I'm in this job."

Despite the dire situation in the town, fortunately the resort's location was fairly secluded. They agreed to hire two additional security crew members, as well as install extra cameras at all entrances. They also chartered private flights from LA and arranged a private security firm to transport cast and crew safely to and from the airport.

Looking back at all the time she had spent on the security plan, Christina could have hardly conceived she would now be standing here with the police on her set. She was eager to prove to Ava that even though things had gone horribly wrong, she was capable of cleaning them up.

They had finally reached the boys' villa, and she opened the door to let Daniela and the officers enter. "Right up this way," Christina said, pointing to the sleek, curved wooden staircase. She followed the four officers up the stairs, indicating that they should turn left at the top to reach Andrew's room.

The five of them crowded into the bedroom, standing between the two double beds. Christina focused her gaze on Nick's empty bed and the vibrant Hawaiian print shirt he'd apparently torn off and thrown over the baseboard after a few too many drinks last night. Though she didn't look at Andrew's body on the opposite bed, she could feel its icy presence creeping across the room toward her, almost as if his soul were clinging to her pant legs and begging her to tell him why this had happened.

Shaking off the chill that crept over her, despite the sunshine and warm breeze sweeping through the large bedroom windows, Christina forced herself to focus. She needed to manage this crisis. She dragged her gaze up toward Daniela, and was surprised to find the chief studying her rather than the dead body.

"Are you alright, Christina?" she asked gently. "You seem quite affected by this."

"Yes, I'm fine. We're all sad. I'm just…trying to figure out what we need to do next. We still need to inform his family, and of course we're trying to minimize any negative press about the incident."

Daniela nodded in understanding. "Well, based on the information shared by the EMTs, I think it's quite clear that this is an overdose. So, you can go ahead and tell his family that. My team will begin photographing the scene now, and then we'll need to take statements from most of the cast and crew, especially anyone who may have been with him last night."

The chief paused, then concluded, "All in all, it should be a straightforward case to close out, but we need to check all these boxes, given the terrible cartel violence going on right now. We'll try to get out of your hair as soon as possible."

"Thank you so much," Christina replied with palpable relief. The network would certainly want to avoid a long, drawn-out investigation.

Chief Martinez turned to her team and began firing off instructions in Spanish when a knock on the door interrupted her.

"*Hola*, sorry miss," came the waitress Maria's voice from behind the partially closed door. Her voice sounded despondent, unlike her normal friendly self. "Sol asked me to bring the coffee for the *policía*."

"Come in, Maria." Christina pushed the door open for the server.

As the young woman walked into the doorway, she looked around the room and startled, tipping the tray and sending scalding coffee sloshing across her hands. "*Ay Dios mío!*" she exclaimed, plopping the tray onto Nick's nightstand and wiping her hands on her crisply ironed white button-down.

"Maria, are you okay?" Christina asked, reaching out to touch the girl's trembling shoulder.

"*Sí, sí*, I'm fine," she replied, her voice shaking. "I'm sorry, *lo siento*," she mumbled, her eyes focused on the floor as she looked eager to escape the room. *She must like dead bodies even less than me*, Christina thought to herself.

Daniela said, "Thank you for the coffee, Maria. That's all for now."

Maria nodded and hurried out of the room without so much as another glance in their direction.

Taking a sip of her piping hot beverage, the chief turned back to Christina, "Now, where were we? I think my team can handle things here. Why don't you and I go downstairs to talk, then we can go meet the cast in the gazebo so I can take some additional statements?"

"Sounds good," Christina said. "Should I have my assistant come up here? In case your officers need anything else?"

"No, I think we're all set."

"Okay, great, let's go then." Christina was relieved to put some distance between herself and the corpse. She started out of the room and down the stairs, with Daniela close behind her.

When they reached the patio, Daniela motioned for her to take a seat on one of the white wicker chairs. "Let's talk here, shall we?" she suggested, pulling a small black notebook and pen from her bag.

Christina eased herself down, sitting up straight and hoping she was projecting confidence and control.

The chief began her questions. "Firstly, why don't you tell me a little about Andrew. What was he like, who was he closest to on set, what was he usually like when he partied?"

"Well, he was very well liked by the cast and crew," Christina answered. *Or most of them, at least*, she thought to herself.

"And you?" Daniela prompted, her tone casual but eyebrows furrowed slightly as if she detected something in Christina's response worth noting.

Clearing her throat, the producer said carefully, "I personally found him to be a bit…entitled. But," she continued with a shrug, "he was perfectly nice to everyone here, so no complaints."

Daniela scribbled some notes before returning her gaze to Christina. "And who were his friends? Who do you think would be best for me to speak with?"

"Definitely Nick. He is—or was," she corrected herself with a wince, "his roommate. He's the one who found him this morning. Totally torn up, the poor guy. He blames himself that he didn't realize anything was wrong when he came to bed last night."

"So, Andrew was already in bed before Nick came up to the room? Was that unusual?"

Christina thought for a moment. "Not really. Most nights they hung out together, but recently Andrew had been spending more and more evenings with Thalia. And Nick was offsite most of yesterday on a date with Ashley, another one of the female cast members."

"Thalia is Andrew's girlfriend, I guess?"

"Yes. They were getting pretty serious." Christina paused. "We usually have one or two couples get engaged at the end of the season, and they looked like they were heading that way."

"That's helpful, thank you. It will be important for me to speak with her as well, to get a sense of Andrew's state of mind." Daniela wrote some additional notes, then asked Christina a few more questions on the logistics of getting a full list of the cast and crew, as well as the hotel staff on duty last night.

"Alright, I think that's all for now," the chief said, tucking away her notebook as she stood. "Let's head down to the gazebo."

The pair walked over the stone path down the hill in silence. Christina was eager to understand more of what was going on in the policewoman's mind, but decided it would be wise not to press her.

When they reached the gazebo, Christina greeted the cast. "Hey, everyone. I know you're all having a really rough time. I want to introduce Chief Martinez from the state police. She needs to ask some of you a few questions."

One of Christina's least favorite cast members, Jake, jumped in angrily. "How about first you tell us what happened to Andrew and why you've been holding us in this gazebo all morning?"

There's a reason the whole crew has been secretly calling him Jake the Jerk, she thought, his entitled tone very familiar to her at this point.

Before Christina could respond, Tae-Hyun's strained voice came from the back of the group. "It was drugs, right? He OD'ed?"

The remaining eight cast members all spun to look at him. Christina shifted uncomfortably, glancing at Chief Martinez. "Unfortunately, we can't share more details at this point in the investigation."

Sitting to her right, Nick had retained his shell-shocked look from this morning. He shook his head, as if emerging from a trance. Finally, he lifted his eyes to Christina's and spoke, still clearly shaken up, but with a look of fierce denial on his face. "There's no way. Andrew didn't do drugs. We've been partying together for a month—hell, we've all been hanging out with him twenty-four-seven for a month—and I've never once seen him with coke or pills, or even heard him talk about it."

Christina shook her head empathetically. "Nick, I know it's hard to accept this possibility, but we have to let the professionals do their job. Who knows? Maybe he was secretly into drugs or maybe he just decided to try something new last night and it all went wrong."

To her left, Christina saw Daniela step commandingly forward. "I think that's enough discussion for now. My team and I need to conduct interviews before we can—"

"No." Nick shook his head more vehemently now, his thick brown curls bobbing along, as he interrupted the chief. "There's something off here. I'm telling you guys, he didn't take any drugs last night. I know it. I know Andrew better than any of you, except maybe Thalia."

The group fell silent as Nick looked toward Thalia, still huddled in her armchair, her gaze fixed on the sea. In a voice shrouded in pain and loss, she said so quietly it was almost lost in the sound of the crashing waves, "Maybe. Or maybe none of us really knew Andrew at all."

Chapter 6: Thalia - 2.5 Months Ago

"Hey, girl, hey!" Thalia's sister proclaimed, greeting her as she stepped into their favorite Thai restaurant for lunch.

"Hi, Sasha." Thalia returned her sister's grin. Ever since leaving the casting call a few days ago, she had been feeling pessimistic about the outcome, but her spirits were immediately buoyed by her sister's infectious energy and orange velour jumpsuit.

"So," Sasha demanded once they had ordered their usual, "tell me everything!"

"I don't know," Thalia began uncertainly. "I feel like it didn't go well. This producer, she seemed kind of bored with me, even though she was really like…weirdly smiley, and made a positive comment to me as I was leaving."

"But that sounds promising!" Sasha insisted.

"I guess so. Maybe. I don't know. You know how important this is to me. I have to make this work."

"Hey," Sasha cut in. "I know how much you want to do this for them. And I still think you'll get in. Anyone who doesn't want my gorgeous, amazing sister on their show is—"

Her opinion was cut off by Thalia's phone vibrating on the vinyl tablecloth. "It's an LA area code!" Thalia gasped.

"Answer it!" Sasha crowed, banging the table and drawing looks from their fellow diners.

Taking a deep breath, Thalia tapped her screen. "Hello?"

"Hi, Thalia!" a chirpy voice responded. "Christina here, from *Love's a Beach.* Listen, we loved you and wanted to officially extend an offer to you to join us this season. I'm sending over the contract now, can you take a look tonight? We want to publish the cast bios in about three weeks, so we're in a bit of a time crunch."

Her lips parted in shock, Thalia stared blankly across the table at her sister, then mumbled what she hoped Christina understood to be her agreement.

"Wonderful!" the producer replied, her tone a shade too bright, and pinched like sunlight peeking through shutters. "Shoot me any questions via email. Talk soon. Can't wait to see you in Mexico!"

"What did they say?" Sasha demanded.

"I...I'm in," Thalia stammered, still processing the news.

"No freaking way!" Sasha leapt up, waving an apology to the owner, who had looked up from the register, startled by the outburst. "I told you," she whispered, trying to rein in her excitement as she sat back down. "I mean, who could resist that face?" She grinned across the table at Thalia. "My sis gonna be on TV, she gonna be famous," she chanted in a sing-song voice, leaning back and forth in her chair.

Thalia smiled briefly at her sibling's antics, before a frown crossed her face. "Maybe I shouldn't do it," she said, apprehension creeping into her voice. As Sasha opened her mouth to protest, she continued quickly, "It's so much time away from work! And the clean energy bill we've been working on is supposed to come up in the Senate within the next few months. What if I miss it?"

"Nope," Sasha said, shaking her head. "We're not doing this. We talked about this *ex-ten-sive-ly* before you even applied. And you decided it was for the best. You spent so much time meditating on it. Please don't doubt yourself now," she implored.

Looking into her sister's eyes, Thalia nodded slowly. "You're right," she admitted. "With the social media exposure I'll be able to get—"

"I know, I know," Sasha interrupted. "And hey," she added slyly, "you may even fall in love."

* * *

Two weeks later, Sasha held up a stringy, hot pink bikini, wriggling her eyebrows suggestively at Thalia. "What about this sexy little number?" she said with a giggle. Thalia groaned and rolled her eyes, pretending to be annoyed with her sister, but secretly thankful they had this time together before she flew off to Puerto Engaño. They were spending the afternoon shopping at a few outrageously expensive boutiques in DUMBO, which Thalia had walked by a hundred times but could never justify even setting foot in. Now, however, she needed her fashionista sister's help to revamp her wardrobe in a few short weeks.

A saleswoman in the boutique approached the girls and cleared her throat. "Hello, ladies," she said smoothly. "Is there anything I can help you with today?" A stiff smile was plastered across her face, framed by blonde hair swept into a neat bun at the nape of her neck.

Thalia's senses were immediately on edge. "No, we're fine. Just browsing, thank you," she replied quickly to the woman.

"Sure," the associate replied. "I'll be right over here if you need me." She stepped to a shelf a few feet away and began tidying up the already neatly folded blouses there. Her gaze flickered between the shirts and the sisters.

Thalia and Sasha exchanged a knowing glance, having both experienced this level of distrust from store employees way too often. "C'mon, let's go," Thalia muttered to her sister.

Sasha shrugged, and looked at the saleswoman again. "Let's go," she announced loudly. "It's such a shame we didn't find anything cute enough for you to wear on *Love's a Beach*. It would have been such great exposure for a local New York brand. Guess we'll have to try another store. We need to really stock up your wardrobe for the show!" Sasha had continued with increasing emphasis and volume throughout her little tirade, making sure the salesperson heard them as they walked toward the door. She returned the woman's surprised look with a small shrug and a deceptively innocent grin.

As they exited onto the busy street, the chic windchimes twinkling on their way out of the store, Sasha burst out laughing. Even in her embarrassment, Thalia had to admit it was pretty funny.

"That was a real *Pretty Woman* move in there," Thalia said, elbowing Sasha in the ribs.

"Hey," Sasha replied defensively. "She started it. She clearly didn't think we had any money to spend there, *and* she was watching us like a hawk. Like I would have stolen her tacky pink bikini anyways," she said, pretending to gag. "I just wanted to let her know she made a big mistake. HUGE!" she giggled.

"I appreciate you speaking up," Thalia said, letting the playfulness of the moment fade as they strolled down Front Street toward the nearest subway station. "That's something Mom would have done, you know?" she said, her throat catching.

"One hundred percent," Sasha agreed. Silence hung heavy between the sisters.

"It's okay to miss them," Thalia prompted her sister gently. While Thalia had spent lots of time in therapy and had become comfortable talking about their parents in the five years since they passed, Sasha had never been good with emotion. Instead, she deflected with her humor and big personality.

Tonight was no different as Sasha nodded curtly then changed the subject. "So anyways, have you told Veronica yet? If homegirl fires you, I'm not giving you a spot on my couch—unless you make me your vegan brownies every night," she teased.

Thalia winced at the mention of her boss. "No," she admitted. "I've been putting it off as long as possible. But I think I need to talk to her tomorrow. This week we'll be starting our social media campaign planning for next quarter, so there's no way I can avoid it any longer. Plus, the producer said the cast bios will be released next week."

"What do you think Veronica will say?" Sasha asked.

Thalia paused to consider. "I'm honestly not sure. I really hope she'll get it and see the big picture. But at the same time, she is an old school activist. So, all this social media stuff is really foreign to her."

"Which is why she needs a brilliant outreach strategist like you to remain a part of her team," Sasha countered.

"True," Thalia agreed, grateful for her sister's incessant optimism. "So, let's see. Two months is a long time to be totally out of pocket, but I think I have some solid ideas for a coverage plan."

"You got this, sis," Sasha said as they reached the entrance to the subway station. She extended her arms, wrapping Thalia in a quick but fierce hug. "Love you. Text me how it goes with Veronica!" Sasha blew her a quick kiss and bounded down the stairs, racing to catch the train they could hear approaching the station.

Thalia began her walk home, pausing on the corner to enjoy the warm spring evening and the bustle of the first outdoor diners of the season lining the sidewalks. She caught sight of a woman about her age having dinner with a middle-aged couple who appeared to be her parents. As the father leaned over to kiss the young woman's forehead, Thalia's throat swelled with emotion and she had to look away. With each step toward her apartment she repeated a mantra to reassure herself ahead of her conversation with her boss tomorrow. *I'm going to make them proud. I'm going to make them proud.*

* * *

When her alarm clock buzzed the next morning, Thalia jumped out of bed and dove into sun salutation, to put herself in the right headspace for the difficult conversation she would have with Veronica today. After a quick shower, she pulled on her favorite work dress, made her daily green smoothie, and began her commute to work.

Thalia loved the vibrancy and energy of New York City. Her neighborhood in Brooklyn had a strong community feel, perfect for lazy Sundays picking out fruits from the farmers market and grabbing a glass of merlot with friends at the cozy little wine bar around the corner from her apartment. But she also enjoyed working in Manhattan, riding along with the buzz like a bee floating together with its swarm, gathering energy from its hive mates.

To ease her nerves about talking to Veronica, Thalia tried to distract herself with some work on the subway. She pulled out her iPad to review her notes on GlobeAction's upcoming social media campaign in which they planned to call out the CEOs of some of the largest carbon emitters. Steven Perkins of

Conch Oil, Rachel Chu of Midwest Airlines, and Bill McKenna of Agracon were all on the top of their list.

Engrossed in her project plan, Thalia suddenly felt the uneasy sensation of someone's gaze on her. She lifted her head to glance around the train, shifting her flowery dress down over her knees. She was surprised to catch the eye, not of a leering man—which happened too frequently on the subway—but of a woman a few years younger than her. Having been caught staring, the stranger blushed furiously, her face matching her frilly pink spring jacket.

"Hey," the woman said with a tiny, awkward wave. "Sorry if this is weird, but I think I saw you on Reality Pete's Insta this morning? Like in the *Love's a Beach* cast bios? He posted them this morning?"

Unsure how to respond to this litany of question-statements, Thalia froze. How had the bios already been released? She thought she had more time. And what if Veronica had seen them before Thalia had a chance to talk to her today?

Pushing her boss out of her mind for a moment, she tried to focus on the newfound adoring fan in front of her. *This is part of the process,* she chanted to herself.

"Yes," Thalia said, pulling on a warm smile. "I leave for filming in a couple of weeks."

"OMG," the girl squealed, attracting a few glances from their fellow commuters. "That's super cool. Makes sense, because you're, like, gorgeous. I hope you find love!"

"Thanks, I hope so too," Thalia replied, touched by the stranger's well wishes.

"Can we take a selfie?"

Thalia nodded, smoothing her hair and saying a silent thanks that she had worn a cute outfit today. As the girl pulled out her phone and positioned herself next to Thalia, she noticed a few other passengers surreptitiously taking photos as well. Even if they didn't know who she was, they seemed to assume she was someone famous, given the selfie request.

The girl snapped a few photos, then looked up. "This is my stop. Thank you so much!"

"No problem!" Thalia replied, trying to match her enthusiasm, and waving as her fan stepped off the train. Once the girl had left, Thalia exhaled the breath she didn't realize she had been holding. Being recognized in public was going to take some getting used to, but she couldn't afford not to be gracious to fans.

As the train approached her office, Thalia weighed her chances of whether Veronica would have found out yet. While it was highly unlikely that her boss would have been cruising Reality Pete's Instagram account or the *#LovesaBeach* hashtag on Twitter, there were definitely other people in her office who watched the show.

In fact, listening to her coworkers Rebecca and Patrick bicker about last season's finale was what had inspired her to apply for the show. "No way, he's totally wrong for her!" Rebecca had declared one day as they walked to their favorite salad place for lunch. "He's such a douche canoe," she added, rolling her eyes.

"Yes," Patrick agreed, "but he's by far the hottest dude on the beach. Who can blame her? And anyways, people still love her. She got a hundred thousand new followers last week alone!"

Until that point, Thalia had been tuning them out, having never watched the show. "One hundred thousand?" she'd asked Patrick in disbelief. She had been working her butt off for the last few months, making painstaking decisions on how to spend the nonprofit's very limited advertising budget, and their social media had barely cracked seven thousand followers.

"Yup," Patrick had said with a smirk. "She'll be raking it in with those skincare partnerships soon. Meanwhile, we're here making the big bucks at GlobeAction."

Now, thinking back to that conversation, Thalia realized that either Patrick or Rebecca almost certainly would have seen Reality Pete's leaked cast bios this morning. She just prayed that neither of them would mention it to Veronica before she had a chance to grab her.

As she dashed up the subway stairs, Thalia did a final mental rehearsal of what she wanted to say to her manager. She was still muttering to herself as she entered the foundation's sustainably designed building, the artwork in the lobby showcasing the locations of each of their partner organizations, from Cairo to Rio de Janeiro to Singapore. As the elevator reached her floor and the doors swung open, she immediately saw a small crowd gathered around Rebecca's desk.

"No, no, no," Thalia groaned, striding across the room.

Patrick swiveled around to look at her as she approached the group. "Is this for real?" he asked, his eyebrows arching in surprise. "I didn't even know you liked the show!"

"Yes, it's real," Thalia replied quickly. "And I would really appreciate it if you could all keep your voices down," she whispered. "The cast announcement wasn't supposed to happen until next week, and I haven't had a chance to talk to Veronica."

"Talk to me about what?" Veronica's rich voice rang out behind them.

Thalia spun on her heels, cursing her coworkers and their stupid obsession with this show.

Before she could respond, Rebecca crowed from behind her, "Ooh, look at this guy, he's super hot! Andrew, age twenty-eight, from LA. You've *got* to hit him up night one of filming, Thals."

Veronica's face remained unreadable. "Filming what, exactly?"

"Well," Thalia began, everything she had rehearsed sloshing around in her mind and slipping over the edges, like when she tried to hold a coffee cup level on the F train. "I have an opportunity that I wanted to speak to you about. That will umm…require some time away from work. To film a show called *Love's a Beach*."

The fine lines on her boss's bronzed forehead etched into deep creases as she furrowed her brow. Her tendency to show her emotions and speak freely was one of the things Thalia admired most about her, though today she found herself wishing that, for once, Veronica would go easy on her.

"My office. Now." Veronica spun and began walking, without waiting for Thalia's response.

As soon as they entered the cozy office, the walls covered with books and art from various indigenous groups across Latin America, Thalia jumped in,

"Veronica, I'm sorry I didn't tell you. I didn't want you to find out this way, but the cast bios weren't supposed to be out until later—"

The older woman held up a hand. "My feelings aren't hurt, Thalia. There's no need to explain." She paused, her deep brown eyes staring intently into Thalia's, studying her. "I just want to understand why you're doing this. A reality show? It seems very…out of character for you."

Despite the many scenarios Thalia had imagined and rehearsed, Veronica's concern for her emotional well-being had not been among them. She was caught off guard, unsure of how to respond, then kicked herself for not planning for this question. Veronica was an amazing manager and invested a lot into the entire team. Of course, she cared about why Thalia wanted to go on the show.

She began slowly, giving herself time to collect her thoughts as she went along. "I can see why it seems odd. I guess the best way to explain it is that it's not necessarily something I want to do, but it's something I feel that I have to do."

Shaking her head, Veronica replied, "I don't understand. You have to do it to find love? I don't think that's true. And what about the clean energy bill? You've worked so unbelievably hard to get this into the Senate, and your outreach strategy is going to be crucial to getting it passed. I've been around the block with legislation like this. We are so close to getting the votes we need, and we're in a better position to make a real impact than I've seen in my thirty-year career. This bill could be the last shot we get."

Veronica paused, her expression softening. "I know this bill is personal for you, too. Your parents…" her voice trailed off, as if she were deciding how to approach the topic delicately. "They would be ecstatic to see what we're about to accomplish. They devoted their lives to this work, and I thought you had, too. Do you not care anymore?"

"Of course, I do!" Thalia insisted, the mention of her parents slicing her heart. "I care so much. That's why I need to do this. It's going to help, I promise. I just need you to trust me." She looked up at her manager, her eyes pleading.

After what felt like an eternity of silent consideration, Veronica nodded.

"Okay. I trust you."

Touched by Veronica's confidence in her, Thalia's voice caught in her throat. With a deep breath, she said tenaciously, "I won't let you down. I won't let any of you down."

Chapter 7: Thalia - Now

"Here you go, Thals," Ashley said, handing her a mug of tea and perching on the edge of the rattan armchair Thalia was curled into under the shade of the gazebo. "I tried to get you a veggie quesadilla too, but Maria wasn't around."

Pulling her gaze away from the shimmering sea, Thalia looked absently at her roommate. "I'm not hungry. But thanks for the tea."

"Well, you have to eat something."

Thalia didn't respond, letting Ashley rub her shoulder in silence, the murmurs of the other cast members audible nearby. Taking a sip of the scalding chamomile tea, she fixed her eyes back on the ocean, wishing she could drift away into the endless horizon. It would be easier than facing this reality.

"I actually loved him, you know," she said abruptly, as if she'd suddenly recalled the evasive lyrics to a song.

"Oh, I know, sweet pea. We all could see it."

"I didn't…" she trailed off, wondering what she could say to relieve some of the pain gnawing at her chest without revealing too much. She tried to focus, but found her thoughts straying back to the last time she'd looked into Andrew's eyes.

"You didn't what?" Ashley prodded gently. "Take your time."

"I don't know. I didn't…get to say goodbye to him the way I wanted to," she finished in a tiny voice that stuck in her throat like honey.

Ashley nodded wordlessly, her eyes filling upon seeing Thalia's emotion.

"*Perdón*, are you Thalia?" Both girls glanced up at the melodic voice that had interrupted the tender moment to find Chief Martinez standing before them.

"Yes, that's me," Thalia replied, wiping her eyes and extending her hand to the police officer, who embraced it in firm grasp. Chief Martinez placed her other hand gently on Thalia's arm.

"I'm very sorry for your loss."

"Thank you, Chief Martinez."

"Daniela, please," she said with a kind smile. "Thalia, could we go and speak somewhere a bit more private? I'd like to hear a little more about your last evening with Andrew."

"Of course," Thalia replied, nerves fluttering in her stomach. "Whatever I can do to help."

As the officer guided her down the path away from the gazebo, Thalia felt the rest of the cast watching her. She glanced at Christina, who was standing a bit away from the group and staring at her as she left with Chief Martinez.

After walking in silence for a few minutes, they reached the girls' villa. "Shall we sit here on the front porch?" Chief Martinez asked, motioning to the two rugged white-washed chairs on the deck. Thalia nodded and sat down, nervous about the questions the chief would have.

As if reading her mind, Chief Martinez leaned forward in her chair. "Now, Thalia, I don't want you to feel anxious. I'm here to understand more about what Andrew was doing last night, and what you have learned about him since you two met."

Taking another breath, Thalia slowly released it. "Okay."

"Let's start with what happened yesterday," Chief Martinez began, poised on her chair with a small notebook in hand. "Can you walk me through the day, right up through when you last saw him?"

Thalia let her mind drift back to yesterday morning. Even though her day had started much like every other day since arriving at Paraiso Maya—waking up early, doing her meditation by the ocean, then coffee and journaling—it felt like a lifetime ago given everything that had happened in the last twenty-four hours.

Twenty-four hours ago, he was alive. She could almost feel the touch of his hand on the smooth skin of her thigh, smell the sharp scent of his aftershave as he leaned in toward her, see his bright green eyes telegraphing a secret to her from across the pool, as if they were in their own little world and not surrounded by castmates and cameras. It seemed impossible that in such a short time, hardly a moment really, all of those million things that made up Andrew could be wiped away.

"Thalia?" Chief Martinez prodded, interrupting her recollection.

"Yes, sorry," Thalia responded, blinking as she refocused. "I woke up and did my meditation. I'm usually the first one awake, so I always have the beach to myself. It's where I go to ground myself, in the midst of all this." She gestured around.

The chief's eyes were sympathetic. "Did you find it overwhelming being here? I can imagine it wouldn't be easy having your life on display all of the time."

With a slight frown, Thalia considered her question. "I mean, I guess the lack of privacy is a bit annoying, but it was worth it. Being here with…him." She couldn't bring herself to bring Andrew's name to her lips, as if his death were a secret and once she said his name, it would become real.

"I understand," Chief Martinez said. "It must be very difficult for you, losing him."

Her throat constricting, Thalia nodded.

"Now, this may not be easy, but can you tell me a little more about your last time seeing him? How were things when you said good night?"

Hesitating, Thalia thought back to last night, fragments of the final conversation she'd had with Andrew ricocheting around in her head. *I want what's best for you, Thals.* She cleared her throat, then looked up into the chief's hazel eyes, her thick lashes still as she held Thalia's gaze.

"We had a few drinks by the pool, then went to one of the cabanas. We were talking and hanging out there for a while, then we wanted a little more privacy."

There was no point in hiding this next part, as the cameras would give them away anyways. Thalia shifted in her seat, fingering the fringe on her swimsuit coverup. The pretty white lace seemed absurd to be wearing now, given the dark events of the day. "There's a spot behind the kitchen where there are no cameras," Thalia admitted. "Nick—another cast member—discovered it, and he told Andrew about it. We went there sometimes so we could have some alone time." She paused, watching Chief Martinez's face, letting her make the assumption that they'd gone there to hook up. If the chief was scandalized by this thought, she didn't show it.

"As you said, it's not easy having your life on camera twenty-four-seven," Thalia added with a miserable, half-hearted attempt at a smile.

"Okay," Chief Martinez said, nodding. "Then, after this little lover's tryst, what happened next?"

"He walked me back to the girls' villa, kissed me good night on the porch, then headed toward the guys' villa." She paused, her lips parting as she remembered that final kiss, Andrew's lips gently brushing hers, and his fingers grazing her hips, before he whispered in her ear, *I'm going to miss you.*

The chief paused, then arranged her features into a gentle expression, as if she wanted to challenge this story without upsetting Thalia. "And are you sure he was heading to the boys' villa?"

"I mean…I don't know for sure, but he seemed tired. We were both ready to call it a night."

Chief Martinez nodded slowly, acknowledging Thalia's feedback while still preparing to press forward with her questions. "I see. But it does seem that all of the evidence indicates a drug overdose. So, perhaps he wasn't actually heading to bed. Perhaps he wanted to have a little more fun?" She waited, studying Thalia for her reaction. "Or perhaps he was feeling stressed and needed to blow off some steam?"

"No," Thalia insisted, her eyes narrowing in annoyance at the questions, which were driving in an uncomfortable direction. "Andrew didn't do drugs. And he seemed normal when we said good night. He seemed happy. He actually…" she trailed off, not wanting to share her intimate moments with this stranger, yet not sure how else to convince the chief of her side of the story. Finally she admitted, "He actually told me that he loved me."

Thalia's eyes welled with tears at the injustice of such a new love being ripped away from her so soon after it had blossomed.

As if she could sense Thalia's distress, Chief Martinez leaned back in her chair, signaling she was finished with her questions. "Thank you, Thalia," she said. "I know it can be painful to think about this. But I promise you I will find out what happened to Andrew, so that you can have some closure."

"Thank you," Thalia replied, her voice barely a whisper as she picked at the hem of her shorts.

The detective's gaze followed her hands down her leg, finally resting on the nasty scrape on her knee. Thalia sensed the slightest shift in her kind energy from a moment ago, as Chief Martinez asked with seemingly forced concern, "That looks like a bad injury. How did it happen?"

Thalia glanced down at the cut, then back up to meet the detective's probing eyes.

"I fell on the rocks at the beach when I heard the commotion this morning. I go down there every morning to meditate," she replied, fighting to keep a defensive tone from creeping into her voice.

"I see," Chief Martinez replied, and Thalia could sense a moment's hesitation, as if she were debating asking a follow-up question, but decided against it. Silence hung between them.

Thalia cleared her throat, then asked, "Do you need me back down at the gazebo? Otherwise, I'd really like to stay here and have some time to myself."

The chief shrugged and shook her head as she answered, "No, that's fine by me. The girls' villa has been cleared. Please take care of yourself." She rose to leave, pulling a small white business card out of her wallet. "And if you think of anything else that may be helpful, please reach out to me. Sometimes people repress memories that are too painful to process at the time, and things bubble to the surface later." With a final nod, Chief Martinez strode back in the direction of the gazebo.

Turning over the card in her hand, Thalia read *Daniela Rosa Castillo Martinez - Jefe de Policía, Estado de Oaxaca,* followed by the chief's email address and phone number.

The contact details served as a painful reminder to Thalia that she hadn't had access to her phone since the start of filming last month. She wondered if the show would make an exception and allow them to use their phones now, or at least once the news of Andrew's death had broken publicly. Even a few minutes of speaking with her sister would make Thalia feel so much better. It was hard to believe that Sasha, whom she told about every minute detail of her life back in Brooklyn—every awful Tinder date, every little triumph at work, every new snack she'd picked up at Trader Joe's—didn't know a single thing about Andrew. Sasha was in the real world where time continued marching on, while Thalia was frozen in a parallel universe, in which the entire beginning, middle, and end to her and Andrew's love story had collapsed into one sliver of existence.

Chapter 8: Blake - 2 Months Ago

Blake lifted his glass, clinking it against Cliff's. "To the best lawyer in LA," he announced, with a mock bow. After waiting for nearly a month, they'd finally received the news last week that Blake's DUI and drug possession charges had officially been dropped. As a thank-you, he was treating Cliff to a steak dinner and the most expensive bottle of red on the menu. "Seriously, man, I cannot thank you enough. You literally saved my life."

Cliff raised his glass again to Blake, and said, "Hey, what are friends for?" He took a long swig of wine. "It sucks about your guy, José, but hey you gotta look out for numero uno, right?"

Blake had to cheers to that. He hadn't seen any news about his dealer being picked up, and also hadn't heard anything from the man himself. In his ideal world, LAPD wouldn't have enough to charge José, but even if they did, Blake couldn't waste time feeling guilty. He had to get on with his life.

In the middle of another generous sip, Cliff raised his eyebrows as if suddenly remembering something. "Hey, I never asked you—how did you manage to keep it out of the press? Isn't that blogger Reality Pete always up your ass?"

Setting down his long-stemmed glass and picking up his brutally sharp steak knife, Blake let out a smug chuckle. "Oh, that part was easy. I gave Pete some tips on the cast for this season in exchange for him not running anything about me. I leaked the cast bios, and gave him the inside scoop on a little problem one of the girls has." Blake mimed sticking his finger down his throat, referencing the cast member's eating disorder.

"Oh man, that's cruel," Cliff groaned.

"Nah," Blake replied, shrugging as he cut into his T-bone, cooked to rare perfection and oozing juices as his knife sliced through it. "He always finds this stuff out anyways." He placed the first bite of beef into his mouth, savoring the tender meat and perfect flavor. This place was worth every one of the many pennies their steaks cost. "Plus," he added after a scrumptious swallow, "this way I can potentially use that storyline in my editing."

"You may be an asshole, but you are definitely good at what you do," Cliff acknowledged, taking another sip. "I still can't believe you didn't get that promotion."

"Thanks, man. I can't either, it was honestly a huge shock. I think it's pretty clear they had a bigger agenda with that hire, but whatever."

"How is the new boss?"

Blake rolled his eyes. "She's fine, just a little intense. Thinks she's saving the world by having a few non-white cast members."

Over the last few weeks, he had been following Tom's advice and lying low, quietly going along with Ava's ideas. It was clear from her first all-hands meeting with the production team and crew that she intended to shake up their usual approach to the show. Even though she never explicitly said she disapproved of the job Blake had been doing as showrunner, her tone always bordered on condescending when she asked him about the old way of doing things. Nevertheless, Blake did his best to smile and nod at every pep talk and new idea that bubbled up out of Ava's mouth. He actually did like some of what she had to say, and he was sure to demonstrate this enthusiasm in the office, though he would never admit it to Cliff or Tom or any of his buddies.

"Anyways," Blake continued, bringing his attention back to his dinner partner, "Tom set up drinks with one of the execs at Paracon for me next week, so I'm sure a better role will come up there."

Cliff looked surprised. "You're really going to make a move from CBC? You've been with the network forever."

"I know," Blake said with a pained look. "I don't want to leave, but this was a slap in the face. They obviously don't value my talent. So, I've got to take it somewhere else."

"Fair enough," Cliff replied.

The two men chatted as they finished their meal, enjoying the atmosphere of the steakhouse—trendy lighting, well-dressed clientele, and impeccable service. Blake listened with great interest as Cliff updated him on an old college friend's business venture, then significantly less so as the conversation turned to Cliff's kids.

As they finished up the bottle of wine, Blake asked, "Can I tempt you with a nightcap at Terrace65?"

Cliff shook his head. "No, I can't tonight."

"Aww c'mon…for old times' sake?"

"No can do. Told Vanessa I'd be home by ten o'clock. You know, some of us have women we've settled down with."

Blake rolled his eyes in jest. "Oh Cliff, why settle down when I can text any one of ten beautiful ladies to come meet me tonight?"

At this, Cliff laughed out loud. "Dude, aren't you the producer of a show about falling in love and happily ever after?"

"Those who can't do, teach," Blake answered with a grin.

* * *

Walking through the door at Terrace65, Blake nodded to the bouncer, bumping fists with him before he climbed the stairs to the rooftop bar with its incredible view of the city. The sparkling skyline was lit up to the east, and the gaping expanse of the ocean sprawled to the west. He spent the next few hours there, chatting with some other guys in the industry who frequented the bar. A generous tipper, Blake always had a full glass of top shelf liquor. As he was cracking a joke with his favorite bartender, he glanced down at his phone and saw a text from Bianca, a twenty-three-year-old spin instructor and one of Blake's latest conquests.

Hey, just finished teaching my last class, let's skip Terrace65 and meet at yours? I could use a shower…and some company in the shower ;)

Looking up at the bartender with a sly grin and a wink, he said, "Well, my friend, duty calls."

"Again? Dude, you've got to teach me your ways. Or, better yet, have your girls bring some friends around here for me!"

Blake laughed. "I'll see what I can do." He slid another twenty-dollar bill across the bar and gave a mock salute. "Thanks, my man. Until next time."

As he walked out of the bar, he ordered an Uber. While he missed having all eyes on him when he pulled up in his Ferrari, the last thing he needed right now was another DUI. He wasn't taking any chances after his brush with the law—at least for a little while. After a few months when things settled down, he'd start driving again, but would be a little more careful.

While he waited for his driver to arrive, he switched over to the messaging app Bianca loved to use. He was getting too old for these apps, but she made it worth his while.

As usual he was not disappointed. He was greeted by a photo of Bianca in the locker room at her gym, her designer sports bra pulled halfway up over her round breasts, with the caption *ready for that shower* emblazoned across her taut stomach. Blake's breath quickened in anticipation of this evening's rendezvous. Where was his driver? He wanted to get the night started ASAP.

As he switched back to the Uber app to check how far away the car was, he felt a sudden presence behind him, and a large hand grabbed his shoulder. Another hand swiped through the air, snatching his phone away. Panic flooded through Blake's body, wiping out the pleasurable anticipation that had been there a moment before.

Shit, I'm being robbed, he thought.

"Hey," he said, attempting to raise his hands in surrender, while keeping his eyes cast down toward the sidewalk. "You can have my phone. And my wallet too." He only had a couple hundred dollars in there, it wasn't worth fighting for. He had a meeting with the marketing department tomorrow, and he didn't want to show up with his face roughed up. Knowing his luck, Ava would probably insert herself in that meeting, too.

The hands pushed him away from Terrace65's bright lights and upbeat music, and into the shadows of the alley next to it. His heart racing, the buzz of the wine and whiskey gone as if the alcohol had evaporated from his bloodstream, Blake stumbled into the narrow passageway. The scent of piss and rotting food flooded his nostrils.

"Look, guys, take everything. I don't want any trouble."

"Oh, we already have some trouble, *Blake*."

At the sound of his name, the producer's head snapped up, his gaze swinging wildly as he willed his eyes to focus in the dim lighting petering from the bulb above the garbage bins. The image finally became clear, and he stared at the two men before him. They both appeared to be Latino, one of average height and the other very tall, his chin hovering at Blake's eye level as he glared down at him. Both of them wore baseball caps, and tattoos lined their bulky arms. Blake was sure he'd never seen these men before in his life.

How the fuck do these guys know my name, he thought desperately, racking his memories for any link to the men, but coming up blank.

"Who are you?" he demanded, trying his best to project confidence and mask the fear and confusion swirling in his head.

The shorter man guffawed, turning to his partner and joking in a thick Mexican accent, "Yo, P, he wants to know who we are. Apparently, this guy is fancy, needs a formal introduction."

His tall attacker didn't return the laughter, his piercing gaze fixed unblinkingly on Blake. "We're friends of José's."

At the mention of the dealer's name, Blake's stomach dropped. *Fuck fuck fuck,* he swore silently. *Are these guys going to kill me for ratting out their friend? Am I really going to die right behind this fucking bar?*

When the producer didn't respond, the first man jumped back in. "Let's say you fucked up, amigo. You thought José was some low-level dealer? Nah. You thought wrong."

Blake felt his face fall and eyes widen in fear as he realized just how badly he had screwed up.

Clearly getting some enjoyment out of seeing the snitch squirm, the man continued, "José is a big deal in the Rodriguez cartel. One of the big *jefes,* you feel me?"

Now Blake's mouth fell open in complete shock. He was very familiar with the Rodriguez cartel. He'd spend the last month reviewing Christina's security plans for how to safely film the season with the very same cartel ramping up violence in Puerto Engaño.

Attempting to regain some composure, Blake began, "Look, I think there may be some misunderstanding—"

The shorter man cut him off. "Oh there's no misunderstanding. You ratted out José and landed him in jail. You cost us one of our best men, and caused some extra heat from the feds that interrupted a very important delivery last week."

"I'm…really sorry to hear that. And, okay, I'll admit I messed up." He raised his hands in admission of guilt. Seeing he wasn't going to be able to talk his way out of the situation, Blake turned instead to what he knew best. "But I'm sure we can come to some kind of arrangement to figure this out, right? I've got cash. I can get it to you by tomorrow."

"We don't want your money. And neither do our bosses," the tall man spat at him, studying Blake with disdain.

"That's right," the smaller one agreed, nodding along, his greasy hair falling over his eyes. "But there is another *arrangement* we can work out."

"Sure, sure," Blake said, seizing the opening to de-escalate the conversation. "What do you need?"

The shorter guy stared pointedly at him, as if to impress upon him that the request he was about to make was not a request at all, but rather a demand. "We need to move a big shipment this summer. Border Patrol and the DEA have been cracking down on our usual routes. And we're behind on our numbers, thanks to the stunt you pulled turning in José."

Blake listened, not clear on what this had to do with him but afraid that interrupting would further anger the man.

Studying his face, the cartel member continued, "José tells us you're some kind of big shot TV guy, and that you have a private charter plane going to and from Puerto Engaño for your show."

Blake's stomach lurched as he finally understood where the conversation was heading. He couldn't stop himself from jumping in. "The security is going to be super intense. And the plane is going to be full of cast and crew and video equipment."

"No," his aggressor said, his eyes flashing with cruel satisfaction at having cornered Blake. "The plane is going to be full of cocaine. Two hundred kilos of it."

Blake flapped his mouth open and closed, shocked not only at the idea of getting involved with drug smuggling, but also the sheer volume the man was referencing. "There's no way to get that back on the plane. No fucking way."

"Well, you'd better find a way, Blake, because our *jefes* are not happy about this situation. Not happy at all. And the only thing that's gonna make them happy is moving two hundred kilos of product to LA by August. Now," he paused, his eyes toying over Blake's frightened expression, "they could probably find another way to move it. But then they wouldn't have any use for you." His arm shot out, seizing the perfectly pressed collar of Blake's gray button-down. As he pulled Blake's head down into a bow, to come to level with his chin, he whispered in his ear, "And if you're not useful to them, you're a dead man." He shoved Blake's head away from him, then straightened his fitted T-shirt. "*Comprende?*"

There was nothing for Blake to do but nod in silent agreement, as he thought to himself, *please, let this be finished.* He just needed to acquiesce for now so he could get away from these two men and have some time to figure out what he was going to do. He couldn't think clearly with his mind racing like this, the sweat pouring down his back and making his expensive shirt stick to his skin.

Apparently satisfied with Blake's response, the cartel member continued, "Good call, *amigo*. Someone will text you more info. Don't worry," he added with a smug grin, "we've already got your number. And your address. And your friend Tom's address." He paused dramatically, letting the indirect threat sink in. "So, we'll be in touch."

With that, the bigger guy gave Blake one final shove for good measure as the pair turned away and stalked out of the alley.

As they rounded the corner, Blake stumbled over to the brick wall, leaning against the cool, rough surface and willing his heartbeat to return to normal.

The faint pulse of music echoed from the rooftop above, rattling in his head as he wondered how the hell he was going to get himself out of this mess.

63

Chapter 9: Blake - Now

Blake took a deep breath, then opened his laptop. While he waited for it to start up, he peered at the reflection on the dark screen, anxiously smoothing his hair and ensuring his suite looked tidy behind him. In a few short minutes, he'd be speaking with the entire C-suite, the global head of PR, and the executive legal team to update them on the situation at the resort.

He logged into the video conferencing link, and was immediately greeted by the CEO, Robert, and the rest of the CBC team, who were gathered in the large boardroom at their headquarters. The only executive not in the room was Ava. Blake was mildly annoyed she wasn't there in person to manage this, especially since it didn't seem like she was sick. *He* certainly would have been there had he been in her shoes.

Ava's composed, elegantly made-up face appeared in a small box next to his, where the stress and exhaustion—and if he was being honest with himself, the last bit of his hangover—were etched across his usually smooth features. Seeing his face squeezed into that small square, while everyone else sat in the spacious conference room, ready to grill him about this tragedy that happened under his watch, Blake felt as if his ego were squashed into its own tiny box.

If Ava felt the same way in her little square, she certainly didn't show it. "Good afternoon, everyone," she said briskly, commanding immediate attention and quieting the chatter in the boardroom. "Thanks for joining so quickly. I've spoken with many of you individually throughout the day, but I wanted to gather this group so that we can all be one hundred percent on the same page before the press release is issued in two hours. Simone, is it ready to go?"

The global PR head leaned forward, smoothing her flowy blouse before responding. "Yes, we've drafted it up, and Legal and Robert signed off on it right before this meeting. Let me flash it up on the screen for everyone to review." With the click of a button on her tablet, Simone shared her screen.

CBC is incredibly saddened to share that one of our cast members, Andrew McKenna, passed away during the filming of the upcoming season of Love's a Beach. *Our hearts go out to Andrew's friends and family in light of this tragic incident. We will be providing mental health support to the cast and crew who grew to know and love Andrew during the last month on set. We ask that the public respect the privacy of Andrew's loved ones as they begin to grieve and heal.*

Nodding his graying head thoughtfully, the CEO said, "I think it's well-written. Short and sweet, expresses empathy, but it distances the network."

With a curt nod, Simone replied, "Thanks, Robert. It's ready to be pushed out on our website and all the social media accounts."

"Speaking of which," Ava interjected, "have there been any leaks on social media? We already had the cast members' phones, and I asked Christina to take phones away from every crew member except herself and Blake."

Simone frowned slightly, her dark eyebrows drawing together. "Nothing on any of the major gossip accounts. Thank God, Reality Pete hasn't gotten ahold of this. That guy is the bane of my existence," she said, rolling her eyes in distaste. "But there is one strange tweet." Simone tapped her long finger on the tablet again, an enormous engagement ring flashing so brightly under the boardroom lights that even Blake could see it through the video. The tweet popped up on his laptop screen, alongside a default avatar where a profile picture normally would have been:

Algo terrible ha pasado a un miembro del elenco de #lovesabeach! La policía de los EEUU debería investigarlo. – @anonimo9285

"Something terrible has happened to a cast member of *Love's a Beach*. The US police should investigate it," Simone translated.

"Seems like it must be a local, right?" Ava asked quickly. "The use of Spanish, and the reference to the 'US police'? Doesn't seem like they know much about US law enforcement."

"Yes," Simone agreed. "The location of the tweet is listed as Mexico. We can't tell much about the person's identity because the account has no followers, isn't following any other accounts, and has no tweets before today. Even though the account is new, it seems like the person is familiar enough with social media to know what a hashtag is. And they clearly wanted the information to be found, as they've chosen a public venue to post this and used the show's hashtag."

Ava absorbed the information, then redirected her attention. "Blake, any thoughts on who it could be? Maybe one of the paramedics who came this morning? Or a member of the resort staff? Legal said we couldn't take their phones, given the local labor laws."

Caught off guard by the sudden question, Blake paused, then shook his head. "I mean…speaks Spanish, familiar with social media…you just described everyone on staff except the chef, who makes some mean *empanadas* but doesn't know how to use a cell phone, as far as I can tell."

Clearly not satisfied with Blake's response, Ava pressed him. "I thought we were controlling phone usage and holding the staff on site since the incident," she said with a frown. "Have any of the crew seen staff using their phones?"

His annoyance growing, Blake responded, perhaps a bit too sharply, "Well, Ava, the resort is over seventy-five acres, so I don't know that our crew of fifty-seven has been able to watch every square inch."

Ava responded quickly, "What about the security cam—"

"Who cares who wrote it," Robert snapped, interrupting the bickering between his two subordinates. "More importantly, is it gaining any traction?"

Shaking her head, Simone confirmed, "You can see there are only five likes so far and two retweets."

"Who are the likes and retweets?" Ava asked, her composure restored, though her eyes betrayed her lingering frustration with Blake.

Clicking her tablet screen again, Simone pulled up the five accounts. "They all appear to be American, and have recently liked other tweets about the show, including posts from CBC's official accounts. They're probably some superfans who were browsing the hashtag and stumbled across this tweet.

And there are no likes on either of the retweets yet." Simone paused, letting the group absorb this information, then continued on, "I could have Legal draft a cease-and-desist letter asking the person to take the tweet down, but sometimes that backfires. They could post a screenshot of it and then it looks like the network is trying to hide something, which is the surest way to spread the story more quickly. There's nothing the Internet loves more than a good conspiracy theory," she finished with a wry smile.

"I agree. Leave it up," Robert said firmly. "Most of America is too dumb and lazy to translate this to English, especially this show's fanbase. No offense, Blake," he added with a glance toward the camera. Blake raised his hands to show none had been taken. "Right," the CEO continued, looking around the room. "What else do we need to cover in this meeting? I have a hard stop at six p.m. I've got dinner with Oprah to try to close the deal for CBC to air her next interview." He grinned, rubbing his fingers together. "I can see the dollar signs now!"

Ava jumped in, rapidly addressing the remaining items on the agenda. "Simone has the production crew on standby and the green room reserved for a press conference in case things start to go awry after the statement is issued. The local police have begun the investigation, and Christina Park is leading as the police liaison. Last but not least, Blake, you've spoken with Andrew's family, correct?"

"Yes," Blake responded, a knot gathering in his stomach as he recalled the shaky voice of Mrs. McKenna.

I don't understand, she'd said in disbelief. *Andrew? My Andrew?*

As Blake waited in silence, listening to her piercing wail, he thought he'd gotten through the worst of it. He wasn't normally a sentimental person, and he'd certainly witnessed his share of heartbreak on the show over the years, comforting a string of contestants with hugs for the women and claps on the back for the men.

However, he'd seen something of his younger self in Andrew, as well as parallels between their families. Like Mr. McKenna, his own father had been a business executive, kind but stoic. When Blake called the McKennas, Andrew's father had taken the phone from his distraught wife, his tone initially calm. But once he grasped what had happened, Mr. McKenna's deep voice cracked. The man's first sob seared into Blake's chest, hot and sharp, shattering something inside of him.

"And?" Ava prompted, interrupting Blake's recollection. "How was it? Anything we should be aware of? Do they seem keen to push this any further?"

Blake shook his head sadly. "No. They just want to bring his body back as soon as possible. They were in too much shock to express anything else."

"Alright then," Ava replied. "I think that's it. Anything else before we close the meeting?" She waited for the team to bring up any additional points for discussion.

Robert cleared his throat. "I think that's all, Ava. Excellent work managing this regrettable incident. On behalf of the entire board, thank you."

"Just doing my job," Ava said, acknowledging his praise with a curt nod. "Thanks everyone, talk to most of you on tomorrow's checkpoint call."

Before Blake could say goodbye to the group, a notification popped up that the meeting had been ended by the host.

Glancing around the room, he spotted his phone on the nightstand. He stood, his fingertips brushing the chair's smooth leather, and walked to the bedside to check whether it had turned back on after charging for the last few hours. The screen remained stubbornly black.

"Of all the days for my phone to get broken…" he muttered to the quiet room.

Through his frustration, he tried to remember exactly how the screen had cracked, walking through the night's events—or at least what he could recall of them—in his mind. He had started the evening here in his room, after wrapping up a full day of shooting.

Even though it sometimes meant longer hours, he had been leading production for most of the off-site dates and letting Christina or one of the other junior producers hold down the fort back at the resort. He felt cooped up and restless when he was here, despite the hotel's lush, expansive grounds. Off-site dates were the only officially sanctioned way to escape and feel like he could breathe again. It was an odd sensation, as he normally loved the relaxation of the resort—drinking margaritas on his sun-drenched balcony, or having a leisurely morning debrief of the prior day's events over some *huevos rancheros* and coffee.

However, this season was different. After the cartel had contacted him outside of Terrace65, he hadn't been sure what to expect. As promised, he'd received a text message a day or two after the alleyway encounter, from a number he didn't recognize.

Hey man, it read. *Good meeting you the other night. Can't wait to see you in Puerto this summer. I'll come say hi at the resort a week or two after you arrive, so we can talk about when I can bring some of my friends around.*

Blake had tried his best to relax up until the flight to Mexico, reminding himself that if he cooperated, he would be safe. And if they got caught, he had the best defense lawyer in LA. He'd debated telling Cliff about the threats, but he knew that his friend would advise him to go straight to the police. After viewing images of mutilated corpses during their security planning for the season, Blake did not want to take any chances in double crossing the cartel. He liked his chances in court much better.

Despite his attempts to reassure himself, he'd still felt nervous traveling to Puerto Engaño, and as filming began, the lingering anxiety permeated everything he did, sticking to his skin like the salty humidity of the turquoise sea he looked out on every morning. Realizing that the cartel knew exactly where he was at the resort made him feel like a caged animal, so he took every chance he could get to leave.

Even though it was strictly against the security plan approved by the network, he'd been sneaking out to the local bar some evenings when he simply couldn't take the claustrophobia. The dive bar, with its cheap tequila and amateur DJ, was a far cry from his usual LA haunts, but something about the energy of having people around him and hearing their chatter—even in another language—gave him a comforting sense of normalcy, as if he could simply return to his life as it was before any of this nonsense with the DUI and José.

Last night had been one of those nights when he had to get away. He'd been off site filming all day, and Raina had been such a diva. Even though she wasn't his usual type, he had to admit she was absolutely stunning, with huge dark eyes, warm brown skin, and luxurious hair cascading in waves down her back. Despite her good looks, he'd rarely encountered a cast member more demanding, and her whining had been incessant throughout the day.

The sun is in my eyes. I need some fresh water. Eww, you want me to eat this crap?

Blake wasn't sure how her date Jake could put up with her, especially since she hadn't even put out for him yet—or at least that had been captured on camera. A farm boy who had never left the U.S. before coming here to film *Love's a Beach*, the poor guy seemed smitten with Raina's "exotic" features and tantalizing curves.

I guess they don't make them like that in Iowa, he'd teased Jake with a smirk and a light punch to the shoulder.

By the time they'd returned to the resort around 8:30 p.m., nearly an hour and a half behind schedule, Blake was famished and ready to let loose. He had ordered some tamales and margaritas to his room, then set up a neat little line of coke on the teak desk. With the music blaring through the speakers of the widescreen TV in his room, he did a line, and then another, the rhythm beating in his chest and chipping away at the cage around him with each thump of the bass.

At ten p.m., he was riding a high and ready to escape. He'd lumbered over to the resort entrance and given a spirited hello and handshake to Alejandro, the resort's head of security. Blake tucked a crisp bill in his hand, which the gentleman grasped and slid into his pocket with a practiced subtlety.

Mumbling something in Spanish to the guard posted at the front gate, Alejandro beckoned to Blake and strode over to his motorcycle, holding his second helmet out to the producer. As they took off down the road, Blake relished the cool, damp wind against his skin, its salty tang settling onto his shirt. They quickly reached their destination, the dive bar a few minutes down the road.

"*Gracias,*" Blake said as he climbed off the bike.

"*De nada,*" his makeshift chauffeur responded. "You call me?" He mimed as if he were holding a phone up to his ear, and then mimed driving his motorcycle to indicate he would come back to pick Blake up.

"*Sí*," Blake answered with a thumbs up, flashing Alejandro a smile. As he drove away, Blake walked into the bar. The decor made it apparent that it had once been a tourist bar, the tiki torches and colorful mural of drinking monkeys on the wall perfectly suited to spring breakers. Even the name of the bar, Señor Tequila, seemed like they'd picked the two Spanish words that drunk Americans were most likely to discover on Google Maps. However, with the recent cartel violence, tourists were sparse and the bar was now frequented mostly by locals, the overpriced cocktails remaining on the menu but ordered much less frequently than the cheap local beer.

He had greeted the bartender Francisco and the DJ Eduardo, both of whom now knew him well, and immediately ordered a few shots, giving one or two away to a couple of guys he recognized from a few nights before. Unfortunately, his memories shortly after arriving at the bar became hazy, swimming in a fog of tequila and cocaine.

Glancing around his hotel room now, he looked for clues of what had happened last night, beyond his damaged phone. His clothes lay in a crumpled pile on the floor, the fitted jeans and Brooks Brothers polo shirt reeking of liquor, but otherwise nothing unusual about them. Though Señor Tequila wasn't exactly the most fastidious establishment for record-keeping, he thought it might be worth checking his pockets for receipts, but came up empty.

He racked his brain for any memory of the night, but he drew a blank after his third or fourth shot of tequila at the bar. He needed to ask Alejandro whether he'd driven him back to the resort, but the staff member's shift didn't start until seven p.m. Glancing at his useless cracked screen again, Blake resigned himself to joining Christina in the production room, where she was preparing the senior staff members for an all-hands meeting later today.

As he pulled on his shoes, Blake became increasingly agitated with his lack of memory. Thinking back on the events of the last twenty-four hours, he felt a sense of unease creep in, the blank spaces in his mind filling up with worry.

If I don't remember breaking my phone, what else don't I remember from last night?

Chapter 10: Christina - 1.5 Months Ago

Curled up on her plush red velvet couch, surrounded by her quirky vintage travel posters, Christina took a deep breath and opened up her laptop. Since the casting day almost a month and a half ago, she had tried to ignore the pit that had wedged into her stomach when Andrew left the room. However, with only two weeks until filming was planned to start, she was now in regular communication with all the cast, and she couldn't leave the feeling to fester in her gut any longer. She needed to know the truth and prepare herself mentally and emotionally before arriving at Paraiso Maya in a few short days.

Andrew McKenna University of Virginia lacrosse, Christina typed into her incognito browser, her pulse quickening as she hit enter. The first link that popped up was an old roster for the team, in which a small photo of Andrew, ruggedly handsome in a navy and orange jersey, appeared next to the stats from his freshman season. Navigating back to the search page, she clicked on the second result, an article from what appeared to be the UVA student newspaper.

A few games away from finishing out a promising freshman season, attacker Andrew McKenna sustained a broken arm during Saturday's match against Duke. The injury occurred a few minutes before halftime. McKenna was attempting a goal when he collided with Duke senior, Griffin Roberts. He is expected to be out for the remainder of the season.

Skimming through the rest of the article, Christina didn't find anything useful about how Andrew's college and lacrosse career had progressed after the injury. She returned to her browser and this time searched *Andrew*

McKenna Los Angeles. After scrolling through a few photos of other Andrew McKennas who were sadly lacking any of this Andrew's facial features, she finally arrived at the right LinkedIn profile. His green eyes shone through the tiny square picture, and his profile showed he currently worked for a very successful West Coast private equity firm. As she scrolled down through his work history and to his education information, above the one-year stint at UVA, she saw what she was hoping and yet fearing:

University of California Los Angeles, 2011-2014, Bachelor's in Finance.

He had been at UCLA the same time as her. She let out a deep whoosh of breath, pausing and closing her eyes for a moment before scrolling down further. Beneath the UVA and UCLA logos, her eyes blurred as she saw the Beta Phi Theta fraternity logo, its bright red letters burning through her tears.

"After all these years," Christina whispered to herself.

Hearing her voice, her dog, Rosie, trotted around the corner, ears perked up in curiosity. "Here, girl," Christina called to her, patting a spot on the sofa. She could certainly use the cuddle right now. In fact, she had rescued Rosie almost five years ago to help manage her nighttime panic attacks.

"I want to meet the calmest, sweetest dog you have," Christina had announced when she entered the shelter. "Literally could not care what they look like, what breed, or anything else. If they'll snuggle with me all night, they're mine."

A few minutes later, one of the volunteers had reemerged with Rosie, her mangy sand-colored fur sticking out in all directions, one eye slightly larger than the other as she studied Christina suspiciously.

"She's a little skittish with strangers," the man had said. "But once she warms up to you, she loves nothing more than to cuddle."

"Same here," Christina had said, feeling something inside of her ease away as she scratched Rosie's lopsided ears.

Now the dog bounded onto the couch, eager to take Christina up on her invitation. After some gentle licks to her owner's face, Rosie curled up next to her with a small sigh, her little body radiating warmth against Christina's leg.

"Good girl," she said, her voice tight as she stroked the small, fluffy head splayed across her lap. The two sat in silence for a few minutes as Christina stewed over her new knowledge about Andrew, trying to focus on Rosie's even breaths in and out.

Suddenly, her Apple watch buzzed, and a notification popped up, reminding her she needed to leave for her group meeting. Honestly, a meeting had probably never been better timed in the history of therapy.

Gently kissing the dog's head and easing it off her lap, Christina stood and began gathering her things into a worn tote from her favorite neighborhood bookstore. "Bye, Ro," she called, blowing an air kiss to the dog as she stepped out of her apartment, locking the door behind her.

Recently, Christina had been listening to her Spanish language learning podcast while driving, but as she started up her car, she searched for something she could zone out to until she arrived at the church where her meetings were held. She clicked on a recent indie playlist her friend had shared.

By some small LA miracle, the traffic was minimal and she arrived a few minutes early. Walking into the recreation hall, she saw Linette, a kind-faced woman with gray speckles in her short, dark hair, finishing setting up the chairs into a circle.

"Hey, Linette," Christina called as she passed through the doorway.

The therapist looked up at her. "Hi, Christina," she said warmly. "Lovely to see you today. How are you doing?"

Christina paused, considering how to answer that question without getting into too much detail before the session officially began.

"Uhh...I've been better," she answered truthfully, forcing a small, strained smile.

Linette's face clouded over with concern as she placed the last chair down and walked over toward Christina. "Tough week?"

"You could say that," Christina replied, her voice dropping to nearly a whisper as she tried to keep it from breaking.

"Oh, it's alright, my darling girl," Linette said soothingly. "Would you like a hug?"

Christina nodded, unable to speak. She felt a tear finally break free and trail down her face as the woman's wiry arms enveloped her.

Growing up with strict Korean parents, there had been so much Christina hadn't been able to share with them throughout her life, but particularly during the last five years. Linette, with her patient voice and gentle eyes that did not judge, had in many ways filled in spaces Christina wished her mother could have.

"Shall we let you share first today?" the therapist asked gently, as a few other women started to file in.

"Yes, please," Christina said, wiping her tears.

To take a moment to compose herself, Christina wandered over to the small folding table with its cheery floral plastic tablecloth and coffee pot, and busied herself with pouring a small cup. Dabbing her eyes with a napkin from the table, she took a deep breath and turned back toward the metal folding chairs organized into a circle, where most of the group had begun to settle. She took an empty seat, greeting the person next to her, a pretty middle-aged woman who rarely spoke but always listened intently to others.

"Alright, let's get started," Linette announced, her voice surprisingly commanding coming from her tiny frame. "It's so good to see all of you today. How is everyone doing?" she asked, glancing around the circle and smiling encouragingly at the nods and mutters she received in return. "Well, I see we've got no new faces today, so let's jump right into things. Christina has asked if she can share first today, so I'll pass the floor to her."

"Thank you, Linette," Christina replied. She paused, trying to muster up her courage. Her fingers traced over the charm bracelet Linette had given her years ago when she first came to the group. The tiny gold anchor was meant to be a reminder that she, like all survivors, was stronger than she felt.

With a shaky breath, she began speaking, turning off her conscious thoughts and letting the words tumble out as she had trained her brain to do over the last few years. "Hi, everyone, I'm Christina. Some of you have heard my story before, but I'll share it again for those of you who haven't. Five years ago I was a senior at UCLA. My friend and I got invited to a party at a frat, and I didn't really want to go because it wasn't exactly my scene, but my friend was really into this one guy in the frat, so she begged me to come along. When we arrived, they immediately gave us some kind of punch, and things got pretty hazy pretty quickly. For a long time, I blamed what happened on myself for drinking too much, but with the help of this group I've finally come to believe that it's *not* my fault. Those guys probably spiked the punch, and even if I did get blackout drunk of my own volition, it's still not my fault."

Christina let her words resonate with the group, gathering strength from the emphatic nods of agreement before she continued. "So, I remember my friend and I were talking to some guys in the living room, then it all is kind of…in and out from there. I do have a couple of pretty distinct flashes of memories. I remember being on my back, I think on a bed, and feeling this pair of gross, sweaty hands on my stomach and my boobs. That actually woke me up and I started trying to curl up in a ball. I just wanted to get my skin away from those clammy hands. But when I tried to put my arms up to block my chest, the hands grabbed my wrists and…"

Christina trailed off. Remembering the feeling of powerlessness was always the most horrifying part of the story for her, no matter how many times she told it. With an involuntary shudder, she steeled herself and continued, "Then the hands pinned down my wrists. I couldn't move. I must have passed back out or blacked part of the assault out, because the next thing I remember was waking up on my sofa."

"I went to the campus crisis center the next day, and was examined by a doctor there. I had bruises on my wrists, and vaginal injuries consistent with…" Christina swallowed. It was still hard to name what had happened to her. "…forced intercourse," she finished instead. "They did a swab, but there was no DNA, so the guy probably used a condom. Since I couldn't remember the name or even anything about what the guy looked like, campus police said there was nothing they could do." Christina paused, still fuming with the injustice of her rapist going unpunished.

"My life fell apart after that. I started having panic attacks and nightmares. I'd wake my roommate up with my crying and screaming. I stopped going to classes, and only managed to graduate because I had a dean who was very understanding. She had survived fifteen years as a woman in the film industry, and had seen some awful things. She let me graduate even though I completely missed finals. I was too depressed to show up."

Christina stopped for a moment, seeing her pain reflected in the eyes of the survivors around her who had also had their lives shattered by someone else's casual cruelty.

"The one saving grace was that I had already done an internship the summer before my senior year, and I had a job offer lined up. Otherwise, I don't know how I would have functioned going through the interview process that spring. I don't know what would have happened to me. Because of that, I had a few months before starting work and I began to get my life back together. The campus counseling center referred me to this group, which has been amazing. It took a while, but I finally forgave my friend for bringing me to the party. I had a lot of anger and misplaced blame toward her for years afterwards, but I reached out a couple years ago and made peace with her."

"Most importantly, I forgave myself, and stopped thinking, 'Oh a good student wouldn't have gone to that party, a good Korean daughter wouldn't have associated with those kinds of people, a promising young filmmaker wouldn't have put herself in that situation.' Because I didn't do anything wrong. The only person who did something wrong, and the only person I haven't forgiven, is that asshole who raped me." Christina spat out the next words, the venom coursing through her veins and escaping through her tongue. "He's a fucking rapist."

"And you know," she continued, the emotions running hot through her voice, "the thing that has pissed me off the most all these years is that this person has had such a profound impact on the course of my life. And despite him having so much control over me, I couldn't remember a single thing about him. The only detail that I can remember is that he was wearing this particular cologne. Kind of cedar mixed with oranges. I swear to God, every time I caught a whiff of citrus for a year after my assault, I completely froze. So yeah, this man basically ruined my entire life, and I knew nothing about him."

Christina bit back her emotions and swallowed her fear of speaking out loud what she now knew. "Until recently. I just found out who my rapist is. His name is Andrew, and now that I know, I can't stop thinking of ways to make him pay for what he did to me."

Chapter 11: Thalia - 1 Month Ago

It was the first night of filming, and Thalia was a bundle of nerves. With a final look in the mirror, she smoothed the front of her dress, then ran her hands down along the red satin fabric hugging her curvaceous hips. Sasha had forced her to buy this ensemble, clapping dramatically when she had walked out of the dressing room.

"Yasss girl! You look like frickin' Beyonce!" Sasha had proclaimed.

Thalia had balked at the price tag—working at an NGO wasn't the most lucrative career—but her sister had insisted it would be a worthwhile investment.

"You *must* wear that night one. The guys will love you. America will love you. You'll be an instant meme!"

Thalia had carefully done her makeup, in a much more exaggerated style than her usual lip gloss and mascara. While she didn't exactly feel like herself, she had to admit she did look fantastic. She found herself wishing the producers hadn't taken their phones before arriving at the resort, so she could send a selfie to Sasha, but then quickly remembered her sister would soon be seeing her outfit on TV, along with the rest of the world. No pressure.

Her thoughts were interrupted as her roommate, Ashley, poked her head out of the bathroom door, her long blonde hair coated in so much hairspray that it didn't move as she leaned to the side. "I think I'm going to be sick, I'm so nervous."

"Don't be nervous," Thalia said, grateful for the distraction from her own anxiety. "This is going to be fun!"

"I guess that depends on your definition of fun," Ashley replied with a sarcastic eyebrow raise. "If there's more of that rosé they had on the plane, then, hell yes, it'll be fun."

CBC had flown all of the contestants to LA, then arranged two separate flights for the charter plane—one with the males, and one with the females. The idea was to keep the suspense as long as possible, and capture their initial reactions to their potential soulmates on camera, even though they had all seen the photos and cast bios in advance.

When the women had arrived at Paraiso Maya earlier that afternoon, they'd been shepherded to their villa and kept there ever since. Thalia had been awestruck by the beautiful villa, with its tasteful tropical decor and striking view of the sea through a huge floor-to-ceiling window. *One night at this villa is probably a whole month's salary for me,* she had thought ruefully.

Despite the incredible accommodations, Thalia had remained anxious ahead of kicking off filming. Her nerves had eased a bit when Christina announced that Thalia and Ashley would be roommates. Ashley's wit, expressed through snappy comments in her thick Southern accent, together with her wide, easy smile, had instantly put Thalia at ease.

"I could definitely go for another glass of rosé," Thalia agreed, laughing. "Though Christina says the margaritas here are bomb. I do love a good spicy marg."

A knock on the door interrupted their planning for the night ahead. Sol poked her head in, the pink streak in her hair falling over her eyes. "Hey, ladies, getting excited? Need you downstairs in five to walk over to the pavilion. Can I check your mics?"

"Come on over," Ashley said, turning toward Sol with open arms. "I hope this isn't the last time I get felt up tonight," she added with a wink at Thalia.

The production assistant quickly checked the positioning of the microphones on each woman, making sure the wires were carefully tucked out of sight and the sound was being captured on the production feed.

"All set!" she confirmed, beaming. "Are you ladies ready?"

Thalia nodded uncertainly. Ashley let out an enthusiastic whoop, but Thalia suspected it was meant to hide her roommate's nerves.

The trio headed downstairs, with Sol knocking on the other bedroom doors as they went. From the first room emerged Karina, a tall, gorgeous Venezuelan woman who apparently worked in some big Wall Street job, and Rachel, a third-grade teacher who was very girl-next-door pretty, and whom Thalia had already heard mention Jesus twice in the last few hours. When they reached the second door, Sol knocked and called out, "Raina? We're ready."

"I need a few more minutes," a voice responded haughtily through the door.

Static crackled on Sol's walkie talkie, and Thalia recognized Christina's voice as it burst through the speaker.

"Sol, where are you guys? Cameras D and E are ready to film the girls' walk to the gazebo."

"Umm," Sol whispered, "we're still waiting on one of the ladies. Raina needs a few more minutes…" she trailed off, clearly hoping the cast member hadn't heard her through the door.

Thalia looked uncomfortably at the floor, shifting from one high heel to the other, not wanting to get involved in any drama before they'd even filmed a minute of footage.

"Let me talk to her." Christina's brusque reply pierced through the radio. Sol eased open the door to Raina's room, and as the other contestants caught sight of the expensive clothes strewn across the floor and the two huge bags of makeup spanning across the bed, Thalia said a silent thanks to the production crew for their foresight to put Raina in the single room. The woman stood in front of the full-length mirror, applying the final touches of makeup to her amber skin, accentuating her high cheekbones and long lashes.

When Raina heard the door creak open, she spun around. "I said I need a few minutes." She shot Sol an icy glare. "Honestly, I'm just not used to getting ready in such cramped quarters," she added dismissively.

Christina's voice crackled over the radio. "Raina, the sun is starting to set and I want to get some footage of you. Your skin is going to look fa-bu-lous in this golden hour."

The woman's eyes lit up at the reminder of her own beauty, then she hastily veiled her excitement with a slight sulk. "Fine, let's go."

With the group now complete, Sol led the contestants down the stairs, each of them grasping tightly onto the railing as they teetered in their high heels. They paused for a moment in the living room as the PA gave them each one last glance over, and then with an enthusiastic thumbs up, waved them out the front door.

It was an absolutely glorious evening. While the sun had beat down on them when they first arrived earlier in the day, it was now softer and gentler, and a cool breeze permeated through the rays, which danced and sparkled across the ocean. The palm trees lining the path to the gazebo swayed in the wind, as if beckoning them to start their journey to love.

Christina stood at the foot of the front deck, gesturing to the camera crew and barking orders into her radio. She stopped when she saw them filing out to the door, and broke into what Thalia sensed was the first genuine smile she'd seen across the producer's face.

"Good evening, ladies! You all look fabulous! How's everyone feeling?" Christina didn't wait for an answer, her enthusiasm picking up steam as she went along. "Alright, let's get some quick one-on-one interviews. Thalia, Rachel, and Karina, let's get you over here by these pink flowers. And Ashley and Raina, over there by the cactus, Sol will do your interviews. Then we'll walk over to the pavilion in," she paused, checking her watch, "seven minutes. Everybody clear?"

The women nodded with varying degrees of confidence, then walked over to their respective places. Christina followed Thalia's group, asking who wanted to start.

"I will," Karina jumped in, her fitted black dress gleaming against her bronze skin in the evening light.

"Perfect," Christina said, taking her place next to the camerawoman. The producer indicated for her to begin rolling. "So, Karina, how are you feeling?"

"I'm feeling great," the brunette said calmly. "I know exactly what I deserve in a man, and I am really hopeful that I'll find it tonight." She remained completely composed as Christina continued to ask her more questions, and Thalia envied her self-assurance.

When they'd wrapped up with Karina, the producer indicated for Thalia to take her place. Stomach lurching, Thalia tried to remember to be herself—just a slightly more upbeat version. As Sasha had said, nobody was going to relate to a Black Barbie doll with no personality, but the show's mostly white fan base also wasn't going to like a Black woman who wasn't "perky" enough for their tastes. She needed to strike the right balance to ensure she'd get the support she was hoping for, if she was going to make this whole thing worth it.

Turning to Christina, she put on a big grin and an expression she hoped conveyed a sense of innocent optimism, despite the nerves fluttering in her stomach.

"Thalia," Christina began, "what are you most excited for tonight?"

"I'm just really looking forward to meeting the guys! It's wild to think that my future husband could be there, waiting for me to meet him." The words sounded forced to her, and she prayed that it came across as genuine on camera. Trying to incorporate some authenticity into her interview, she added with a laugh, "Oh and I'm pretty pumped to eat some tacos, too."

Christina looked pleased that Thalia was opening up and showing a bit more spunk than she had in her casting call. "And that future husband…how are you envisioning him to be? What would be the most important qualities for him to have?"

"I definitely want someone who is kind. That's probably the most important thing to me. And passion. Not only for me and our relationship, but for life and for making an impact. Those things are really important to me."

The producer smiled. "That's perfect, thank you."

Christina moved on to the interview with Rachel, who unsurprisingly mentioned she was looking for a man of faith. Then, suddenly in a blur, it was over and they were walking toward the pavilion. Even though it was a short walk, Thalia's feet ached, protesting the change from her usual flats or sandals to the strappy heels she currently wore. *Please don't let me trip on my dress or do something else stupid on camera,* she prayed.

Even though Thalia didn't really have romance on the brain, she had to admit as the pavilion came into view that the set looked absolutely stunning. Lush green plants, cacti of all shapes and sizes, and bright, tropical flowers framed the plush cream couches dotting the pavilion. Rugged driftwood coffee tables stood in front of each seating area, with candles of varying heights flickering on their tops. Across the ceiling, rattan pendant lamps glowed, and fairy lights streamed down like shooting stars. The view looked out over the ocean, where the sunset basked the entire scene in a warm, orange glow. It looked like a wedding venue. It looked magical.

Amidst the perfectly crafted set, Thalia saw five men standing in the center of the pavilion, and immediately tried to match their faces to the cast bios. She hadn't looked more into the men after reading the initial leak by Reality Pete, but Sasha had repeatedly been sending her posts from the guys' Instagrams, with comments like *Oooh okay he could get it* in response to Jake's latest shirtless post, or *Umm he can cook for me any time* when Tae-Hyun shared a mouth-watering image of his homemade bibimbap. Looking at the group now, she spotted those two men, as well as quickly identifying Marcus, who was in a quirky button-down print shirt with tiny Batman icons all over it, and Nick, who seemed to have just finished saying something that caused a burst of laughter to punch its way out of the pavilion. Finally, Thalia's eyes landed on the last man, Andrew. He was every bit as handsome as his picture, but perhaps a bit too much so for her taste. Guys like that always *knew* how hot they were, and it showed in how they treated you.

The men turned to look at the female contestants as they reached the threshold of the pavilion, and Nick let out a little whistle, garnering a giggle from Ashley and a coy smile from Raina.

Blake emerged smoothly from the bar in the back corner, looking flawless with his wind-rustled blond waves, a white linen suit accenting his tan. Tapping his glass with a delicate fork, he motioned for the waitstaff to serve a glass of champagne to each of the ladies.

"Welcome, welcome everyone! We are so excited to welcome you all to *Love's a Beach.* As you know, this is a very special place, where many couples before you have found love, and even their forever. We're so excited for you to begin this journey." Blake looked appreciatively between the men and the women. "Your future husband or wife could be in this room tonight. And over the course of the next eight weeks, you'll get to grow closer to that person, and maybe even finish this journey with a proposal." He paused again, as if to let these momentous words wash over the contestants, then broke into a grin. "Now, that's enough from me! I know you're all dying to meet your soulmates, so I won't keep you waiting another minute longer. Let's do a quick toast, then get the night started!" Raising his glass high in the air, Blake announced, "To love!"

Each of the cast members followed suit, and ten enthusiastic "To love" calls echoed the producer's, punctuated by clinks of glasses.

As the noise died down and Blake drifted back to the bar, Thalia shifted in her heels. The rest of the cast looked excited, but equally unsure what to do next.

"Well, I for one feel very inspired in my journey for love," Andrew broke the silence with a good-natured jab at Blake's speech.

Thalia looked up in surprise, having expected his voice to be different somehow, and her lips curved up reflexively. Her gaze caught his vivid green eyes, which reflected the dancing fairy lights above them, and he returned a soft smile.

Clearing his throat, Andrew said, "As Lao Tzu said, the journey of a thousand miles begins with a single step. So, I guess someone needs to take the first step. Thalia, would you like to go chat?"

Thalia glanced around, confused as to why he'd singled her out amongst this gorgeous group of women and thrown off by the speed in which he'd made the invitation. Ashley gave her an encouraging wink, while Raina's lips pulled into a pout and Jake wrinkled his nose in annoyance.

Trying to recover quickly and display enthusiasm for the dozens of cameras hovering around the pavilion, she smiled sweetly. "Yes, I'd love to."

Andrew extended his elbow to Thalia, his forearm muscles defined under a white linen shirt with the cuffs rolled up, and a simple black leather bracelet adorning his wrist.

I'm surprised a guy like him isn't wearing a Rolex, she thought as he guided her toward one of the couches overlooking the sea. In her peripheral vision, Thalia saw a camera crew following them, while another waited in front of the couch Andrew was steering her to, already in place to film them once they'd been seated.

Focus, Thalia, she thought to herself, trying to retain her cheerful expression while she concentrated on walking in these ridiculous shoes.

They reached the couch, incident-free, and Thalia lowered herself gingerly onto the smooth cream surface. Remembering the coaching Christina had given them earlier about angling themselves halfway between the camera and the person they were speaking with, she tilted her body toward Andrew and tried to forget about the camera guy standing a few feet away.

"So," Andrew began, "let's get right down to the important stuff."

Thalia's stomach clenched in anticipation of some awful question about what she saw her life like in five years, or how many children she wanted.

"Are you a cat person or a dog person?" Andrew asked.

A burst of laughter escaped from Thalia's lips, fused together with a little sigh of relief at not having to bare her soul on national television—or at least not quite yet. This guy wasn't a total jerk like she'd expected, which unfortunately might make the next few weeks even more difficult. "Dog. One hundred percent."

"Oh, thank God," Andrew quipped. "A beautiful girl like you, it would have been such a waste if you'd said cat person. I would have had to get right up and leave." He pretended to grab his drink and rose an inch off the couch, then sunk back down with a laugh, his thigh settling an inch or two closer to Thalia's than it had been before.

She felt the heat radiating from his body and noticed the flickering candlelight reflected in the jade of his eyes. She let her gaze travel down to his strong jaw and soft lips.

Okay, Sasha was right. He is really freaking hot, she thought to herself. *But you're here on a mission, you need to focus!*

His lips parted, startling her as he teased, "Okay, your turn to ask a very deep and meaningful question."

"Hmm," Thalia replied thoughtfully. "Favorite food?"

"A woman who appreciates food," Andrew said dreamily. "My kind of woman. But that's an unfair question, making me pick just one. How about five?"

Thalia raised an eyebrow at him. "I'll give you three."

"You drive a hard bargain, lady. Alright three. Well, my mom is Ukrainian, and her perogies are my clear number one, all-time favorite food." Thalia warmed at his clear affection toward his mom. "Unfortunately, when she makes them it often devolves into a wrestling match between me and my brother, but that's besides the point." He paused, thinking. "Okay, number two would have to be tacos, I am going to crush a pound of tacos a day this summer. And last but not least, Thai food."

"Thai is a category, not a food, you cheater," Thalia protested, giving him a little push on his shoulder. "You have to pick a specific dish!"

"Alright, alright," Andrew conceded, nudging her in return before settling his hand over hers. Thalia's pulse quickened at the warmth of his strong fingers. "Can't get anything past this one. If I *must* pick one favorite Thai dish, like someone has a gun to your head and I have to pick one in order to save your life…I *guess* it would have to be Panang curry."

Forgetting completely where she was and the pressure of the cameras, Thalia felt her face split into a wide, genuine grin. "That's my favorite food," she replied, flooded with wonderful memories of Sasha and their leisurely lunches at the local Thai joint.

"You have good taste," Andrew replied softly, biting his lip. Thalia found herself involuntarily leaning towards him, guided by the butterflies in her stomach. Seeing Andrew's expression reflecting her desire, she suddenly felt almost shy with the intensity of the moment.

His smile softened as he pulled in closer to her, and right before his lips gently touched hers, he whispered, "Well, then I guess I'll have to take you to my favorite Thai place in LA when this is all over."

Chapter 12: Christina - Now

Christina awoke, spreading across the king-sized bed in the suite she'd managed to finagle for herself, after spending the last few seasons rooming with the same snoring sound tech. She glanced at her phone, and seeing it was only seven a.m., was ready to drift back into a dreamy sleep when she suddenly remembered yesterday's events. Shooting upright, she felt bile threatening its way up her throat.

"It's fine, Christina. It's going to be fine. Get it together," she muttered to herself, grateful she didn't have a roommate to witness her monologue.

She walked to the bathroom, pulling her long dark hair into a messy knot at the top of her head. Turning on the water, she splashed the cool liquid over her face, then patted it dry with one of the fluffy white towels housekeeping had refreshed for her yesterday.

Glancing at the sink, she saw the expensive Korean face cream her mom had brought back for her after visiting her sister and cousins in Seoul earlier this year.

"Please, Christina," she'd implored, "just use it. You're getting wrinkles. And you're not even married yet!"

Despite all the healing she'd done over the past five years, she still hadn't managed to tell her parents about the sexual assault. How could she get married when being alone with a guy made her pulse start to race? Or, when the first man she'd tried to be intimate with, nearly a year and a half after the assault, hadn't returned her calls because she'd had a panic attack mid make-out session? Or, when she'd finally found someone who she started to trust, but when she told him her story, he brushed it off as a "drunken college thing" and didn't see what the big deal was? She couldn't explain all of this to her mother, couldn't bear the disappointment she imagined she'd spot behind her mom's stoic gaze.

So, instead, she threw herself into her job, and while her parents didn't exactly love her non-traditional line of work, they had to admit she was doing well for herself. And they definitely enjoyed showing off the photo of Christina from last year's CBC gala when she'd met Eun Hye Song—or Eunice Song as the American audience knew her—a famous Korean actress who'd been drafted to star in the network's new sitcom about an immigrant family.

Her passion for her work seemed to pacify her parents most of the time, but the occasional comment about her love life still crept in and did make her feel a small burst of guilt for not doing this one thing to make them truly happy. It was part of the reason Christina so badly wanted to get closure from her incident; so she could move on with her romantic life, and find happiness for both herself and her parents.

Looking now at her reflection in the mirror, she frowned at the bags under her eyes and her pallid complexion, despite spending the last month in the Mexican sun. She looked terrible, which pretty much matched how she felt. With a sigh, she conceded that perhaps her mother was right, and liberally applied the smooth cream from the pretty little round container.

After brushing her teeth and pulling on some clothes, Christina grabbed her phone and room key, and headed toward the restaurant. She wanted to get some coffee and try to eat something before meeting with Chief Martinez, who was due to return to the resort at eight a.m. with an update on the medical examiner's report.

As she passed the boys' villa, she saw Nick and Tae-Hyun sitting outside on the balcony, huddled in hushed conversation. They gave her a small wave as she passed, then turned back toward each other, making it clear they didn't want to initiate a conversation with her. Overhead, a patch of gray-white clouds covered the sky, blocking out the sun and giving a dull, dark appearance to the normally sparkling sea.

Christina reached the restaurant, bending down to scratch the ears of the black and white spotted cat who was always hanging around. His coloring was reminiscent of Rosie's, and as he rubbed his soft fur against her calves, Christina's heart panged with longing for her dog. With everything going on, it would be so nice to have her here for comfort.

Giving an affectionate pat to send the kitty on his way, Christina straightened up and saw Maria, who was wiping down a table at the far end of the seating area.

"*Buenos días,*" she called to the waitress, who jumped at her voice, dropping the rag onto the table as if it were hot to the touch.

"Good morning, Señorita Christina," the young woman replied.

This morning, Maria's usually cheery countenance was clouded over, her pretty, gentle eyes framed by creases and dark circles. She looked exactly how Christina felt, which, frankly, was like shit.

"How are you? You don't look so good," Christina ventured.

"I am okay. Yesterday was very bad. I feel sad for Señor Andrew. He was a very nice man." Christina stiffened, and the waitress must have read something on her face, because she quickly shifted the tone of the conversation. "It's also umm…a lot of stress because…well, I hope I'm not rude to say." As Maria fumbled over her words, Christina waited with bated breath, sure the waitress was going to bring up the incident that the producer had stumbled upon a few days ago. Though she had tried to forget about it, anger and anxiety swirled in her chest every time her mind drifted back to that afternoon.

But instead, Maria asked, "I want to know, will I still get my salary? Even if you don't film anymore?"

"Oh," Christina sighed, relieved she had at least one easy topic to address today before the police arrived and things got complicated again. "Yes, of course. We've already paid the resort for the whole original filming period. So, you will get your paycheck, no worries." She felt confident promising this, since the PR mess of a headline like *CBC stiffs poor Mexican resort workers of their salaries* did not seem like something they needed on top of managing the press around Andrew's death.

Maria relaxed slightly, the corners of her lips turning up, though the usual light still hadn't returned to her eyes. "Thank you so much, Señorita Christina. My family really needs the money. I earn the most money for my family," she said with a bittersweet combination of pride and sadness.

Between this admission and what she'd seen going on with Maria the other day, Christina's heart ached for this woman. "Of course, I totally understand. I'll ask the manager to let you all know officially, okay?"

"*Gracias,*" she replied with a slight inclination of her head, then she scurried away to the kitchen.

Finding a seat for herself, Christina pulled out her phone while she awaited Chief Martinez's arrival. She opened up Twitter to a deluge of tweets about Andrew's death. CBC's tweet announcing the incident and linking to the official press release had over 20,000 likes and nearly 3,000 replies, which she began browsing through.

Oh no! He seemed like he was going to be my favorite guy this season! Prayers for his family and the #lovesabeach cast and crew - @beachpodgirl

Tbh he seemed like kind of a douche but this is still really sad - @coribear

OMG! I wonder what will happen with the season…do you think they'll cancel it? It's been filming for a month so maybe they'll just show that footage. Would be super sad to watch though, especially if he had started to fall for someone :(- @labfan89

She scrolled quickly through many similar posts, mostly expressing how sad the situation was. Many of the tweets from prior contestants had already garnered thousands of likes. Right as she was about to close out of the app, one reply sent a few minutes ago caught her eye.

No murió de una sobredosis. La policía son mentirosos. - @anonimo9285

Given her limited knowledge of Spanish, Christina wasn't sure exactly what it said, but didn't have a good feeling. She hit the "Translate Tweet" button, clenching her phone in anticipation.

He didn't die from an overdose. The police are liars.

Christina gasped. Who could have written this, and why? The cast still didn't have access to their phones, though last night several of them had started to raise a fuss about it. She combed through the crew in her mind, considering each of her colleagues like a seashell on the beach, before tossing each one back into the ocean. No, she didn't think any of them would jeopardize the show and their own livelihoods by tweeting something like this. It didn't make any sense.

Lost in thought, she was startled by a voice behind her.

"Hello, Christina."

She spun to see who had spoken her name. Standing there in wide-legged white linen pants, a coral silk blouse tucked in elegantly at her waistline, dark skin glowing in the morning sun, was Ava.

"Oh, hi," Christina stammered, jumping to her feet and turning her phone face down on the table. "Ava, what are you doing here?"

Her boss's brow furrowed, the usually smooth skin around her eyes now showing the faintest trace of creases. With a sigh, she admitted, "I'll be honest, Christina, I was a little worried about how things were going."

Christina's heart dropped at hearing her mentor's disappointment, and she scrambled to hide the emotion from her face, but could tell Ava had seen it.

The executive interjected, "Now, you've really stepped up and done a terrific job. Please don't think that's what I'm saying, because it's not." The knot in Christina's stomach loosened slightly at this reassurance. "But this is an incredibly tough situation for the network, and frankly, the more *senior* leadership on set is what I was worried about." Blake's unspoken name hung heavily in the air between them, their mutual frustration with him politely hidden from their faces but crackling in their energy. After a pause, Ava continued, "So, when you reported that you were meeting with the police again this morning, I decided to come down."

Christina processed this information, hoping that Ava meant it when she said she'd done a terrific job. But if that were the case, why had she come down in such a rush? It had been nearly ten p.m. last night when Christina had sent Ava an email update, carefully reading and rereading the sentences through the exhaustion of the day, before finally hitting send and collapsing onto the fine sheets of her bed. Maybe something else had happened with Blake, unrelated to her email, which prompted Ava to come. Christina clung to this hope and vowed to double down on her efforts to manage this crisis in a way that would make Ava proud.

"Makes perfect sense," Christina said amenably, recovering her composure. "In that case, let me make sure you're up to speed before Chief Martinez arrives in a few minutes. Blake isn't joining us because he's dealing with a bit of a cast mutiny about still not having access to their phones."

Ava raised her eyebrows but didn't comment, which Christina took as an indication she should continue. She proceeded to give Ava a summary of the status in interviewing the cast, the mental health services they'd provided so far, and the evidence the police had gathered from Andrew's room yesterday.

"So, today," Christina concluded, "they should be bringing a report of the tox screen and medical examiner's findings from the autopsy. That will be independently audited by a consultant that CBC has arranged, with an airtight nondisclosure agreement."

Ava nodded thoughtfully, taking in this information. Christina felt the executive's eyes boring into hers, sensing a personal question was coming before the older woman even opened her mouth. "Thank you, Christina. You've handled everything very…professionally. But how are you feeling? We capture emotions on screen, but we're also allowed to have them ourselves, you know."

With a tight-lipped smile, Christina gave what she hoped seemed like an appropriate response. "Yes, I mean of course I'm sad. Andrew was such," she cleared her throat, absently twisting her watch around her wrist, before recovering, "a great guy." Looking at Ava's expectant face, she continued on. "So much of the cast loved him," she said truthfully. "So yeah, it's really sad. But I just want to help make sure his death is treated appropriately. That he gets the investigation he deserves, you know? I think that's the best way to respect his memory."

Seemingly satisfied with the producer's emotional state, Ava nodded. "Alright then, let's get to work."

No sooner had the words left her mouth did Chief Martinez enter into the restaurant. The lead detective's long hair was pulled into a low ponytail today, and despite her simple tailored trousers and short-sleeved white blouse, she was still striking.

"Good morning," Christina called, rising to shake Daniela's hand as she approached the table. "May I introduce you to Ava Taylor-Washington? She is the executive vice president of Reality Segments at CBC. *La jefa,*" she added in a nervous attempt at humor.

"It's a pleasure, Ms. Taylor-Washington," Chief Martinez said, introducing herself in turn.

"Please, call me Ava." The executive motioned for them all to take a seat. "Thank you so much for your support to close out this investigation quickly and discreetly. Christina has briefed me on all your excellent work yesterday. What updates do you have for us today?"

Extracting a file from her expensive-looking leather briefcase, her manicured fingertips brushing over it like butter, Chief Martinez carefully placed a few documents in front of them for Ava and Christina to review.

"Given the sensitivity of this case and visibility in the American media, we put the medical examinations on top priority and our teams worked through the night last night to complete everything. As I told Christina yesterday, this is merely a formality and we want to conclude this as quickly as possible, as I'm sure you do as well." Shuffling through the papers, she pulled one on top and indicated to it. "Our medical examiner has completed his initial review, and we sent the results to you and your legal team this morning. To summarize, the findings are consistent with a drug overdose. The toxicology screen indicated that cocaine was present in Andrew's bloodstream, and the autopsy indicated cardiac distress in line with excessive drug consumption."

Ava nodded. "I don't think that's a surprise to anyone. I'm sure Christina told you that the network is having the bloodwork independently audited, right? We should have results later today."

A glimmer of some undetectable emotion appeared across Daniela's expression before she responded. "Yes, she mentioned it. Though I have to admit, I'm still not sure why that's necessary. We already confirmed the drug levels were sufficient to cause the overdose."

"I get that," Ava replied curtly. "But I want to know whether this was a case of partying gone wrong or something intentional."

Christina jerked her head in Ava's direction, heart leaping into her throat.

"What do you mean 'intentional'?"

"I mean," Ava said with a bit gentler tone, "I want to know if he committed suicide. It matters for how we are presenting this in the media. Is the story one of a culture crisis on the show, with partying and sex running rampant? In which case we need to think about how this can still be spun as a show about true love. Or is it a troubled young man who couldn't handle the stress of filming? In which case we need to announce steps to perform stronger mental health screening of applicants, and provide better counseling services on set."

Christina nodded, understanding the lens from which Ava was viewing this. She was trying to protect the network—and her own job—from the blowback, which made sense. But Christina couldn't help feeling a tiny bit surprised at the calculated nature of Ava's reaction.

Chief Martinez also did not appear entirely pleased with this take. "Ms. Taylor-Washington," she began.

"Ava, please," the executive interjected firmly.

"Ava," the chief corrected herself, her lips curved graciously, "I can assure you that many Oaxaca state resources are being devoted to this case. But we need to be able to come to our own conclusions, and not to be steered in a certain way just to make your CEO happy." Daniela paused, while Christina waited anxiously to see how Ava would respond. From everything she had seen so far, Ava was fair but tough, and was used to running things her own way. Christina wasn't sure how she would handle being told to back off, especially when she'd come down here herself to handle things, probably at Robert's direction.

After what seemed like an eternity of the two women locking eyes, Ava's expression softened. "Of course," she demurred. "It's your jurisdiction. I have the utmost confidence that you'll bring the investigation to a quick and thorough closure."

I guess she's realized she'll catch more flies with honey, Christina thought to herself, breathing a tiny sigh of relief as the moment of tension passed.

However, her reprieve was short-lived, as Ava's gaze slowly froze back over, never breaking its connection with Chief Martinez's big, hazel eyes.

"You know, one of my dear friends is a US senator, and is a member of the Foreign Relations Committee. They are briefed on all high-profile deaths of Americans overseas, and in cases where the investigations are not getting proper attention, they have to get the FBI involved. It would be such an inconvenience for everyone if the US asked the Mexican Federal Police to invite the FBI down here, wouldn't it?"

The chief's gaze held steady, her chin lifting almost imperceptibly in response to Ava's thinly veiled threat. "Of course," she replied, her tone conciliatory. "I'm sure that won't be necessary."

"I'm glad we're on the same page," Ava replied, standing and smoothing her blouse with one hand, as she extended the other to Daniela. "Thank you so much for your time today, and we will share our consultant's evaluation of the tox results as soon as it's available."

"The pleasure was all mine," Chief Martinez responded, before turning to leave.

Once the chief was out of earshot, Christina turned to Ava, desperate to get her read of the situation. But the executive's gaze was focused not on the policewoman's shrinking figure in the distance, but rather on her phone screen. Her wide eyes and ruby red lips pursed into a tiny *o,* immediately tipping off Christina that something had rattled Ava.

"What is it?" Christina asked.

Ava cleared her throat and began, "I just received the review of the medical report from CBC's independent medical examiner. They agreed with the Mexican police that he died between midnight and three a.m. However, their analysis indicates that the drugs in Andrew's system were *not* pure cocaine, but rather a mix of cocaine and fentanyl, as well as another opioid that is rarely available in street drugs. And the levels were significantly higher than typical recreational usage. About ten times higher."

Ava studied Christina soberly, before continuing to summarize the contents of her screen. "Additionally, the way the chemical compounds were metabolized, coupled with the fact that the medical report doesn't indicate any residue in his nostrils, indicates that the drugs were likely administered either orally or injected, which is less common in recreational use. They said it could have even been dissolved into a beverage. Given all of these facts, it is the opinion of the independent examiner that," she paused for a moment, her nostrils flaring as she struggled to regain her composure, "there is a high likelihood that Andrew was murdered."

Christina let out a gasp, glancing nervously around the restaurant. When Daniela left, Christina had felt relieved that the investigation would be quick and straightforward, making this more of a PR issue than anything else—which she knew Simone and her team would handle flawlessly. However, this new information changed everything. A full-fledged murder investigation was going to make things way more complicated. Christina shivered uneasily despite the tropical sun streaming into the restaurant.

"Obviously the police here have no idea what they're doing," Ava said, throwing up her hands in exasperation. "I'll need to share this with them. But I only want to share this with the police, the CBC Board, you, and Blake. We need to keep this absolutely secret, because every single person in this resort just became a suspect."

Chapter 13: Christina - 3 Weeks Ago

Christina wasn't sure exactly what had driven her impromptu decision to cast Andrew, or what she planned to do with her discovery. All she knew at the time was that as a producer, she wielded power over the lives of the cast members—deciding their wardrobes, dictating what they drank and when they slept, steering them toward and away from romantic connections, and ultimately controlling how their story unfolded on the show. She'd spent years since her sexual assault feeling helpless, and the idea of finally taking back control of her life *and* that of her attacker made something swell deep inside of her.

As the start of filming approached, she'd felt giddy, almost reckless, with the possibilities of exerting this newfound power. He had taken everything from her, and it dawned on Christina that she had an opportunity to take from Andrew what seemed to matter most to him, despite it being built on a lie: his perfect reputation.

Now that the season had begun, Christina sought out opportunities to film and edit footage that would expose Andrew to all of America as the asshole he really was. She felt a secret thrill the first few days, nearly drunk on the prospect of capturing him making some off-color remark to one of the guys, or making a fool of himself after having too much to drink, which she could leverage to edit him as the villain on the show.

Yet as the first week of filming passed, he hadn't done or said a single thing that Christina could use. This guy acted like he was in some sort of competition with Mother Theresa. He picked up after himself when they were done having a few beers by the pool. He was kind and gracious when interacting with the crew and even the resort staff, greeting them by name in Spanish each morning. He listened attentively as his best friend Nick talked about his developing feelings for Ashley, showing emotional maturity when giving him advice and ending the conversation with a bromance hug so wholesome Christina could already hear the Midwestern Moms demographic producing a collective "awww!" when it would air.

And most importantly, while other men on the show usually tried to juggle multiple relationships, or sneakily hooked up with other women besides the one they were supposedly pursuing, it was clear from night one that Andrew only had eyes for Thalia. His swoon-worthy green eyes lit up every time she came into view, and he spent every moment on camera either with her, or talking about her with the guys, telling them how much he liked her and how he really felt they had a future together after the show.

At first, watching the two of them together had made her anxiety skyrocket, warning signs flashing in her mind as she saw him approach Thalia. Every time the couple interacted, Christina felt like she'd been plunged into an ice bath, her heart stopping as she waited in fear he would hurt another woman like he had hurt her. Only once they had physically separated could she breathe easily again.

As filming went on, that paralysis and fear slowly warmed into a simmering rage that this man was fooling not only Thalia, but the rest of the cast and crew, and soon the six million people who would watch this romance unfold on their screens. They'd all think he was a total sweetheart, rather than seeing him for the rapist asshole he truly was.

Soon, Christina could hardly contain her anger and frustration. She needed to go to greater lengths to sabotage Andrew's appearance on film. The first step, she knew, was to ensure that any slip-up she managed to induce needed to be captured on camera.

On the eighth day of filming, Christina greeted the camera crew at breakfast. "Good morning, team!" she chirped.

The introverted group mumbled a response to her, heads down over their plates of *huevos rancheros* and equipment lying carefully on the table, ready at a moment's notice to begin filming the cast once they were up for the day.

Even though most of the team was quiet, she knew they took great pride in their work, and might not take kindly to the feedback she was about to share.

"Listen, I've been thinking…we need more eyes on Andrew." As several heads snapped up in defense, she forged ahead. "I know you all are understaffed. And there's a lot of ground to cover with ten cast members. But Ava and Blake agree that Andrew is the golden boy of the season, the husband material! We really need the spotlight on him at all times, from every conversation he has with Thalia or other cast members, down to him walking to the pool. He's our star and we can't miss a minute on tape."

The crew nodded in agreement, acknowledging they would make more of an effort. Professing her gratitude, Christina turned away, grinning inwardly at how easily her excuse had gone over with the crew.

The next morning, Andrew was chatting with some of the male cast members at breakfast, the group getting into a heated discussion on the merits of college versus professional football.

Boys, Christina thought in annoyance, sipping her steaming hot coffee. As the discussion became more animated with shouts of NFL players' stats and waving of arms, an idea struck her. She quickly confirmed the camera crew was in place, with one lens focused in tight on Andrew, then made her way through the metal swinging door into the kitchen.

"*Hola,* Juan!" she said, apparently catching the lanky, pimply teenage waiter off guard by knowing his name.

"*Buenos días, señorita.*" His voice jittered with nerves. "Can I get something for you? Some eggs or coffee?"

"No, I've had my breakfast, thank you. I actually have a favor to ask you."

"Yes, of course," Juan replied, clearly eager to please, "what can I do?"

Keenly aware of how ridiculous this would sound, she looked him squarely in the eye and plunged in. "I would like you to go spill some coffee on Andrew. The one in the white shirt. Make it look like an accident."

Juan's angular features pulled into a confused frown. "You want me to… spill the coffee? On Señor Andrew?"

"Yes," Christina confirmed. She was certain this would elicit an angry reaction from Andrew—something, anything she could use to edit and slowly build the storyline of him as the villain.

"But the coffee is very hot! And *señor* is very nice!" Juan protested.

"Let's see about that," Christina snapped, pulling out a hundred-peso bill from her pocket. "Just do it."

"Uh…okay," he agreed reluctantly.

Striding out of the kitchen, Christina reclaimed her seat a few tables over from the male contestants, and waited in anticipation.

Juan exited the kitchen door and approached Andrew's table, reaching between him and Jake the Jerk to refill his mug. As if on cue, Jake threw his hands up in exasperation at Marcus's professed love for college game days, his elbow knocking the carafe, which Juan then tipped sideways, emptying coffee all over Andrew's white linen shirt.

Barely able to contain her glee, Christina watched as Andrew sprung up from his chair in surprise. But rather than getting angry at the poor waiter, he elicited hearty laughs from the table as he whooped, "And here I thought I could never have too much coffee!" Much to Christina's chagrin, he stripped off his stained shirt and tossed it casually across the back of the chair. He then grabbed some napkins to help the waiter clean up the spill, his perfectly taut pecs and biceps rippling as he wiped the floor.

Christina sulked off and locked herself in the production room for an hour so she could plot her next move. As she replayed her failed attempt at breakfast, Christina realized Andrew was too well-heeled to slip up on something like simple manners in front of a crowd. She needed to dig deeper and target his vulnerabilities.

What do I know about Andrew? She knew that men like him thought very highly of themselves, and assumed every woman they met would be enamored by them. She knew that men like him were addicted to the feeling of power over women, that they needed to make themselves feel important. And she knew that men like him were often very good at putting up a facade of respect for women. She hoped that if she poked at the right places, it would crumble and leave him open for his character to creep through.

* * *

The next morning after breakfast, she pulled Raina aside first for taping the female contestants' daily confessionals.

Squeezing into the small space and taking her seat behind the camera, Christina readied herself for the interview. She eased into the conversation by asking Raina a few questions about how she was feeling and what she was most looking forward to today.

Her nerves raced knowing she was potentially about to put Raina into harm's way, but she steeled her resolve, reminding herself of the conclusion she'd come to yesterday: that it was better for a woman to flirt with Andrew in this controlled environment rather than out in the real world where Christina couldn't protect them. And more importantly, that this was all for the greater good to expose him for who he really was.

Clearing her throat as Raina finished up a complaint about the metallic taste of the bottled water in her room, Christina whispered conspiratorially, "I think Andrew was checking you out at the pool yesterday. I mean, duh, you're gorgeous."

Raina's eyes lit up, raw vanity streaking across her face as her lovely lips curled into a smug smile. "You think so?" she asked, sweeping her long hair to one side. "I thought he and Thalia kind of had a thing going."

"Hmm." Christina feigned being deep in thought. "You know, I thought so too, but I heard him telling Nick today that it's more of a casual thing to him. So fair game, right?"

"Right," answered Raina with a salacious smile.

Later that afternoon, most of the cast was hanging out by the resort's main pool. The men drank beers as they swam around, and the women perched on the ledge, their long legs extended gracefully as their toes grazed the cool water.

Thalia and Karina had been pulled away by Sol to get their sizing for the mariachi-themed date that was coming up next week. The contestants were going to dress up in traditional Mexican clothing and perform a mariachi song with their own lyrics for their love interest. "Wow, that's not stereotypical at all," Sol had said when Blake presented the idea. Christina didn't disagree, but she was too distracted by the Andrew situation to argue with her boss, so it was going ahead.

Now, Christina and the camera crew hovered at the fringes by the pool, waiting to capture something interesting. Raina's dark eyes suddenly caught hers, and Christina gave her an encouraging wink, glancing pointedly at Andrew, who was chatting with Nick in the shallow end.

When Nick got out to refresh his drink, Raina slid into the water and flounced up next to Andrew, her tiny bikini barely hanging on as she moved toward him like a shark seeking her prey.

Christina's heart leapt. With Thalia not around, this was the perfect opportunity for her plan to kick into gear.

"Hey, focus in on Andrew and Raina," she muttered to the camerawoman next to her, who immediately shifted her position to get the best shot of the pair.

From where she stood, Christina couldn't hear what Andrew and Raina were talking about, but their body language was like a megaphone. Raina acted exactly as she'd expected, leaning in and laughing breathily at some stupid joke he'd made, her voluminous eyelashes fluttering madly. But to Christina's dismay, Andrew simply gave her a polite smile and held even-toned conversation, his eyes never drifting down toward her plentiful cleavage.

When Nick returned with a fresh Corona for Andrew, Raina sulked away, clearly insulted by his lack of interest. She shot a venomous glance at Christina before lowering her huge sunglasses down over her eyes and reclining on a pool chair apart from the group.

What the hell, Christina fumed. She was shocked he'd rejected Raina's advances, and frustrated she'd blown her chance to tempt him with arguably the most attractive woman in the cast. Raina was far too prideful to pursue him again, she knew that for certain.

Maybe he knew Ashley would tell Thalia if he strayed, she thought, eyeing the blonde cast member chatting nearby with the other ladies. Again, he'd been too smart to get caught doing something wrong. She needed a way to confront him more directly.

Suddenly, an idea came to her. It would take some convincing to get Blake on board, but she instinctively knew Ava would love it. And most importantly, that it would force Andrew to show his true colors.

* * *

"Hey, everyone!" Christina's chipper voice greeted the entire cast as they lounged in the pagoda where they'd been asked to gather after breakfast the next morning. "We have a really exciting group date planned today."

"A spa day?" Raina piped up hopefully, her hair gleaming in the bright morning sun.

"Bungee jumping?" Jake the Jerk suggested, his voice coursing with adrenaline.

A broad grin spread over Christina's face. "No, this is something that's going to help you get to know your potential partners on a deeper level. As some of you may know, historically this show has shied away from bringing up 'big topics' on air, but our new executive has a different take on this. She believes that by discussing things like politics and religion and technology early on, we can not only help build more lasting relationships on this show...but also make some great TV."

Christina clapped her hands in gleeful anticipation, then pointed to five sleek, low tables spaced throughout the pagoda, each with two white wicker chairs facing each other on opposite sites. "This is going to be a speed dating type setup. Please take a seat at the spot where you find your name, across from your first 'date,'" she instructed.

The cast shuffled into place, most of them eyeing Christina with trepidation. The production team had placed pitchers of mimosas and two tall champagne glasses on each table, which Ashley reached for immediately when she saw that she was paired with Jake the Jerk. Andrew took his place across from Rachel, whose gold cross dangled just below her collarbone. Out of all the contestants, he was the only one who looked unruffled.

Let's see how long that lasts, Christina thought smugly.

105

Thalia was seated at the table next to Andrew and Rachel, her first match set with Nick, whose typical boyish grin was replaced by a strained expression. He ran his hands nervously through his dark, floppy curls.

"Alright," Christina began, knowing she needed to ease the cast in with some softball questions before hammering them with the meaty ones. "The first question to discuss with your partner is: How many children do you want, and why?" She didn't even bother listening to the responses, knowing that Andrew would give some perfect, gag-worthy answer.

Once the camera leads indicated to Christina that all the pairs had wrapped up their responses, she moved on to the next question, turning the intensity up a notch. "What religion are you, and what religion do you want to raise your children?"

Andrew and Rachel studied each other a moment, before the female contestant responded, "I'm a proud Christian woman. And it's very important to me that my partner and children share my faith."

"I respect that," Andrew replied. "I'm Christian as well." Rachel nodded in approval, her bright blue eyes focused on his handsome features. "But I'm open to having a partner of another faith. And I guess how our children would be raised is a question that's best left for me and her to discuss."

Christina studied Rachel's reaction closely, and as she'd hoped, saw the first flicker of conflict between the two amicable contestants. Rachel's back straightened almost imperceptibly at Andrew's response.

Now Christina was ready for the real question, the reason she had paired Andrew and Rachel. This *had* to produce some good footage she could use.

Clearing her throat, she said to the group, "The next question is: Who did you vote for in the last election, and why?" This time she hovered hungrily near Andrew and Rachel's table, ready to pounce on any juicy morsel she could use on air.

"Ladies first," Andrew tilted his head toward Rachel.

"I voted for Margaret Reed. I think she would have revived the soul of our nation," Rachel said, her voice the most assertive that Christina had ever heard it, edging on defensive, as if daring Andrew to challenge her. This was no shock, given the contestant's prior comments about her faith, and the candidate's pandering to the religious right. "Instead, we're stuck with President Ferris," she grumbled, wrinkling her nose in disgust.

Christina noticed Andrew's sharp jawline tense. "Well, we'll have to agree to disagree," he said magnanimously. "I voted for President Ferris and am a big fan."

Out of the corner of her eye, Christina swore she saw Thalia give a little sigh of relief.

Andrew explained, "I agree with her positions on racial justice, workers' rights, and climate change."

Rachel bristled, and Christina could hardly help herself from taking another step toward their table, in anticipation of Andrew laying into the conservative contestant. "And what about her views on abortion?" Rachel demanded.

"Yes, I'm pro-choice, like President Ferris," Andrew replied firmly.

Rachel's usually demure features twisted in hatred, and she spat out, "So, you're okay with killing innocent babies?"

Christina waited eagerly for Andrew to return a flash of anger. He paused for a moment, eyes trained on Rachel. When he finally responded, Christina let out a gush of disappointment at his gentle, even tone. "I can see that we have some differences of opinion here. But yes, I support a woman's right to choose. Unequivocally."

Rachel startled everyone by standing up suddenly from the table, knocking her champagne flute askew. The rest of the cast pivoted in their chairs at the sound of splintering glass. "I'm done here. I have nothing else to discuss with this *murderer*," she announced, her tone edging on hysterical. With that, she turned and fled from the pagoda, her cornflower blue dress flying behind her as she stormed toward the girls' villa.

The rest of the cast looked around, stunned at Rachel's outburst. Rising from her chair, Thalia crouched next to Andrew, whispering something in his ear as she caressed his shoulder.

Her gaze fixated on the glass shards strewn across the floor, Christina felt a panic gripping her as she realized Rachel's exit had not only put an end to this date, but also an end to her ideas for retribution against Andrew. Her hopes had shattered like the champagne glass, and she knew the manipulation tactics she had honed as a producer were not going to work. There was nothing she could possibly do to reveal Andrew's true character on camera; he was too careful, too polished, too well-practiced at putting on a front as some successful nice guy. She had failed. She had one chance that so many survivors never have—to extract justice on her own terms—and she had failed. She had let him win again, and now he would never pay for what he'd done to her.

Hanging her head despondently, she looked down at her hands, her eyes catching on the glinting gold anchor dangling from her wrist.

You are stronger than you think, she heard Linette's words echoing in her head. A little flicker of determination sparked inside her, and Christina picked her head back up, staring at Andrew's handsome face across the room. The spark expanded into a fire inside of her, blazing hot and bright, and she promised to herself that she was going to find a way to make him pay for ruining her life, whatever the cost.

Chapter 14: Blake - 2 Weeks Ago

After a long day at an offsite date with Karina and Marcus, Blake was absolutely famished. They had run behind schedule after filming and re-filming scenes a million times, thanks to Karina being incredibly stiff and apparently having never watched a romantic film in her life. The first half of the date had been fine, as the zip-lining took up most of the couple's focus, but when they sat down to a beautiful cliffside picnic, the conversation turned disastrous.

Karina talked about herself for thirty minutes, going on about her high-powered job in private equity and a major deal she'd recently lost to a West Coast firm. She quizzed Marcus about why he'd chosen his career as a comic book artist, and even asked him if he'd gotten a stock buyout when his company got acquired last year, announcing that she expected her partner to be on her level intellectually and financially.

After four takes of the same scene, Blake was watching the sun begin to dip toward the horizon, at a loss for how to salvage this date and already building a villain storyline for Karina in his mind.

Thankfully, Christina jumped in and pulled the woman aside for a few minutes, while Blake quietly told Marcus, "Hang in there, bud—I promise I'll get you on a date with Ashley soon. She seems much more focused on finding a hubby and less on finding an…investment partner." He flashed a sporting grin at Marcus, who begrudgingly returned the smile and then headed back to the picnic blanket to start filming again.

When Karina returned from her chat with Christina, it was like she was a different person. She began giggling at Marcus's nerdy jokes and even asked him about whether he wanted children.

"What the hell did you say to her?" Blake muttered to Christina, whose face lit up with smug satisfaction as they stood together behind the cameras.

"I told her that she was going to die alone if she didn't start focusing on men's hearts and not their pedigree," Christina replied, her eyes never leaving the contestant. "And, also, that her eggs were shriveling up."

"No fucking way."

"I swear," Christina replied with a grin, turning to Blake. "Some people just need a kick in the ass. It's all about knowing who they are, and how hard to kick."

Finally back at the resort, Blake walked toward the kitchen, hankering for a snack and mulling over the day's events. As much as he hated to admit it, his junior producer *was* good at her job. He didn't want it to go to her head, but he also needed her talent in order to keep the season on track and save his own ass. He'd have to handle her more carefully going forward.

As he reached the restaurant, his stomach grumbling at the thought of the chef's famous tamales, he waved hello to the pretty waitress, who was arranging silverware in preparation for breakfast the next morning. "Hey," he called to her. "Can you bring me out some tamales?"

She jumped at his voice, sending a fork clattering on the table. "Okay, sir, I will ask the chef right away," she said, not quite meeting his eyes. She started to walk to the kitchen, then turned around and added hesitantly, "Someone was looking for you, sir. They said they come to fix the cameras."

Peeved his production crew wasn't handling this issue, Blake shrugged. "Okay, I'll let my equipment guy know to come down here."

The waitress shook her head, insisting, "No, sir. They asked for Mr. Blake. They are waiting in the storage unit to show you the problem with the cameras."

Running his hands through his hair, Blake tried to hide his annoyance. "Fine, let me go see what they want. Get the tamales ready for me. Please," he added as an afterthought. He turned and went back the way he'd come, heading toward the storage unit where they kept the spare cameras, away from the enticing odor of the kitchen. His stomach protested as he walked, and his mind drifted to that waitress…what was her name again? She was pretty hot. If only the resort manager let them wear something a little more flattering than those black pants and white button-downs…he'd have to make a suggestion to him tomorrow. Only made sense to get the whole resort in the right vibe.

As he rounded the corner and pulled open the door to the storage unit, a familiar voice greeted him, washing over him like a sheet of cold water.

"What's up, Blake?"

Blake was instantly transported back to the alley beside Terrace65, and felt the same pit in his stomach as he looked at the face of the shorter man from that night. The man's hair was now a bit longer but still as greasy, and his sinister smile glinted in the dim lighting. Blake had pictured that face a million times since that incident, but after a few weeks on set with no contact from the cartel, he'd let himself be lulled into a false sense of security.

Maybe they were just trying to fuck with me, he'd thought to himself only this afternoon. *Maybe they really don't plan to have me traffic any drugs.*

Any hope he'd allowed to swell now deflated as he saw the man in front of him, here on his set, confronting him without a care in the world.

"How did you get in here?" Blake demanded, his voice projecting more confidence than he felt. There were cameras covering every inch of this resort—surely the cartel member wouldn't hurt him here? The fact that his much larger accomplice was missing tonight gave Blake a bit more reassurance.

"Oh, I got some connections," the man shot back. "Helps to have friends in high places, you know what I'm saying?"

Blake didn't respond, waiting to hear what the man was going to demand.

"Relax, Blake," he said, with exaggerated kindness. "*Tranquilo.* It's all good. You know, I think you and I got off on the wrong foot. I never even introduced myself properly. But since we're going to be working together for the next month or two, I think we should get to know each other, right?" Ignoring Blake's sulking silence, he continued, "Well, I already know a lot about you, thanks to my boy, José. He says whatsup, by the way. But you don't know anything about me! So let me introduce myself. I'm Manuel. It's nice to officially meet you," he said, offering his hand to Blake.

Staring at the spiderweb tattoos creeping up Manuel's hand and forearm, Blake hesitated, then extended his hand.

I guess I don't have a choice, he thought defeatedly. *I came to their home turf like an idiot. I should have let Christina run this damn season, said I had kidney stones or some shit and stayed home.*

Manuel grinned as they grasped hands, apparently amused by Blake's frustration at being caught in this situation.

"Now, like I told you in LA, you're going to help us bring a lot of *special* items back on your plane. I'll see you a few times a week and bring some more goodies to store in here each time." Blake's eyes widened anxiously, and Manuel held up his hands with a little shrug as if to say, *Don't blame me! You got yourself into this mess.*

"But I have crew members in here all the time," Blake protested, attempting to fabricate some reason why this couldn't be happening. "They're going to notice some sketchy boxes in here."

"Don't worry, my man," Manuel replied. "We are *very* good at hiding stuff. How else do you think we became the best in the biz? We're gonna have coke hidden up inside lights and microphones and all kinds of crap—we good, man."

"But," Blake stammered, scrambling to see how he could stop this inevitable ball of shit from rolling down the hill. "What about the resort security? They're very strict. They'll notice you coming and going. And they'll know you don't work here."

Manuel grinned, clearly taking pleasure in seeing Blake squirm, whether because he had screwed over his friend, José, or because the cartel member probably viewed him as a rich entitled asshole, he wasn't sure. "Like I said, *amigo*. Friends in high places. And when you see me around, you can pretend I'm a gardener or something." He paused, then added with a trace of bitterness, "All your American crew members will have no trouble believing that anyways."

Blake didn't respond. For once, his charm and ability to finesse any situation fell short.

Manuel's jawline hardened. "So, we're all good then. See you around, bro." And with that, he turned and exited the storage facility, leaving Blake in stunned silence.

Taking a few moments to compose himself, Blake tried to process the fact that he was actually about to become an international drug smuggler, but simply couldn't wrap his brain around the idea. Should he call Cliff to see if he could help him? He considered the idea for a moment before his pride bubbled up. His friend would tell him he was a complete idiot for getting himself into this situation—and he wasn't wrong. Blake couldn't bear the embarrassment.

A deep rumble in his stomach interrupted Blake's thoughts, reminding him that the waitress should have his tamales ready by now. With one big deep breath, he walked out into the quiet evening, the darkness and an eerie calm enveloping him despite the turmoil he'd just experienced inside the storage building. The sound of laughter tinkled over from the main pool area where the cast was hanging out.

At least someone is having fun tonight, he thought moodily. As he rounded the corner to head back toward the restaurant, he ran straight into Andrew, nearly spilling the margarita the cast member held in his hand.

"Oh, hey, Blake," he said, smiling with a lightness that the producer noted enviously. "I'm grabbing a spicy margarita for Thalia—they ran out of the peppers at the poolside bar. The girl knows what she likes." Andrew laughed, his eyes twinkling with affection. He glanced in the direction Blake had come from. "Doing some late-night equipment inventory? And here I thought you'd be enjoying a beer by now," he teased, his tone jovial. "Tae-Hyun told me today was a little rough."

"Yeah, yeah," Blake said with a quick forced laugh, wondering if Andrew had seen Manuel exiting the utility building just moments before him. "All done with work now, so I'm gonna grab that beer. Have a good night." He sidestepped Andrew, ignoring the look of confusion on the contestant's face at the short response from Blake, who often joked and chatted with him.

"You too," Andrew called after him.

Blake sped away toward the restaurant, pushing the interaction out of his mind. All he wanted was to crush some tamales, then go drink some whiskey in his room. The night's events had ruined any ideas he had of heading to Señor Tequila. In any case, it was probably for the best, since last time he'd visited, he'd gotten a little handsy with a local girl, and the bartender, Francisco, had gotten pretty pissed at him.

What was that chick's name again? Blake tried to think back to that evening, bringing her luscious lips into focus in his mind. *Lucia? Maria? Wait, no—Maria is the waitress here at the resort!*

Feeling pleased with himself that he'd remembered her name, he felt his mood buoy slightly at the prospect of getting her into his bed. He thought he should have a pretty good shot at it by the end of filming—yes, he could make it a little goal for himself by the end of the summer.

Approaching the restaurant, he prepared to turn on the charm. As requested, Maria had the tamales waiting for him on a small table near the entrance to the open pavilion. The waitress was finishing up for the night, and the lights were already off in the kitchen, with the lamps along the adjacent walkway casting creeping shadows into the seating area.

"Thanks for this. I guess I should say *gracias.*" Blake gave her a winning smile and appreciative glance.

Maria had startled at his voice, as she had when he first arrived at the restaurant this evening.

She's jumpy, he thought. *Bet I can think of a way to help her relax.*

"Yes, sir. No problem, sir."

"All good with the cameras, by the way," he replied. "Thanks again for your help."

Her large brown eyes stared at him unblinking, and her head tilted ever so slightly as she responded, "Sure, sir. Glad everything is okay with the… cameras."

Blake had an unsettled feeling she could sense his shaken nerves beneath his suave facade. He considered probing Maria about whether she knew the man who had asked for him. Puerto Engaño was not a huge town, so it wasn't outside the realm of possibility that they knew each other. On the other hand, Maria seemed quiet and a bit naive (and Blake had to admit her innocence was a total turn-on), so it seemed unlikely she was mixed up with hardcore cartel members. Even if she did know anything about Manuel, what would come of it? It's not like this girl had any power to help him out of his shitty situation. After a moment's pause, he decided that the fewer people who could connect him to anyone from the cartel, the better.

"Well, thanks again for the late-night tamales, Maria. I owe you one," he said with a wink. "Have a great night."

Her face was impassive as the lamps cast shadows over it, giving an almost haunted appearance to her normally beautiful features. "You too, sir. Take care."

Chapter 15: Thalia - Now

Thalia had slept miserably, tossing and turning all night and waking up soaked in sweat, despite the cool sea breeze swaying through her window. When she'd finally prepared herself to get up, she opened her eyes to find sunlight streaming into the room, and Ashley propped on her bed reading a copy of *People en Español*.

"Hey there, sleepyhead." Ashley's rich drawl rang across the room.

"I thought you didn't speak Spanish?" Thalia grumbled, squinting at her roommate.

"I don't, silly. But I'm fluent in the language of sexy Latin men." She cackled, pleased with her own joke. "How you feeling, sweet pea?" she said more seriously, her blue eyes fraught with concern.

"As good as can be, I guess," Thalia answered truthfully.

"Fair enough. Well, you missed some big news. Apparently, Blake's boss, some big CBC executive, is here. Karina saw her at breakfast when she was up early to do her usual workout." She paused, rolling her eyes. "Freaking weirdo. Who has the energy for Pilates after yesterday?"

Thalia smiled, grateful for the distraction of Ashley's warm humor.

"Anyways," her roommate continued, "we're supposed to be down there for a meeting with the head honcho at eleven, so get your butt out of bed. Maria brought some coffee up, by the way." She pointed to a tray sitting on top of the wardrobe, a colorful pitcher and delicate mugs arranged carefully next to a plate covered with aluminum foil.

Despite the turmoil in her mind, Thalia felt her body respond instinctively to the thought of food. She couldn't remember what—or even if—she'd eaten yesterday. "What's on the plate?" she asked tentatively.

"Chilaquiles and refried beans. That woman is a freaking saint."

Nodding in enthusiastic agreement, Thalia stretched and rose from the bed. She grabbed the tray, letting herself enjoy the aromas as she lifted off the foil and began to eat.

Ashley continued to distract her with her chitchat, and since she couldn't read the captions in the magazine, made up her own random stories about the Latin celebrities who were featured.

"And this guy," she said, pointing to a devastatingly handsome middle-aged actor who Thalia recognized but couldn't place, "his wife is divorcing him because he is obsessed with corgis. They had seventeen corgis, and he had little corgi faces printed all over their bedsheets, custom paintings of each of their dogs hanging all over the walls, corgi coffee mugs, the whole nine yards. Poor woman couldn't take it anymore."

Thalia listened half-heartedly, appreciating Ashley's efforts to lift her spirits, even though her thoughts continually drifted elsewhere. She'd attempted to meditate last night, but couldn't tame the thoughts swirling wildly through her mind: Andrew's face, the mounting pressure she was feeling as filming remained stopped, and the disappointment she would bring to everyone. Ashley was wonderful, but Thalia desperately needed to talk to Sasha—the only one who would truly understand.

"What are you thinking about?" Ashley interrupted her thoughts.

Thalia's eyes brimmed with tears. "Wishing I could talk to my sister, that's all."

"Why don't you ask at this all-hands meeting to get your phone back? Ask this senior executive woman. It's ridiculous that we're all going through this trauma and we can't even speak to our families. I'm sure the news has been made public by now anyways, so what's the point of keeping us away from the outside world?"

Thalia picked at a loose string on her bedspread. "I really doubt she'll say yes. I'm sure this is a PR nightmare for them."

"Hey, at least you can try, right?" Ashley encouraged her. "Worst she can say is no. Chin up, sweet pea."

After finishing her breakfast, the caffeine and food boosting her energy, Thalia made her way to the pavilion with the rest of the cast and crew for the meeting. The sustenance, in combination with Ashley's pep talk, left her feeling confident enough to ask to speak to Sasha. Thalia knew she probably felt worse than any other cast member, but Ashley had reminded her that all of them were struggling and could benefit from the comfort of speaking with a loved one. She would use her position as Andrew's grieving girlfriend for the good of the entire cast, not just herself.

As they entered the pavilion, the mood was tense among the nine cast members and fifty-some crew members. Looking around the crowd, she spotted Christina and most of the AV crew she'd become friendly with, their faces tense. Thalia was sure that, on top of the stress of this crisis, having their boss in town and being uncertain of how she would react couldn't be easy.

She felt a pang of sympathy for Christina, whom she'd come to admire over the last few weeks. Blake was a fun guy, if a little schmoozy with his dimples and the non-stop winking, but it was pretty clear to Thalia that Christina did a lot of the heavy lifting on the production team. *This whole thing has probably been a mess for her*, Thalia thought.

Blake arrived shortly after them, entering not with his usual easy confidence, but rather a sort of disengaged stance, his posture curved as if he'd been bent into the shape by the sheer weight of yesterday's events. Christina tersely waved him over to her, pulling him away from the rest of the crew into a private discussion.

Before she had a chance to wonder what they were talking about, Thalia felt a poke to her side, just as a hush swept over the pavilion.

"That's the head honcho," Ashley whispered. "I saw a picture of her in *Elle* magazine when she got hired."

Thalia's eyes swept to the entrance of the pavilion, where a striking middle-aged Black woman strode assuredly to the front of the crowd.

Tropical executive chic, Thalia thought to herself, trying to categorize the woman's outfit as she admired the authority her presence commanded.

"Good morning, everyone," the woman addressed the group. "Thank you for gathering here. Many of you know me, but for those of you I haven't had the pleasure of meeting, I'm Ava Taylor-Washington, and I lead the Reality Segment for CBC. Let me start by saying that my heart goes out to the cast and crew who came to know and care for Andrew over the past month." She paused, surveying the room, and Thalia squirmed as she felt Ava's intense brown eyes settle on her.

Of course, she knows who I am, Thalia thought to herself. Her shoulders tensed as she realized this woman she'd never met had been watching her on tape for weeks, getting to know her through the footage, and seeing her fall for Andrew.

Ava continued, "I know that my team here has been doing an excellent job handling this situation, and I want to reiterate that I'm here to provide support, not because anything is wrong or anyone is in trouble. This is a terrible tragedy, and the network and I want to get closure for Andrew's family, while ensuring the safety and mental wellbeing of everyone here. Now," she said, glancing around the crowd, "I know a lot of you must have questions for me. I'm an open book," she added, her arms spread wide, palms up.

Nick's hand shot in the air, his eyes fiery in preparation to again defend his belief that Andrew had not overdosed.

"Yes, go ahead Nick," Ava said.

The cast member lowered his hand, brushing it through his curls. His face reflected the same unease that Thalia had felt at Ava knowing so much about her.

"I know Andrew wasn't using drugs," he said fiercely, his voice strained with emotion, but supported by a quiet confidence in his relationship with his late friend. "So, I want to know what the hell happened to him, and why you guys are lying to us."

Ava remained calm in reaction to Nick's outburst, her face radiating gentle concern without betraying any sign of anger or defensiveness. "Nick," she began. "I know it can be difficult to process these things. And to find out new things about someone we cared about and thought of in a certain way, after they're gone. We want to keep the image that we have of them with us forever." She paused, watching for his reaction. "But the fact is, Andrew *did* die of an overdose."

"Where's the proof?" Nick demanded.

The executive's composure didn't waver for a moment. "Christina and I have met with the police, and the initial toxicology screen confirms that there was enough cocaine in his system to cause his death."

Thalia sat frozen, hardly able to process what she was hearing.

Ava continued, "The autopsy shows heart failure, which is consistent with the strain that this level of drugs would cause to your internal organs. The police gave us a copy of the reports, and I'll be happy to review them with any one of you, if you think it will help you with your grieving process."

It felt surreal to Thalia—like her brain was swimming through murky water, and the image of Andrew's stiff body angled across his bed kept surfacing to the top. As Thalia glanced around the room, everyone else looked as dazed as she felt absorbing this information.

The one exception was Christina, whom Thalia noticed shuffling uncomfortably in the corner, not looking at anyone else in the room. *Why's she acting so weird?*

A silence swelled among the cast and crew, filling in the gaps between bodies and stifling the room. No breeze filtered in from the ocean, and even the waves seemed to have calmed from their usual crash to a dull rumble, as the reality of Andrew's death settled over the group.

Ava let the quiet expand like a balloon, until she finally released the pressure with the soft pop of her voice. "Well, does anyone have more questions for me?"

"I do," Thalia responded in a tiny voice. "I want to know," she hesitated, feeling everyone's eyes upon her. She glanced sideways to Ashley, who gave her an almost imperceptible nod of encouragement. "I want to know," she repeated, gaining confidence, "whether the cast can have our phones. We are all really struggling with this, and it would make a huge difference to be able to talk with our loved ones."

Ava studied her, as if trying to judge how hard Thalia would push on this topic before deciding what her answer would be. Thalia set her jaw in determination, and Ava finally responded, "We can't give you open access to your phones, as we're still dealing with quite a lot of media and PR issues related to this." Several of the cast members opened their mouths as if to protest, and Ava continued, "But…we can allow you to make one supervised video call per day. So, after this meeting, Christina and Sol can begin organizing those time slots right away."

Relief swelled in Thalia's heart at the thought of seeing Sasha's face. She wouldn't be able to say everything she wanted to with the producers listening in, but just being able to tell her sister that Andrew existed, and that she had fallen in love with him, would make Andrew's death feel more real. As painful as that might be, it had to be better than the fog she was drifting through. She had learned that lesson in the aftermath of her parents' death.

Ava's brusque voice interrupted Thalia's thoughts. "Alright, anyone else have questions?" No one spoke or raised their hand. "In that case, let's wrap up for now. Everyone, please try to stay calm while we finalize the details and our next steps. We'll have another update for you by this time tomorrow." With that she gave the group a small nod, then walked out of the pavilion, already pulling out her cell phone to make her next important call—she probably needed to update the bigwigs at CBC.

As Thalia's gaze followed Ava, Ashley nudged her. "Hey, there's Christina," she said, pointing to the back corner. "Go grab her and tell her you want to talk to your sister ASAP!"

Thalia nodded, giving Ashley's leg a quick little squeeze to show her appreciation before she hopped out of the chair.

"Hi, Christina," Thalia said as she approached, watching the producer pull her dark, shiny hair into a bundle atop her head. Over the last few weeks, Thalia had been grateful for all the airtime Christina gave to her and Andrew's burgeoning relationship, and had felt that she and Christina were developing a good rapport. But now it seemed like the producer wasn't quite meeting her eyes. When she finally did, Thalia recoiled at the pity she found there.

With what she hoped was a gracious smile, Thalia reminded herself that this was exactly the emotion that would spur Christina to help her. She braced herself and asked, "Could I talk to my sister now, please? I'm really struggling, as you can imagine."

"Oh, my God, of course," the producer replied, relief washing over her face. Thalia got the sense that Christina was happy to be able to help her in some way. "Let's go to one of the confessional rooms so it's quiet. Hey, Sol," Christina called to the production assistant, who was speaking in hushed tones with one of the cameramen a few feet away. "Can you please organize times with the rest of the cast to call their families? Let's do thirty-minute slots, and bring them to confessional room B."

"On it," Sol confirmed, touching the cameraman on the arm before walking off toward the couches where most of the cast members were still seated.

"Let's go," Christina said to Thalia, leading the way out of the pavilion and across the grounds. The pair walked without speaking, and Ava's words replayed in Thalia's head. *Enough cocaine in his system to cause his death. The autopsy shows heart failure.* The description of what happened felt hollow and clinical, at odds with Thalia's complex swirl of emotions leading up to and following Andrew's death.

"I'm sorry," Christina said abruptly, after a few moments of silence. "I could tell that you really liked him. But I know you'll be okay. You're strong, and you'll find a wonderful relationship."

Thalia swayed on the spot, Christina's unexpected words almost knocking her off balance. It had been just over twenty-four hours since her boyfriend was found dead, and the producer was already talking about how she would move on? While in her heart Thalia knew this was true, it seemed to be an odd time to talk about it.

As if sensing Thalia's discomfort, Christina backtracked. "But of course, I mean right now you're going through a lot. Which is why I'm so glad Ava gave the okay to talk to your families."

They finally reached the confessional room, a makeshift space that usually acted as the resort's spa, but had been decked out with woven tapestries and rattan furniture for filming individual cast interviews. Thalia was grateful for the end to their awkward conversation.

"Here you go," Christina said, opening the door and letting Thalia walk through first. Christina grabbed a tablet and punched in a passcode to unlock it. Only the producers knew the codes—a control used to ensure the contestants remained in their little bubble of romantic bliss, isolated from contact with the real world. Each of the cast members' emergency contacts were saved in the tablet, and Christina scrolled down until she found Thalia's sister.

"Sasha, right?" Christina asked.

Thalia nodded eagerly.

"Okay, just press this button to call when you're ready. News of Andrew's death has been published in a press release by CBC, so you can tell her that, but the police have asked us not to share details about the crime scene or the investigation. So, nothing about who found his body, the tox screens, or anything like that, okay?"

She paused, waiting for Thalia's acknowledgement. "I have to listen in, unfortunately. So, I'll be sitting right outside here, and I'll come get you in thirty minutes." With that she stepped backwards out of the small space, and nudged the door halfway closed, giving Thalia some semblance of privacy while also ensuring she could hear through the crack.

Sinking onto the fluffy cushion of the chair, Thalia forcefully gripped the tablet, which was now her sole lifeline to the outside world. With a slight shake in her hands, she dialed her sister, praying she would answer. Relief flooded over her like a warm shower when she saw her sister's face pop up on the screen.

"Sasha!" she cried, her voice breaking with emotion.

"OH, MY GOD!" Sasha screamed when she realized who was on the line. Behind her, Thalia saw the exposed brick of the graphic design office Sasha worked at, and flashes of other employees' faces as her sister hurried past them to dive into a conference room. "Thals, are you okay? I saw on Twitter that someone died, is that true? What happened?" In her typical style, she hurled questions at Thalia, her mouth struggling to keep up as her brain bounced in a million different directions. Once she had finished this barrage, she stared impatiently at her sister, waiting for her to respond.

Usually, Thalia fed off her sister's energy, rising to match it until the two were chirping over each other or collapsing into hysterical giggles or breaking into a spontaneous dance on the subway. This time, however, she couldn't muster a response, and Thalia could tell from the look on Sasha's face that she sensed how much this news had impacted her. After a pause, she continued, more gingerly this time, "Thalia? Are you okay?"

Shaking her head, Thalia replied, "No. Not really. I mean, physically, yes. But emotionally…" her voice trailed off. "We were dating. Me and Andrew. I…" she stopped again, knowing that putting it into words would make it more real, which would make it hurt worse.

Thalia looked at the uncharacteristically patient expression on her sister's face, whose features so closely mirrored her own. She realized that this person knew her better and loved her more than anyone else left on this Earth, and if she didn't share how she was feeling with her, then she would only continue to spiral downwards.

With a shaky breath, Thalia continued with the easiest part of the truth. "I was falling in love with him. We were in love."

The expression on Sasha's face nearly broke her heart, seeing her own pain reflected and magnified through the lens of love for her.

"Oh, Thalia," her sister whispered, her eyes welling with tears.

Feeling tears fighting to escape her own eyes, Thalia continued, "And now filming is paused indefinitely, and I don't know what will happen with, you know…" She trailed off, conscious of Christina being right outside the door. "I don't know if you've been following the news, but it's made things a little bit umm…complicated," she hinted, hoping Sasha would get her reference and recognize why she'd needed to do what she did. Thalia believed her sister would understand she'd had to make a choice—a choice that cracked her heart open.

"Don't worry about that right now," Sasha chided her. "Tell me everything about Andrew."

And so, Thalia spoke for the next twenty minutes, telling Sasha the story of meeting Andrew the first night, how he'd singled her out and the instant crackle of chemistry she'd felt between them. How they'd spent long, lazy sunny days together in the cabana talking about movies and music and what were the worst names for dogs, and dreamy evenings together curled next to the fire pit, sharing their deepest hopes and fears. Sasha listened wordlessly, and though Thalia knew her well enough to realize it was probably shocking for her to hear about her pragmatic, level-headed sister plunging into a fiery romance, she was grateful Sasha listened without interruption or judgment on her face.

When she finally reached the point of the story where she'd had her last conversation with Andrew, Thalia hesitated, coming back into the moment in this tiny room, and remembering that Christina was still sitting a few feet away. She couldn't tell Sasha the full truth—not with the producer listening—and yet her heart was heavy with the weight of her secret.

"The last night I saw him, he told me that he loved me. He gave me a kiss good night," she swallowed, his words echoing in her head, "and then that was it. The next time I saw him he was…gone."

"What happened to him?" Sasha asked in a hushed tone.

Thalia eyed the crack in the door, certain Christina was listening intently, especially now. "I'm not allowed to talk about it." It was an honest—if convenient—excuse to avoid answering her question.

"Okay," Sasha replied, studying her sister's face carefully. Thalia knew she was trying to guess what she was insinuating. "But there was nothing…off? Like he was all good physically, emotionally when you saw him last?"

"Yes," Thalia insisted. "He was great." She paused at the thought of Christina waiting nearby, the secret Andrew had revealed in his final night catching in her throat.

No, she couldn't share that yet. It wasn't her secret to tell.

But Sasha's question caught on something in her memory, like a snag in a thread. "Well, he was a little…*off* when we first met up for dinner that night. He said he needed to tell me something weird that had happened. But then I had something umm…important I wanted to talk about with him. So, he said he'd tell me later, but then I forgot to ask him." She frowned at the screen, her eyes glazing over as she concentrated, trying to remember if he'd mentioned any more details. Had he been referring to the same secret he had told her, or something else entirely? She needed more time to think.

Glancing at the time on the screen, she realized she only had a minute or two left with her sister and pasted on a smile. "I'm sure it was just something dumb his roommate had done, or something like that. He's always acting a fool."

Reading her guarded expression, Sasha replied brightly, "Yeah, that was probably it."

"Anyways," Thalia said, "I have to go now. But I feel a million times better after talking to you, sis. I love you so much. I'm hoping they'll let me call you again soon."

"Call me anytime you can, day or night. Love you, sissy."

The phone disconnected and Thalia sat in silence, wondering what Andrew had been trying to tell her right before he died.

Chapter 16: Thalia - 1 Week Ago

Andrew and Thalia sat tucked away on a cabana bed, having found some semblance of privacy as the rest of the cast played a game of volleyball farther down the beach.

Jake had tried and failed to goad Andrew into joining, apparently keen to beat him in some sort of competition. Last night Andrew had told her his suspicions that Jake had set his heart on Thalia and was still salty over Andrew snagging her on night one. While she had balked at the idea of men fighting over her, it was obvious that Jake wasn't Andrew's biggest fan. It didn't help that Jake's new love interest Raina still threw fruitless flirty glances in Andrew's direction every chance she got. With his bulging biceps and country star good looks, Jake probably wasn't used to losing when it came to getting women's attention, and it clearly wasn't sitting well with him.

Enjoying some alone time now—or as alone as they could get with Christina and the camera crew set up a few yards away—Thalia and Andrew collapsed into a fit of laughter at a joke she had made. As Andrew reached across the daybed, his muscular arm now a glimmering golden tan after spending a few weeks in the sun, his strong hands ever so gently brushed a dark curl from Thalia's face.

She felt a shiver at the base of her spine as he whispered almost inaudibly, like a silent caress, *You're beautiful.* Her smile lit up at the admiration in his eyes, and she pulled him into a deep kiss.

Swept up in the moment, Thalia was startled by the sound of someone clearing their throat insistently.

"We need some dialogue, you two," Christina reprimanded them.

As they disentangled their limbs, Andrew spoke first. "I had a lot of fun with you today," he said, the light from a few strategically placed lanterns reflecting in his bright green eyes as he smiled at Thalia. She was stretched across the cabana bed, her head reclined against a colorfully embroidered pillow, and her long, toned legs tucked up beneath her.

"Me too," she replied, her lips upturned shyly. "I didn't think bungee jumping was my scene, but you made it worth it."

"Totally worth it," he grinned. "Yeah, you mentioned today that this was out of character for you, and that your sister would have loved it. What's she like? You haven't told me much about her."

"She's wild," Thalia replied with a laugh. "Always getting up to something, chatting with strangers, making a scene. Totally infectious personality." She paused, forcing a small smile as she braced herself for the conversation she knew it was time to have. "We have always been really close, since we were little. My parents both worked a lot. My dad was a lawyer with a killer commute to the city, and my mom was a biology professor, so she spent long hours researching, grading papers, the whole deal. They were both very committed to environmental causes and traveled all over speaking at conferences and stuff. So, Sasha and I had a lot of time just the two of us."

Andrew's expression brimmed with compassion as he grabbed her hand and leaned forward. "You spoke about your parents in the past tense," he noted gently.

Thalia nodded slowly, her full lips pressed together as she tried to contain a flood of emotion. When she finally spoke, her voice came out as barely a whisper. "They died in a car accident five years ago."

"Oh, Thalia. I'm so so sorry," Andrew said, his eyes searching hers. "That must have been awful. Especially losing them so suddenly."

"Yeah, it was pretty umm…not ideal." Thalia tried to force a laugh as she dabbed a tear that had escaped from her shining eyes. "We didn't exactly end on good terms. Like I said, they worked a lot. And the night before they died I—" her voice broke and she hung her head, ashamed to share the rest of the story.

"It's okay," Andrew whispered. "You don't have to tell me if it's not the right time. Or place," he added, glancing at the camera.

Thalia's heart ached with gratitude. "Thank you. I really appreciate you listening."

"Of course." Andrew exhaled sadly. "I care about you. I'm here for you."

Thalia felt her body relax into his solid frame, relieved that he'd really listened to her and hadn't pressured her to open up further. Stealing a glance toward the camera people to see how they'd reacted to her opening up about her family, she was surprised to see Christina standing apart from the crew, her eyes narrowed and lips pursed.

"Do you want to talk about something else?" Andrew prompted, before she had a chance to consider what the producer might be upset about. "I'd love to know more about your work. You mentioned you work at a nonprofit, right?"

Thankful for the change of subject, Thalia smiled widely, hoping it would hide the sadness echoing in her heart. "Ironically, my work is still related to my parents because I ended up working at an environmental and climate change advocacy group. We lobby for world governments to take legislative action to protect the environment. I just…I really want to make my parents proud. It's the most important thing in the world to me now." She heard the desperation she'd fought to keep out of her voice, but Andrew seemed to miss it, or chose not to press the issue.

Andrew nodded. "I get that. What's the organization called?"

"GlobeAction."

"I've heard of that!" he exclaimed. "They had that really cool social media campaign last year with the politicians dressed as endangered animals, right?"

Thalia beamed with pride. "Yes, that was my idea. I'm the director of social media."

"Seriously?" Andrew's eyes widened in shock. "That's amazing!"

"Thank you. I love it. I'm super passionate about it."

Thalia hesitated, collecting her thoughts. This was a critical juncture; how much she revealed now and how she framed things could change everything.

She continued carefully, "And I'm so bummed right now because there is some major legislation being discussed in Congress, which we've been working on for years, and I don't even have a way to find out how it's going. And it's *really* important to me that it passes. I'll be…devastated if it doesn't."

Andrew was eager to console her. "Wow, that must be so frustrating. After all your hard work! I have faith though. I'm sure everything you've done up to this point will make it a success."

"Thanks." Thalia smiled, his genuine confidence in her affecting her more than she cared to admit. Wanting to shift away from the topic of her work, she asked, "So, what about you? Tell me about your family."

"Well," Andrew replied slowly. "I already told you I'm close with my mom. My dad and I have had some…disagreements over the years that have made our relationship a little rocky." His face clouded over, and Thalia bristled at this information.

"But," Andrew continued, his expression brightening, "on the sibling front, like you, I'm the oldest and I'm also super close with my brother, Michael. He has Down syndrome. He's my best friend. Michael is obsessed with football—like, can name every player on the Patriots kind of obsessed—and he loves playing jokes on everyone. Especially our poor mom." Andrew's expression was wistful, as if some happy memories were floating serenely through his mind. "But he loves her so much, and he watches this show religiously with her. It's kind of their bonding thing. It was my mom's idea for me to come on the show, but he convinced me. He said to me, 'The girls on there are really beautiful.' I wrote him a letter yesterday and told him he was right," he added with a grin. Thalia's pulse quickened as he winked at her. "He made me this bracelet for good luck on the show. He's wearing a matching one at home as a way for us to stay connected."

Thalia glanced down to Andrew's wrist, a black leather braided bracelet circling his forearm. "I was wondering about that the first night!" she said, touched by this display of love between siblings, which reminded her so much of her own. *Focus, Thalia,* she reprimanded herself.

"Yeah, Michael is the best. He's been a huge inspiration for me. Because of him, I started to volunteer with an organization in LA that provides job training and opportunities for people with Down syndrome, and now it's the absolute highlight of my week. They recently asked me to take on a board seat. And, of course, Michael has been my biggest cheerleader."

"He sounds like a wonderful brother," Thalia replied, overwhelmed by the wave of affection she felt for Andrew. "It seems like you guys have an amazing relationship." She paused, letting her feelings wash over her instead of fighting them—just for a moment—then said softly, "I'd love to meet him someday."

His voice a husky whisper, Andrew replied, "I'd love that, too." His strong, tanned arms pulled Thalia into a slow, tender kiss as her hands rose to stroke his sharp jawline.

When they finally pulled apart, Thalia caught a glimpse of Christina out of the corner of her eye, the producer's expression fuming before she turned and stormed away toward the production room.

Chapter 17: Blake - Now

After their meeting with the cast ended, Ava had asked Blake and Christina to meet at her suite at one p.m. The junior producer had gone off to monitor Thalia while she spoke with her sister, and Blake had once again been delegated the task of dealing with the whiny crew complaining about being bored sitting around the resort. Once he'd suffered through an hour of talking to them, he politely excused himself for his meeting with Ava. This might be the first meeting he had been early for in a long time.

Approaching the door to Ava's room, he saw Christina striding up the path just a few steps ahead of him. Turning at the sound of his footsteps, she gave him a curt wave, then knocked on the heavy coral wooden door as he joined her on the patio. When the entryway opened to reveal a basic room with a view of the gardens rather than the ocean, Blake felt a twinge of awkwardness. He had offered to trade Ava for his presidential suite when she first arrived, feeling like it only made sense for the boss to have the nicest room in the resort. However, she had refused, retorting bluntly, "I'm not here for vacation, Blake. I'm here to clean this mess up."

Now, as they entered the room, he glanced around, noticing the two large suitcases in the corner, and the nearly full closet where various items from the woman's impeccable wardrobe were carefully hung. *She packed quite a bit to fly down here on short notice,* he noted, before refocusing his attention on the matter at hand.

She indicated for them to take a seat. Blake perched himself on the mahogany desk chair, unsure that he wanted to hear what was coming next. He had a sinking feeling it would only make his life more complicated.

Thinking longingly of the last night before this mess had started, he wished he could be carefree at Señor Tequila again, chatting with the bartenders and local girls, sipping tequila on the rocks. With a sigh, he pulled out his laptop to give the impression he was focusing on work, but really, he wanted to check if Manuel had responded to him. His cracked phone screen made using the device impossible, so he had logged into iMessage on his laptop to send messages to the cartel member, who was saved in his contacts as 'AV Repair'.

Ava's expression was grim. "Blake, Christina and I found out some major news this morning, and unfortunately, we didn't have time to tell you before the meeting with the cast."

Annoyance prickled on the back of his neck, but it lost a battle against the curiosity and nerves clawing their way up his throat. "What is it?"

"CBC's review of the toxicology report revealed that Andrew was very likely murdered."

Blake's stomach dropped as he tried to process what she was saying. "Murdered? But I thought he overdosed?" A million questions swirled in his head. Who would want to hurt a nice guy like Andrew? Was it one of the cast members? Or worse, one of his own crew? Another possibility crept into his mind, but he forced it down, not liking the idea at all. It couldn't be related. *No way,* his brain insisted.

Ava shook her head and proceeded to share more details on the CBC examiner's findings with him. "This changes everything. Until we have more info, we need to keep this very close to the chest. Only the three of us, the police, and the board. And we need to ramp up our review of the security footage. I know we were already working on it, but now we need faster and more thorough review. Where are we with that, Blake?"

As he was about to respond, a notification on his laptop screen alerted him to a new message from AV Repair. Blake's heart began to race. He had enough on his plate with this news—couldn't Manuel have chosen a better time to finally respond to him?

"Uhh, yes. Was just checking an update from our...offsite coordinator," he said, slamming the laptop closed. "Canceling all dates for now, obviously."

Across the table from him, Christina rolled her eyes, clearly seeing through this fib, although she probably suspected he'd been busy messaging girls on Tinder, not dealing with an epic crisis.

"Obviously," Ava said dryly, raising a single eyebrow. "So, have we reviewed all the camera footage? The hotel manager confirmed they're reviewing all of their security footage, but have we started going through our own cameras?"

"Yes, we have," Blake replied, clearing his throat and sitting up straighter, brushing off Ava's condescending tone. *I have bigger issues on my mind right now*, he thought as his eyes darted to his closed laptop. "We have all the PAs going through footage."

"From what date to what date? And how many of them are working on it? Is it enough? If we don't show our cooperation quickly, the police may subpoena us to turn over everything. And I know there are some things we don't want out in the public. No one needs to see Raina's little performance for Jake last weekend."

Blake snickered, then stopped at Ava's impatient expression. "Well, umm, we thought we'd start like a day before. And I think we've got about…five PAs working on it?"

Ava let out an almost imperceptible sigh of frustration.

Christina cleared her throat.

Blake could hardly stop himself from rolling his eyes. *Always eager for a chance to make me look bad.*

The young producer said, "Actually, we've got six production assistants reviewing footage from twenty cameras around the resort. We've collected all the footage starting thirty-six hours in advance of Andrew's body being discovered, and up to twelve hours after. So, a forty-eight-hour period in total. Also, I thought maybe to expedite things, we could upload some of the footage to the cloud and have interns back in LA work on it as well. Thoughts?"

Blake suppressed a gag at the puppy dog expression in her eyes, so desperate to impress her new idol.

Ava nodded. "Excellent idea, please go ahead. Thanks for taking the lead on this, Christina."

Taking the lead? Blake fumed. *Has she forgotten who is in charge here?*

"Alright," Ava continued, "is there anything else we need to cover in this meeting?"

Blake shook his head, anxious to end the meeting so he could respond to Manuel.

Christina shifted in her chair. "I think we should consider looping Sol in, too." When Ava began to protest, she insisted, "I know she's junior, but she's trustworthy and knows how to get stuff done. She speaks Spanish, so she could help talking to the resort staff. Plus, she's more tech savvy than any of us."

Ava paused, considering. "I'll think about it."

Blake noted how Christina's shoulders eased at Ava's response.

"Great," the executive concluded, "let's reconvene tomorrow morning. Christina and I will share the CBC tox report analysis with the police then, and we can see what direction they want to take the investigation."

Breathing a sigh of relief, Blake stood from his chair, slipping out the door and hurrying toward the privacy of his room. He had spent all day yesterday frantically texting Manuel, his anxiety through the roof as police swarmed the hotel grounds.

We have a problem...call me, Blake's first message had read, a few hours after they'd found Andrew's body. Then later that afternoon, he'd written, *Seriously, a guy died on the set, there are police here.* And then that evening, he messaged him again, *They told us he overdosed, so they are gonna know there are drugs here at the resort! Wtf am I supposed to do?*

When Blake had been trying to fall asleep last night, the heart-wrenching sound of Mr. McKenna breaking down on the phone played over and over in his mind. Giving up on sleep, he'd gotten up out of bed, opening his laptop to message Manuel once again. *I'm not going to Mexican jail. You need to figure this shit out.*

Despite the increasingly desperate tone of his texts, Blake had gone all of last night and most of today without hearing back from the cartel member. He'd thought to himself this morning that Manuel had probably seen the news as well and was trying to figure out how to best deal with the law enforcement presence at the resort. Some small part of him had taken pleasure in imagining Manuel freaking out, too, even if they were going down on the same sinking ship.

Yet, when he finally settled back at his desk and read the response now, it didn't seem Manuel was stressed by these developments at all.

Be cool...it's all good, the message read. Short, simple, and no acknowledgement of the monumental shitstorm that could be coming their way.

What did that even mean? It's all good? *It is NOT all good,* Blake thought angrily.

He paced around his room for a few minutes, considering what to do next. Over the last few weeks, Manuel had made several trips to the resort, always alone, and carrying a large box with tools, cameras, or some kind of lighting in tow. He knew that these boxes were filled with cocaine, but never looked inside, figuring it was better if he didn't know and could more easily feign surprise if they were ever discovered.

Blake considered whether he could try to move the drugs out of the storage unit, maybe even out of the resort grounds. But after wracking his brain, Blake couldn't come up with a way to move the goods without attracting attention. If anyone saw him lifting a finger to move a camera box, they'd immediately send a PA to go do it for him, which was the last thing he needed. He couldn't risk anyone on set finding out what he was doing or his career would be over. This kind of scandal would not be easily swept under the rug by moving to Paracon or some other network.

Thinking through his options, Blake also considered whether there was a way to get rid of the drugs. Maybe he could toss them in the ocean, perhaps at night time when it was too dark to see anything on the beach. But just as Blake was getting excited about this plan, a sudden realization hit him: if he destroyed millions of dollars' worth of product, the cartel would surely come after him. Manuel had become less scary to him, but his presence still implied the ongoing threat from the cartel. Even if they didn't kill him immediately, he'd never be able to stop wondering when they would be coming for him again. Whatever he did, he needed to make sure the cocaine ended up safely back in the hands of the cartel.

Staring down the abyss of these three dead ends—being thrown in Mexican prison, losing his career, or the risk of bodily harm by some cartel lackey—Blake was at a loss. His muscles tight from pacing the room, he collapsed onto the bed, bringing his hands to his face. He was used to taking quick, decisive action and getting the outcomes he wanted, but this time there was nothing in his control he could do to make this problem go away.

Demoralized, he admitted to himself that he was totally dependent on Manuel and the cartel to fix this situation. They had the resources here on the ground, and much more experience with this type of clandestine work. With a glimmer of hope, he realized the cartel also had a vested interest in ensuring the drugs weren't discovered, because even if they weren't tied back to the cartel and Blake took the fall, the goods would be seized as evidence and the cartel would be out of a lot of cash. Yes, he'd convince Manuel that it was in his own best interest to ensure the cocaine was moved to a safer location.

Out of habit, he reached for his phone, then put it back down at the sight of the cracked screen, annoyed he still couldn't remember how he had broken it. He turned back toward his laptop instead, and bracing himself, hit the dial button to video chat with Manuel. After only two rings, the man's long face appeared on the screen, his eyes squinting suspiciously.

"Yo, why are you calling me?" Manuel exclaimed.

"I told you, there's an emergency here. We need to figure this shit out!"

"No." Anger flashed across Manuel's sharp features. "I told *you* that it's all good. I—"

Blake interrupted, his frustration erupting, "Dude, I don't think you get it. There are police coming here every day. They originally said this kid died of an overdose, but now it looks like he was *murdered* with drugs. There are going to be questions about where the drugs came from. They're going to search the resort." Remembering to focus on what the cartel had to lose, he appealed to Manuel's personal interests. "I don't think your bosses will be too pleased if the police seize however many pounds of cocaine you've already brought here."

Manuel's features screwed up, his mouth twisting as he rolled his eyes at Blake. "You're really dumb, bro, if you think we're pulling some amateur shit like that. If I tell you it's all good, then it's all good. Those bosses you're so worried about got it under control."

"I don't think so," Blake retorted, shaking his head in disbelief. Why was Manuel refusing to do anything to stop this train from going off the rails? "Let me talk to them, then. I want to hear it directly from them."

Laughter taunted him from the other side of the screen. "You think I'm gonna let you talk to the head of the cartel? You wild." Manuel chuckled to himself before his face grew serious again, as if to impress upon Blake what he was about to say. "You talk to *me*. And you don't do *shit* until I tell you to. If you can't be chill, I'm gonna have to be paying you a different kind of visit. Is that clear?"

Despite his small frame and lean face, something in Manuel's eyes sent a flash of fear coursing through Blake's veins. *This guy will not hesitate to kill me,* he realized with a jolt.

"Yes," Blake replied, finding his voice. "I'm chill. We're good."

"Aight, then. Wait for my text. And don't call me again."

As the screen went black, Blake's heart thumped in the silent room. He didn't trust Manuel and the cartel one bit. He needed to find a way to ensure the police didn't discover the drugs, and most importantly, his connection to the cartel. But the question was, how?

Chapter 18: Thalia - 3 Days Ago

Thalia splayed across a fuchsia unicorn pool float, a spicy margarita in her hand, as Ashley floated a few feet away from her on a giant pineapple, gripping a glass of rosé.

"Soooo," the blonde began, angling her slim body on the raft so she could see Thalia's face, "seems like you and Andrew are getting pre-tty serious." She raised one eyebrow under her wide-brimmed hat, awaiting more details from her roommate.

"Hey, I could say the same about you," Thalia teased, deflecting the question as she kicked at the water, her hot pink pedicure bright against her warm brown skin.

She made a conscious effort to look at Ashley, and not toward the crew at the poolside. It still hadn't grown easy for her, this act of being natural while also trying to be someone the fanbase would love, all while pretending that the cameras—which had become a constant presence—didn't exist.

"Me and Andrew getting serious?" Ashley guffawed. "Nah, but I do think Nick is pretty great." Some genuine emotion pierced through the facade of humor Thalia had become so familiar with over the last few weeks.

"Did you ever think this would happen?" Thalia asked. "I mean, when you came on the show…did you actually think you'd find someone?"

Ashley paused, as if she hadn't really considered the question before. "I guess I'd hoped," she said slowly. "I mean, I was so sick of the rat race on the apps, one guy after the other sending you gross messages. And then even the ones who say they're looking for something serious end up telling you later that they think it would be better if you 'keep things casual,' " she said, her hands forming into air quotes. "So yeah, I hoped it would happen. But did I honestly believe it would? I'm not sure." Taking a sip of her wine, she returned the question to Thalia. "Did you?"

Thalia considered how to reply. She was aware of the camera crew sitting four feet away on the edge of the pool, which made it impossible to be honest about why she'd come on the show. The truth was that even though falling in love hadn't been her motivation, Andrew *was* a pretty great guy. Perhaps a little too great, since she felt her thoughts often drifting to him, when what she needed was to stay focused on her goal.

Looking at Ashley's expectant face, she decided to go with a partial truth. "Doesn't everyone want that fairytale ending? It's surprised me, how much I care about him. I've had boyfriends before, but no one who I ever clicked with instantly like this, and respected so much. He's incredible."

Ashley chuckled to herself. "Aww look at our little Thals, all grown up and falling in love!"

"Hey, I didn't say love!"

"You didn't have to, darling," Ashley replied with a wink. Glancing toward the path leading to the restaurant, she shifted her attention as the cameras swiveled in that direction. "Speak of the devil!" she called gleefully, as Andrew's broad shoulders appeared from around a tree blooming with huge orange flowers.

"Hi, ladies," he greeted them with a wave, his smile lighting up as his eyes landed on Thalia. She returned his gaze shyly, hoping he hadn't overheard their conversation. "Sorry to interrupt this girls' pool day, but I have something I wanted to talk to Thalia about, and it's kind of time sensitive."

"Oh," Thalia exclaimed, a little flutter in her stomach catching her off guard.

"Ooohh," Ashley echoed, drawing out the syllable. "I know what that's code for. I'll leave you to it, then." She wiggled her eyebrows in her roommate's direction.

"Oh, my God," Thalia replied with an eyeroll, splashing some water in Ashley's direction. "Go cheer on your boyfriend at the frisbee match the guys are having."

Ashley eased herself off of the raft and onto the steps of the pool, letting the water come up over her long legs as she wrapped her hair into a low bun. "That's the plan, lady. Catch you later," she said, blowing a kiss as she walked away in the direction of the beach.

Turning her attention to Andrew, Thalia asked, "So what did you want to talk about?"

He extended his arm to help her out of the water, his lips turned up and eyes sparkling with mischief. "Actually, it's something I wanted to show you. But I knew if I said that, we'd only get more wisecracks from Ashley."

Thalia let out a little burst of laughter. "Alright, so what do you want to *show* me, then?"

"C'mon, it's down at the restaurant." He took her hand, guiding her back down the path he'd come from, and glancing at his watch. A flash of anxiety crossed his face, and his gait quickened.

"Everything okay?"

"Yes, but we need to hurry. It's almost noon. And I don't want the camera crew to follow us."

After living with no commitments, no place to be, and no sense of time for the last several weeks, Thalia was thrown off by this sudden rush, and couldn't imagine what it was that Andrew wanted to show her. Still, given how invested he seemed in the surprise, she picked up her pace to match his. Glancing behind her, she saw the camera crew that had been assembled lazily next to the pool still scrambling to pack up and move their gear to follow her and Andrew.

When they arrived at the restaurant, Thalia noted the clock read 11:58. She waved as Andrew greeted Maria, who jumped up to meet them.

"*Hola, Maria. ¿Está lista? Es la hora, no?*"

"*Sí, Señor Andrew. ¡Ven conmigo!*" Glancing around furtively, the waitress seemed satisfied with the empty restaurant, then beckoned them back through the kitchen doors, which Thalia had only ever seen employees enter.

"Is the chef making me some tamales?" she guessed, as the smell of fresh chiles hit her nose. "Because I could really go for some of those right now."

"No, even better," he replied, barely able to contain his grin. They passed by the chef standing at the stove, who gave Andrew a conspiratorial wink as he stirred a pot of something that smelled delicious, steam clouding his round face.

They reached what appeared to be an employee break room, with a small round table and two shabby folding chairs squeezed inside. A tray with a coffee carafe and two mugs had been placed upon the table, a trail of steam rising up from the jug toward the dim overhead light. On the wall, a tiny, ancient TV was mounted, two antennae sticking up at odd angles from its top. It was playing a local news station, the anchor speaking at a speed that was way beyond Thalia's Spanish comprehension levels.

Maria looked between them, smiling as she said, "*¡Qué lo paséis bien!*" before walking away.

"So," Andrew said, excitement shining on his face. "I know you said that you're frustrated you didn't know how your environmental bill was progressing in Congress."

"Right…" Thalia confirmed, still not understanding what this had to do with the closet-like room they were now standing in.

"Well, I found out from talking with Maria that the local news station switches to CNN International at noon every day. So, I'm guessing, and hoping, that they'll be covering this on CNN, since it's a major piece of legislation."

Thaila swallowed as her throat constricted with emotion, overwhelmed at his thoughtful gesture. "I can't thank you enough, Andrew. This means the world to me."

The corners of his lips turned softly up, he replied, "And *you* mean the world to *me*."

Hearing those words full of passion and sincerity in this dingy room, when they were finally out of sight of the cameras for the first time in almost a month, Thalia felt her heart warm and knew that Ashley was right—she was falling in love with this man.

A blast of music from the TV interrupted their moment, indicating the CNN International news segment was about to begin. Andrew stepped behind one of the rickety chairs, pulling it out away from the table, and motioned toward the seat. "My lady."

"Thank you, good sir," she replied, easing herself down onto the wooden frame.

He grabbed a mug and poured her a cup of coffee, the rich aroma pervading the tiny room. Reaching for the remote, he turned up the volume so that they could hear what the announcers were saying, thankfully in English with Spanish subtitles.

"Good afternoon, ladies and gentlemen. This is your CNN World News report. I'm Bill Myers. Lawmakers in Washington DC have been engaged in fierce debate over a piece of environmental legislation that has been sponsored by Senator Cooker, Democrat from Pennsylvania, and Senator Landers, Democrat from Maine."

Thalia's heart leapt at the mention of her bill. She leaned forward, desperate to catch every word of the update, but nervous about what it would reveal. She glanced at Andrew, expecting his eyes to be on the TV, but instead they were fixed on her, awaiting her reaction.

The announcer's smooth voice swelled. "This is the most progressive and ambitious climate change bill that has ever been put forth in the US legislature, seeking measures such as capping carbon emissions from manufacturing and agricultural producers, investing nearly two trillion dollars in clean energy sources, and providing additional protections for US national parks and other environmentally sensitive areas."

"Most ambitious climate bill ever! That's you!" Andrew whispered, giving her two corny thumbs up.

Thalia flashed him an anxious smile, then refocused on the screen as the anchor continued, "Since the Democratic party currently controls the Senate, but not the House of Representatives, they will need to convince at least five US representatives to vote for the bill in order for it to be made into law. The bill was originally expected to come up for a vote during the fall session, but Democrats are now trying to pass it before the summer recess."

"No," Thalia gasped. "It's happening too soon!" During the last conversation she'd had with her boss, Veronica shared she had been meeting with several senior congresspeople. Veronica's intel indicated it wouldn't be pushed through until the end of the year, as they were working on negotiations with the few key Republicans who were considering reaching across the aisle on this issue.

Trying to retrain her swimming focus on the TV, Thalia heard the anchor say, "Unfortunately…" Thalia's stomach lurched at this machete of a word. "Public support for the bill remains low, as the American public seems skeptical of this level of financial investment. With a significant portion of the public still not believing in the man-made effects of climate change, particularly those in the five states which these congressmen and congresswomen represent, it's looking like it will be challenging for Democrats to pass this bill. That would be a major blow to President Ferris's administration. Unless there is a major shift in public opinion before the vote in a few weeks, CNN's political analysts project the bill will fail. Next up, we have a special report on the scandal involving the Prime Minister of—"

The sound and image disappeared as Andrew clicked off the television, gently placing the remote back on the table. "Thalia," he said, his voice soft, "I'm so sorry. I feel terrible that you had to find out this way."

Her hands felt like they had gone numb around the coffee mug, her grip nearly slipping as she tried to set it back onto the table. Looking up at Andrew, she stared at him shell-shocked, wondering how she could have been so happy three minutes ago, and so utterly crushed right now. Andrew was incredible, but the entire reason she'd come on the show, the whole reason she was here, was to get a following she could leverage to get this bill passed. Thalia had imagined she'd have time for the show to air and to build up her following well in advance of the public debate and media attention on the bill. Yet, something must have happened to rush it onto the floor, and unfortunately, it didn't seem that GlobeAction had all their ducks in a row. She couldn't believe the deal was on the brink of collapse.

Thinking of all she could be doing if she were at work now, she chastised herself for taking this time away. Despite the enthusiasm of the social media team she'd built, they were all basically fresh out of school, and would be scrambling in this kind of crisis without her leadership. Veronica was a veteran in the field, but she was old school—calling in favors with connections to get meetings with politicians, working with scientific experts on drafting legislation, writing speeches, that kind of thing. Social media and the court of public opinion were unfamiliar territory for her. Veronica respected her, but Thalia sometimes needed to work very hard to convince her that it was worthwhile investing their resources into the digital campaigns Thalia had designed. Thalia felt a pang of guilt thinking of how her boss and the entire GlobeAction team needed her right now, while she was wasting away her time on a tropical vacation, cozying up with some guy. She needed to focus on her task and stop getting distracted by her feelings for him.

"Thalia? Are you okay?" Andrew's voice eased her away from her thoughts.

Her eyes brimming with tears, Thalia looked up at the exposed pipes in the ceiling, holding in a breath for a few seconds before letting it out.

"I told you that my parents died suddenly," she began slowly. "But I didn't tell you what happened the night before they died."

She studied Andrew's expression, trying to gauge whether he was ready to hear this, and was relieved to find his gaze fixed steadily on hers. He reached across the table, the smooth pad of his thumb stroking the top of her hand. With this reassurance, she proceeded with her story.

"My graduation from Georgetown was coming up, and my parents called to tell me they were going to miss it because of an environmental conference they needed to attend. After years of them missing my basketball games and Sasha's dance recitals and my holiday weekends home from college…I was so frustrated. So, I don't know, I just lost it. Totally flipped out on them. I told them that they cared more about their work than their daughters. That I wasn't even sure they loved me. That—" her voice broke on a jagged edge of the painful memory. She continued, her voice rasping, "that I didn't care if they came to my graduation, or if I ever saw them again."

Emotion shone in Andrew's eyes as he watched her break down. "Oh, Thalia," he breathed, pulling her into a tight embrace.

She fixed her eyes on the now black TV screen, too full of shame and regret to meet his gaze. She said flatly, "I never talked to them again. Twenty-four hours later they were gone. And I made a promise to myself then that I would do whatever it took to make them proud. To honor their memory. That's why I started working at GlobeAction, and that's why I *need* to get this bill passed. I need to make things right," she finished, her tone almost pleading.

"Wow," Andrew replied, stunned. "That is a lot to put on yourself. And a lot to process." He let out a big breath. "I know we need to talk a lot more about this, and I absolutely want to do that with you. But right now, we should probably go back out there. They've probably told Blake we disappeared, and I don't want Maria to get in any trouble."

Blake, Thalia thought, her brain still heavy with the weight of the crushing news. She drew in a deep breath to ground herself and clear her mind, so she could figure out how to salvage this.

Slowly, the gears began to turn, and she felt every pulse of her heart as the fog lifted and the shape of a plan began to form in her mind. It was drastic, but the severity of the situation called for it.

"You ready?" Andrew prompted again, extending his hand to her as he rose from his chair.

With Andrew's bright green eyes studying her, Thalia returned his gaze. Her voice full of resolve, but tinged with sadness at knowing what she knew she had to sacrifice, she replied, "Yes. I'm going to make this work."

Chapter 19: Christina - Now

Christina tapped her foot, waiting to see how Ava would break the news of CBC's analysis of the tox report to Chief Martinez. The chief sat across from them at a narrow desk they'd rearranged in Christina's suite to accommodate a more private meeting place than the restaurant. Ava had asked her to lay low during the discussion and let her take the lead. While she wasn't used to taking a back seat, Christina was nervously anticipating the sparks that would fly as the two powerhouse women faced off. *I am a reality show producer,* she thought wryly. *Always living for the drama.*

"Thank you for coming here," Ava began.

"You're welcome," Daniela responded, "though I have to admit I'm a bit puzzled as to why you wanted to meet here instead of at the restaurant again."

Ava cleared her throat. "Well, that's actually the main topic we wanted to discuss this morning."

Raising one perfectly arched eyebrow, the chief replied, "Go on."

"After completing an independent audit of the toxicology screen, our CBC medical consultants found that the levels and types of drugs in Andrew's bloodstream were not consistent with an overdose. In fact, the levels were so high that they think it's highly unlikely the drugs could have been administered by Andrew himself. They are of the belief that," she paused, and Christina felt her breath catch, "Andrew was murdered."

A tiny "oh" of surprise formed on Daniela's full lips. "Well, that is… certainly unexpected." She paused, and Christina could see her processing this information. Snapping back into focus, Daniela looked at Ava. "I'll have the forensics team review the data again. It seems they may have missed something. Thank you very much for bringing this to our attention."

"Of course," Ava said with a nod.

"Now," the chief continued, gathering momentum as she recovered from her initial shock, "assuming our team confirms CBC's analysis, we will obviously need to shift the focus of the investigation. I will assign extra units to work on this case and begin identifying potential suspects and reviewing additional evidence. Thank you for your help so far. My team will take it from here."

Ava leaned forward in her chair, her posture stiffening as her features puckered into a slight frown. "To be honest, Chief Martinez, given the events so far, I'd be much more comfortable if my team remained involved. I'd like to have personal oversight into every development on the case."

Christina felt a slight bristle on the back of her neck. Something about Ava's tone implied there was more going on than just a distrust of the police's competence. Christina couldn't quite pinpoint the emotion laced in her mentor's voice. *She sounds almost…defensive?* Brushing away the thought, Christina reasoned, *she's had to deal with people not taking her seriously her whole career. She has to be overbearing to get shit done.*

Regardless of Ava's intent, it was clear Daniela was a proud woman who didn't take well to her authority being questioned by a civilian, and an American one at that.

A flash of defiance sharpening her smooth features, Daniela replied with feigned nonchalance, "We'll be happy to have your team involved to the extent that our department deems appropriate. For starters, that involves providing us with all of your camera footage."

Ava's composure faltered as she was caught off guard by the request, which didn't seem to be a request at all, but rather a demand in retaliation for her questioning the police department's capabilities. Christina could practically see Ava fuming as she retorted, "That footage is the property of CBC. We won't be sharing it without a subpoena. I'll share the contact details for our general counsel with you."

"Is that really necessary?" Chief Martinez's hazel eyes flashed. "We're all working toward a common goal, so I'm surprised by this lack of cooperation."

Ava's jaw tensed. "We have been conducting our own reviews of the film, and will alert you to anything suspicious. Our teams are working tirelessly on the review. We discovered an additional camera last night, so all footage—including that one—should be reviewed by tomorrow evening."

"An additional camera?" Christina's surprise at this revelation let the question escape from her lips, despite Ava's orders to stay quiet. The last update Sol had given her was that they were aiming to finish the footage review by tonight.

"Yes, from the pathway between the crew housing and the boys' villa," Ava replied, shooting Christina a warning glance. Her tone made it clear that this was not to be discussed further in front of the chief.

"With all due respect," Daniela interjected, "your team are not detectives. They make reality TV." She waved her hand dismissively, her bracelets jingling. "The video needs to be reviewed by professionals."

"Well then I guess you'd better get working on that subpoena," Ava said, her chin lifting haughtily as she held the chief's gaze.

Daniela returned the withering look, her full lips pressed together as she considered how to respond. After what seemed to Christina like an eternity, the chief said, "I'll be in touch," then stood and left the room without another word.

As Daniela walked away, Ava turned to Christina, her expression serious. "I consider you my mentee. So, I want to share this feedback with you. Don't *ever* let you or your team appear disjointed in front of your opponent, or anyone for that matter."

"I'm sorry," Christina sputtered, pulling at the hairband around her wrist. "I was just caught off guard. I...I thought I was on top of the review process. I want to take personal responsibility for reviewing every second of footage."

"No, no. Don't apologize. That's my second piece of advice for you today," Ava said, the frown lines around her eyes softening. "Look, we are women in this industry, and it's tough. And on top of that, we're women of color. We have to build loyal teams, we have to be twice as tough as everyone else, and we have to do whatever it takes to create our own success—however unconventional that path might be." She paused, studying Christina. "Now, are you on my team?"

"Of course," Christina answered with certainty. "One hundred percent."

"Good. Now let's get the PAs on that footage from the last camera."

"No," Christina insisted. "I'll do it myself. I want to…to make sure this gets done right."

"Okay, as long as you can finish it by this evening. I don't want to give Chief Martinez any window of opportunity to claim we haven't cooperated fully."

Christina nodded to show she understood.

The executive glanced down at her watch, the fine gold glinting on her wrist, the only jewelry on her hands. "Now, I've got to go find Blake and prep with him before the next all-hands meeting."

As Christina headed toward the production room to begin the long slog of reviewing the last camera footage, she decided to take a detour to the restaurant to grab more coffee for fuel. Her mind was racing as she wondered what additional evidence the police would be looking for, and how they'd begin putting together a possible suspect list.

Approaching the restaurant, she spotted Maria clearing a pile of abandoned plates from one of the tables. "Hey, Maria," she greeted her. "How are you doing? You know with…" she trailed off, unsure how to raise the topic on her mind.

"I'm fine," the waitress confirmed with a curt nod. "Oh, and thank you for talk to my manager. He tell us we get all our money soon."

Relieved that the resort manager had followed through on their conversation yesterday about the staff's pay, Christina smiled. "I'm glad to hear that."

As Maria continued stacking the dishes, she hesitated, as if debating whether to say something. Apparently having made up her mind, she lifted her gaze from the table up toward the producer. "That woman, Ava…she your boss?"

"Yeah," Christina replied, pouring herself a coffee from the fresh carafe the staff kept on hand for the crew. "She came to Mexico to help us because of Andrew."

A slight frown crossed the waitress's pretty face, the morning sunlight streaking half of it in sun while the other remained in the shadow of a beam to the pavilion. "She only come here after he die?"

"Yes," Christina answered, confused by the question. "She lives in LA. She's a big boss, so she doesn't stay here for the whole season."

The wrinkles on Maria's forehead deepened as she paused, then uttered a quiet, "Oh."

"Why do you ask?"

Glancing around as if to see whether anyone was in earshot, Maria replied, "I work at a different hotel as housekeeping. I think I see her there last week. But probably I'm wrong, it's another lady." Her shoulder shrank into a shrug, as if sorry she'd brought it up.

Christina hesitated, unsure of how to respond. "Yeah, probably." Avoiding the waitress's gaze, she took a sip of steaming coffee then announced with false cheeriness, "Alright, well I've got to get to work. See you later."

"*Adiós*," the waitress replied, her large brown eyes clouded with an expression Christina couldn't quite read.

Heading to the AV room, Christina wondered about Maria's comment. *It's probably just someone who looks like her, right? Maria must be confused.* She wasn't sure why Ava would have been in Mexico the week prior. Up until they had discovered Andrew's body, the season had been going very well, with Ava regularly sharing positive feedback on their updates and the clips she was seeing. There would have been no reason for her to come to Puerto Engaño before the incident. And even if she had, wouldn't she have been staying here at Paraiso Maya? They were using less than half of the available beds at the resort. It wouldn't make any sense for her to stay at a different hotel, especially with all the super strict security measures that had been put in place at this property. Even if for some reason she had come earlier, and had stayed at another hotel…why would she lie about it?

Are you on my team? Ava's question echoed in her head. It seemed this team kept secrets from each other.

Arriving at the AV room, Christina tried to brush the thoughts from her mind, as she had a more important task at hand. She desperately needed to find and review the footage from this last camera that had been discovered. How had she missed it?

Fortunately, Sol was in the room already, and Christina asked the PA to quickly pull up the new film, then settled into her favorite chair to begin a long day of combing through the footage. She hit play and bumped up the speed to double time, wanting to get through it as quickly as possible, without missing anything important.

Christina watched as the thirty-six hours prior to the discovery of Andrew's body unfolded on film. She noted the comings and goings of the crew from the building where their rooms were all located—except for Blake who, of course, had a suite, and herself as she'd miraculously managed to finagle one for herself this season. A group of cameramen walked along the pathway, equipment in hand. Before the season started, Ava had proposed that they sleep with it in their rooms to ensure they didn't miss any juicy action that might happen very late at night or early in the morning.

As Christina continued watching, the camera captured the sun rising high in the sky, beaming down on the staff, all of whom Christina recognized. Each of them passed along the path to enjoy their breaks in rotating shifts. Nothing out of the ordinary so far.

When the time stamp on the footage read 2:37 p.m., her stomach grumbled loudly, interrupting her focus.

"Sol, can you bring me a chicken burrito, please?" she requested over the radio to the PA, who had disappeared hours ago, after realizing Christina was going to review this last tape herself.

"On it." The staticky reply cut through the silence in the room as Christina watched in fast forward. The PA appeared fifteen minutes later with a warm, foil-wrapped burrito in hand.

"Thanks," Christina said, refusing to peel her eyes from the screen.

For the next three hours, Christina diligently reviewed the tape, the mind-numbing boredom of watching her coworkers walk back and forth wearing on her. She occasionally stood up to stretch, reaching her hands up over her head, her midriff exposed beneath her plain black tank top.

The film showed a time stamp of nearly 10:15 p.m. when something caught her eye. Scrambling for the keyboard, Christina rewound the tape by a minute, then pressed play in normal speed, heart pounding as she waited to confirm what she thought she'd seen.

Thirty seconds later, a lean figure with broad shoulders, clothed in casual shorts and a light-colored tank top, made its way down the path. The dim lighting along the path glinted against the sandy blond hair atop his head. Though she couldn't see the person's face, it was clear from the build and gait that it was Andrew. He passed by the camera, his stride determined and confident, but then went out of view. Where was he heading?

Christina scanned through the list of the cameras, trying to figure out which one would capture the end of that path. That trail diverged at the restaurant and the spa, where they had set up the confessional rooms. Reviewing the details, Christina determined that camera nine should pick up at the end of the path, assuming Andrew hadn't taken any random detours. She pulled up the footage and jumped to the 10:15 p.m. time stamp from the evening before his body was found.

"C'mon," she muttered, waiting to see Andrew emerge on the screen. She leaned forward, gripping the mouse in anxiety.

After two minutes that seemed to stretch into eternity, Christina saw his athletic frame appear. At the fork in the path, he seemed to hesitate, then headed toward the spa where the confessional rooms were set up. He went out of view again, but it was likely that had been his final destination.

Christina wondered why he hadn't pulled in a crew member before he went in. At the start of this season, Ava had asked that they instruct the cast on how to film confessionals on their own, sharing her experience from one of her previous shows where she'd gotten some very raw, vulnerable footage when the pressure of having a producer staring at you from behind the camera was taken away.

Even though they'd complied with her request, so far she didn't know of any confessional footage that had been filmed without a producer there. In fact, the cast usually preferred to be hanging on the beach or drinking at the poolside bar, rather than stuck in a tiny, windowless room speaking to a producer. Typically, they had to drag in the stars and practically force them to talk about their feelings, so she was surprised to see Andrew voluntarily heading toward the confessional. She had no idea what he might have spoken to the camera about.

As her mind wandered through the possibilities, her fingers scrolled through the folder containing all the confessional videos, until she finally found an unnamed file dated 10:26 p.m. that evening, which hadn't been opened. She guessed that after the body was found, no one had been bothering to review the confessional tapes, as they were too focused on the security footage. It seemed like Andrew had needed some time to prepare himself, because there was a five-minute gap between when he arrived at the spa and when he started to record. Her spine tingling in anticipation, both excited and nervous about what he might have said, she hit play.

Andrew's fine, golden features appeared on the screen. Even before he began speaking, Christina could tell that something was off. The usual sparkle of his eyes was dull, and instead of the relaxed confidence that often played across his face, she noticed the tension of his angular jaw, his rosy lips pursed into a thin, straight line.

He opened his mouth, cleared his throat, then closed it again, staring into the camera. When he began speaking, his voice seemed strained, forced somehow. "This has been an amazing experience for me, and I'm so glad to have met Thalia. She is incredible, and I'll always cherish the time we had together here on *Love's a Beach*. But I have been doing some real soul-searching, and as amazing a person as she is, I have realized that she isn't *my* person." He paused, clenching and unclenching his jaw, his gaze drifting away from the camera. When he looked back to it, his emerald eyes were twinkling, but now with tears. "I know she is going to be crushed, but…I have to do what's right. For me. And for her. Because we both deserve to find our forever love."

Christina sat dumbfounded as she watched Andrew lean in toward the camera, his features illuminated larger than life in this close up view, her long-forgotten burrito now cold on the desk next to her.

His voice husky, he completed his confessional with a somber announcement: "And that is why I plan to break up with her tomorrow."

Chapter 20: Blake - 2 Days Ago

"Good morning, Blake!" Sol greeted him at breakfast. "Ready for today's *amazing* mariachi date?"

He detected the sarcasm in her voice, but his head was pounding from last night's tequila, and he couldn't be bothered to address it. "Pumped," he mumbled.

"Before you kick that off, I wanted to show you this confessional I taped with Karina this morning," the PA ventured.

Blake barely contained a sigh. He did not have the energy for this before he'd even finished his breakfast burrito, but he knew Sol was like a dog with a bone when she had an idea, and if she kept hounding him all day, then he *really* would not have any energy.

"Fine," he responded, taking a much-needed swig of coffee.

"Great," she said, whipping her tablet out of her bag and onto the table before Blake could even set his mug down. "So, the interesting part starts right about…here."

The showrunner watched as Karina's lean frame filled the screen. "I'm very good at what I do, you know. And my firm, Trinity Fund? It's one of the largest private equity firms in New York. I closed half a billion dollars of deals last year. But one got away from me." Her voice hardened at the memory.

"*Por favor,*" Sol's voice interrupted timidly in the background of the video. "Can we try to stay on topic? We were talking about Christina's suggestion that you and Andrew might be a good match?"

"It's related," Karina snapped, and next to him Blake saw Sol jump a bit at her sharp tone, even watching it now. "As I was saying, there was a big deal that should have been all mine. A big movie production company was spinning off its comic division and we were set to buy it. Do you know how big my bonus would have been? Anyways, it doesn't matter." She hurried along with a wave. "The point is, I'd worked on that deal for years, countless hours and tons of dinners buttering up their sleazy CEO. And at the last minute it was stolen away by another firm, Westfund. And do you know who works at Westfund?"

"No, I don't," Sol stammered faintly, off camera.

"Andrew," Karina spat out, a bitter smile on her face. "He led the deal. So no, I will not be pursuing a relationship with that *hijo de puta*."

"Oh, okay…" Sol's voice trailed off.

"And one more thing," Karina added with a smirk. "You know who else you may want to ask about this? Marcus. His division was the one that got spun off. And I don't think he was happy with the changes that Andrew's firm made," she said, her voice glinting with malice.

"Whoa," Blake said as Sol paused the tape. "That's…a lot. I mean, if we're going to use this, we gotta go full villain edit on Karina. I think we have enough to make it work, between this and her interrogation on her date with Marcus. I mean no one likes a chick who is this hardcore about her career, right?" Ignoring the indignant expression on the PA's face, he continued, "But it's not like she's going to come to blows with him over this. Let's dig into the Marcus angle and see if we can stir up some drama and get him to confront Andrew. Who knows, maybe we'll even catch some punches on camera," he mused.

"Copy that," Sol replied. "I'll talk to Marcus tonight."

* * *

Later that night, Blake bounced on the balls of his feet, checking his phone again. It was 10:17, and Manuel was supposed to have arrived at the storage unit at ten p.m. There had been no offsite dates today or the day before, and Blake could feel himself itching to leave the resort, the restlessness rattling around inside of him like a loose pin, subtle but persistent. He desperately wanted to go to Señor Tequila tonight, but if this guy didn't show up soon, he was going to have to postpone until tomorrow night. At least if he couldn't go out tonight, he could have a glass or two of the whiskey back in his room, maybe do a few lines. That would take the edge off for the next twenty-four hours.

Tomorrow, he had to do an offsite with Raina and Jake, who miraculously didn't seem to mind her whiny voice and had picked her when he'd finally been given the chance for a date, despite her obvious interest in Andrew.

Blake had tried to charm Raina and coax her into saying something, *anything*, positive throughout filming, just so he could have some B-roll that didn't make her look like a total wet blanket, but the closest he'd gotten was that the coffee at the resort was "okay" and that Jake "wasn't bad-looking." Spending the day with the two of them tomorrow was going to be rough.

After a few more minutes that stretched lazily into the dark, humid evening, Blake finally saw a figure emerging down the dimly lit pathway from the restaurant. Manuel came into view, his angular features casting shadows across his face. Behind him, he pulled a trolley that had clearly been borrowed from the hotel reception, stacked with eight long boxes displaying images of camera tripods.

"What's up, bro?" Manuel grinned, his teeth glinting in the lamplight.

Blake shivered as the image gave him a flashback to the first night Manuel had cornered him outside of Terrace65, when this whole mess had started.

No, he thought bitterly, *this all started when I decided to rat out my drug dealer to avoid a DUI charge, like an idiot.*

"Hey, man," Blake replied, his voice strained. "That's…a lot of boxes."

"Well, we got a lot of powder. And we're almost halfway through your little vacation, right? So, I thought we'd speed things up a little."

"This is hardly a vacation," Blake shot back, his nerves grating. "Number one, I'm working for my actual job. And number two, I'm having to deal with this shit." He gestured at the trolley in annoyance.

"Hey, you're living in paradise. Seems like a vacation to me. Especially compared to a prison cell, am I right?" he asked pointedly, reminding him why they were here in the first place. Sulking in the shadows, Blake didn't respond. "Alright then, let's get these little camera standy things inside," Manuel said.

He rolled the trolley into the storage unit, then launched into the same lecture he'd given Blake at every drop-off for the last month, about how they were setting the contraband boxes in the back of the space now to ensure no one from Blake's crew accidentally opened them, but that when they were loaded onto the plane, it was critical to mix the fake equipment in with the real equipment.

The producer still hadn't figured out how exactly he was going to insert himself into the process of loading cargo when the rest of the staff knew damn well his usual flight routine was to park himself in the front of the plane with a glass of whiskey and his noise-canceling headphones, but he'd sort that out closer to the time. Maybe he'd make up some bullshit excuse about wanting to be more hands on under the new leadership, or something like that. Most of the team seemed to love Ava, so they'd probably lap that right up.

Glancing around the room, Blake spotted the prior set of boxes Manuel had dropped off—a pair of microphones that time—sitting inconspicuously in a corner, behind several other boxes of actual lighting equipment. Given the size of this new delivery, he wanted to bury the boxes under some others. He saw a few boxes of screens, which he knew would be easier to move than some of the heavier items, and indicated to Manuel to wheel the cart in that direction.

"Under these," Blake grunted as he began to shift some of the lights out of the way. "No one will dig through this. Should be a good hiding spot. And the boxes look pretty legit, too," he said with forced enthusiasm, as if he were trying to convince himself.

As Blake finished clearing a space and reached for the first box of illicit material, he heard a rustle outside, almost indistinguishable from the evening breeze, but quietly betraying movement in the bushes along the side of the building. He lifted his head, thinking that, in his paranoia, he may have imagined it, but Manuel swiveled toward the open door too.

Blake's mind went blank. He had prepared for a moment like this, rehearsing a thousand times with excuses for why he would be in the storage unit with Manuel. But they all seemed to have escaped him right now. He began to panic, but as quickly as the footsteps had approached, they faded away. A wave of relief washed over him.

However, when Manuel turned back toward Blake, his face displayed a very different emotion. Eyes cold and hard, his voice cutting like a razor, the cartel member declared quietly, "They probably heard us talk about hiding boxes. They might have even seen us through the door."

"No way," Blake insisted. "I'm sure they were just passing by."

The cartel member shook his head, long hair falling into his eyes. "Not taking any chances, bro. We need to know who that was so we can take care of it."

"Take care of what?" Blake asked, fighting to keep his voice steady.

Manuel did not answer the question, studying him with those piercing eyes. "You figure out who that was and tell me. By tomorrow."

Blake didn't respond, knowing this wasn't a request. As if sensing the gravity of the situation, Manuel exited silently, leaving Blake alone in the storage unit to realize what an even bigger disaster this was.

Feeling claustrophobic in the small space, Blake hurried outside to clear his mind so he could figure out what the hell he was going to do next. He knew exactly where all of the show's cameras and resort's security cameras were placed around the grounds, and there wasn't one on this path. He could check back to see who had been passing by the restaurant around this time, as that was the closest camera, but tons of resort staff, cast, and crew were always hanging around there. It would be difficult to narrow it down. And he needed to be one hundred percent certain before he told Manuel anything. He knew what sharing a name with him might mean, but what choice did he have? If he didn't let Manuel take care of the issue, then he wasn't just risking potential exposure of his schemes, but also the cartel taking it out on him.

As Blake walked back toward the restaurant, wondering how he was going to sort this out, his shoe caught on a small object near the edge of the path, sending it scattering into the bushes. He glanced around, ensuring nobody was in sight, then squatted down to retrieve it. Holding it up under the dim lanterns, he squinted to make out what it was. His fingers ran over the smooth, buttery material, and he felt a wave of nausea rise in his stomach as he recognized the item he was holding. The last time he'd seen this black leather bracelet, it had been around Andrew's wrist.

Chapter 21: Thalia - Now

Thalia breathed deeply, the tangy scent of the ocean air abrasive in her nostrils. Her arms stretched up in salutation to the non-existent sun. Though her eyes were closed, she could sense that the dark storm clouds in the distance were drawing nearer, based on the feel of the wind whipping more quickly now, tiny grains of sand prickling against the few inches of her calves exposed beneath the hem of her yoga pants.

Speeding up slightly through the last few poses of her routine, she tried not to worry about the impending rain but rather keep her mind focused on the sensations of her body: her calves loosening as she stretched, her hips opening and releasing the tension she'd been carrying the last few days.

Speaking with Sasha yesterday had certainly helped her mental state, but she also needed to care for herself physically, as Ashley had reminded her this morning, a plate full of fresh tropical fruit and cup of coffee in hand.

As a sudden crack of thunder startled Thalia out of her breathing flow, her eyes flew open. The sky had darkened significantly, and the storm clouds were casting an eerie green light across the beach, transforming the pristine sand from a sparkling white to a lifeless gray. It was only four in the afternoon, but it felt much later without the usual bright sun bearing down.

Thalia wanted to resume her yoga session so she could finish it before the inevitable rain began. However, she spotted Christina walking toward her on the beach, accompanied by Chief Martinez, who had interviewed her the morning of Andrew's death.

Christina's dark hair was piled on top of her head, bobbing as the pair approached her, while Chief Martinez's long amber waves flowed freely, streaming behind her in the wind. Despite the chief's high heels, she made her way gracefully across the sand.

Thalia couldn't pinpoint the emotion on Chief Martinez's blank face, but something about her posture made Thalia uneasy. With the chief's back ramrod straight, shoulders squared, and head held almost unnaturally high, a sudden image came into Thalia's mind of a jaguar preparing to pounce on its prey. Seeing Christina hanging back behind the chief, staring at the ground, did not give her any more comfort.

Thalia straightened up to meet Chief Martinez, maintaining eye contact as the two drew closer, and hoping that her features didn't betray her apprehension.

"Thalia?" Chief Martinez greeted her. "Nice to see you again."

"Same to you, Chief Martinez," Thalia responded. "Is there any news about Andrew's investigation?"

The chief didn't respond, her eyes penetrating as her lips pressed together. A slightly puzzled look spread across her face, but it felt forced to Thalia, as if she were playing a game of hide and seek with a toddler, and was pretending that she couldn't find them.

"Actually, Thalia," Chief Martinez said, "We were hoping that you may be able to help us with that. We have some new information we'd like to discuss with you."

"Of course," Thalia answered. "I'm happy to help however I can."

"Thank you, Thalia. I appreciate that. Shall we walk over to the restaurant? I'd hate for us to get rained on."

The chief wore an accommodating smile, but again Thalia got the sense that it was disingenuous, and an uncomfortable pit began to grow in her stomach. She nodded, falling into step behind Chief Martinez as she and Christina made their way toward the seating area. The producer was still averting her gaze, looking down at her scuffed black Converses as they walked in silence.

When they reached the restaurant, Thalia scanned the room, hoping Maria could bring her a cup of coffee to help clear her mind, or at least provide a distraction for her hands while she spoke with the chief. However, the waitress was nowhere in sight, and Thalia resigned herself to the discomfort of the situation as the three of them sat down at a rectangular table. She studied a hairline crack in the mosaic tile of the tabletop, jaggedly dividing one side from the other just as her life had now split into before Andrew and after Andrew.

Chief Martinez cleared her throat, then began, "Thalia, there's something I'd like you to watch. And then I'd like you to tell us what you know about it."

Puzzled, Thalia nodded in agreement. Christina pulled a tablet out from her bag and angled it toward her. Thalia glanced down at it, and was surprised to see a frozen image of Andrew, huddled into what she recognized as the tiny confessional room, with its familiar backdrop of turquoise Mexican blankets draped artfully behind him.

The producer's finger, with its nail chewed down to almost non-existence, reached across the table and hit the play button.

"She isn't my person…" Thalia's eyes immediately blurred over as she heard Andrew's familiar voice out loud for the first time since she'd said goodbye to him. "And that is why I plan to break up with her tomorrow."

Christina touched the screen again, and the silence at the table was so absolute that Thalia felt it bearing down upon her, pressing like an ever-expanding balloon.

Chief Martinez's voice cut through like barbed wire, its spikes threatening to violently pop the tension. "Did you know about this?" she demanded. "It's certainly not the picture you painted of your relationship with Andrew. You said he'd told you that he loved you the night that he died." Her voice was thick with accusation.

Thalia shivered in the cool wind, which blew the first drops of rain nearly horizontal as they began to fall. "I can explain," she replied. Her efforts to keep her tone calm resulted in it coming out as hardly more than a whisper, though the voice inside her head was shouting a warning signal: *Why are they asking me about this if he overdosed?*

"You'd better," Chief Martinez threatened, her volume escalating over the raindrops that were now falling fast and heavy onto the roof of the restaurant.

Thalia was at a loss. Clearly something was going on here beyond what she'd been told. If she decided to be honest, it could land her in significant trouble, and ruin everything she'd worked for. But based on this conversation and the ominous gleam in Chief Martinez's eyes, it seemed like she was already headed for trouble. Thalia made a decision in that instant to come clean.

"I am an eco-activist," she began slowly. Registering the look of confusion on the chief's face, she explained, "I am pushing for legislation to prevent climate change and protect the environment. It's my passion and it was my parents' life's work before they died."

Chief Martinez's eyebrow arched with impatience. "What does this have to do with Andrew?"

"I'm getting there, I promise," Thalia replied, her voice gaining confidence as she refocused on her purpose in being here. "When I applied to be on this show, I wasn't really coming to find love." She glanced nervously at Christina. "I kind of said whatever I needed to in order to get selected, because what I really wanted was to build a following to promote my organization's climate legislation, and other environmental action."

Turning now to face the producer, whose face flickered with dismay at being used, she continued, "I'm really sorry, Christina. I wasn't trying to hurt you, or the show. It's just…this is literally a once in a lifetime chance to get this legislation passed. I had to try to take it."

The producer's mouth opened as if to interject, her narrowed eyes glaring at Thalia, but Chief Martinez held up a hand, her long, manicured nails pointing skywards. "Let's focus on the topic of this investigation, please."

"Right, so…" Thalia paused, trying to collect her thoughts as she processed Christina's reaction. She had grown to like the producer over the last few weeks, and felt a pang of guilt for tricking her, even if she knew in her heart that the cause was justified.

"Umm the thing is, I didn't come here for love, but I did end up falling in love with Andrew. He is so…" her voice broke as she thought back to their brief but intense time together. "Easy to love," she finished with a weak smile.

Dabbing at a tear that had escaped from the corner of her eye, she continued, "I had told him all about GlobeAction and the legislation, and how important it was to me to pass the bill and honor my parents' memory. Even though we don't have our phones, he found a way for me to see the US news, and it turns out the bill is heading toward failure." She left out the details of how they'd gotten the news, not wanting to get Maria into trouble for helping them. "So, I kind of freaked out when I found that out, and Andrew was so amazing and supportive. We were thinking about how we could get me as many followers as possible, to help increase public support for the bill. And actually, we kind of took inspiration from Blake."

"Blake?" Christina jumped in, her head tilted quizzically, as if she couldn't believe her boss was capable of inspiring anyone.

"Yeah." Thalia nodded with a small sniffle. "You know, he got dumped on his season and it made him one of the most popular contestants ever. So, I thought, maybe if Andrew pretended to dump me on the show, it would get us more air time, and get me a lot of sympathy support. Then I could use all of that influence to help get the legislation passed."

She turned toward Chief Martinez, her tone shifting from the apologetic to pleading. "That breakup confessional you saw was fake. Andrew was just pretending that he planned to dump me. It wasn't real. We loved each other."

Chief Martinez's face was impassive as she studied Thalia. "An interesting story," she pondered, as if trying to see where she could poke a hole in it. "And would you like to explain to me how you managed to keep this supposed plan a secret, in the middle of a TV set where your entire lives were being filmed?"

Thalia frowned, recalling the earlier interview she'd had with the chief. "Like I told you before, there's a spot behind the kitchen with no cameras. I already told you that we went there the night he died."

"You did mention that," Chief Martinez agreed. Her smile twisted into a taunting expression. "But you failed to mention that you hatched this elaborate plan together."

"I was afraid," Thalia admitted, her voice imploring the officer to understand. "I didn't want it to look like I had a reason to be upset with him. Because I really and truly didn't. Plus, the plan wouldn't have worked if the producers knew about it." She hung her head, sneaking another guilty glance at Christina, whose mouth was taut, as if trying to hold herself back from jumping in. "We needed it to be believable on screen that he broke my heart. So, we kept it completely off screen, removed our mics and everything when we were in the camera dead zone."

"I see," Chief Martinez replied. "So, what you're saying is that you have no proof that this plan actually existed?" Her eyes flashed with the thrill of catching Thalia in a trap where she couldn't prove her side of the story.

The contestant shook her head slowly but firmly. "No, I didn't say that. I do have proof. I have a note from Andrew." She looked between the producer and the chief, whose triumphant expression soured. "He slipped a note into my pocket when we were saying goodbye that night. I didn't even realize it at the time—I only found it when I got back to my room." She paused, a bittersweet smile spreading across her lips at the memory of Andrew's fingertips brushing against her hips after their final embrace.

Chief Martinez's lips were pulled almost into a pout, and Thalia could practically feel the chief's adrenaline deflating as she realized that the new suspect she thought she'd identified was a false lead after all. Turning toward Christina, the chief demanded, "We'll need to see the note, of course. And do a comparison to a handwriting sample from Andrew." She seemed to be desperately grasping for a last shred of evidence to invalidate Thalia's story.

Christina nodded. "Yes, I have some letters he wrote to his brother. He had asked us to scan and email them a few times during filming, since he couldn't be in contact with him via phone." She paused, then swallowed, as if trying to clear her throat. "His mom wrote me back last time thanking me for sending them. She said his brother read them every night before bed."

Her gaze landed on Thalia, who was surprised to find a mix of unreadable emotions wavering across the producer's face. Christina's eyes glistened, hinting at tears, which Thalia found surprising from the usually no-nonsense woman—especially since she had never really seemed to take to Andrew the same way everyone else on set did. It was almost as if she had seen his perfect persona and distrusted it rather than being drawn to it. Knowing that she'd spent a few years in this business, Thalia couldn't blame her. She probably saw fake people trying to get likes and followers all the time.

And I'm one of them, Thalia thought bitterly to herself.

A heavy silence hung over the table, as the rain slowed to a quiet hum against the tin roof.

"I promise you," Thalia whispered, her voice breaking as she turned to Chief Martinez, "I would have never wanted to hurt him. And I can't think of anyone else who would, either."

"Umm, actually…" Christina interrupted. Her expression was pained, as if she were debating whether to say what would come next. In a strained voice, so low that Thalia and Chief Martinez leaned forward to hear her, the producer finally said, "I do think there may be someone else who had a reason to be mad at Andrew. Maybe even mad enough to want to hurt him."

Chapter 22: Christina - 1 Day Ago

Christina slammed her laptop shut after spending the early morning holed up in her suite, combing through another few hours of footage of Andrew and Thalia. She was good at her job, and she could anticipate the fandom's reactions very well. Watching back scenes with Andrew comforting Thalia about her dead parents, talking about his brother, and planning to introduce Thalia to his family, she knew the viewers were going to fall in love with this apparent real-life Prince Charming.

Only she would know the truth. Every time she saw Andrew touch Thalia, an uncontrollable rage coursed through her, and she was hardly able to restrain herself from pulling his disgusting hands off the woman's body.

A week ago, she'd nearly lost it watching them on a daybed and had to walk away. Since then, she'd kept her distance, claiming since their relationship was so far along, it didn't need as much attention from her. She told Sol to run point on them while Christina focused on the contestants who were falling behind in fostering connection. She had three solid relationships forming for the season, but Ava had been pressuring them to ignite the flames for a fourth.

Ava had also been pushing them to capture something more dramatic. "This footage is all fine," she'd said. "No, it's good. But it's not *enough*. This will help our ratings, for sure. But it won't fix them overnight. And if we don't see a huge jump this season, we may not have another shot. I need some sort of inciting incident, something to elevate the entire storyline. We need to make this show the talk of the town, something people can't resist."

No stroke of genius had come to Christina around creating a dramatic event, but she did have an idea for a fourth relationship. She realized that Tae-Hyun was probably awake now and she could go talk to him. It had been almost a month and he seemed to have almost given up on making a connection with someone. As she packed up her laptop, she caught herself involuntarily checking her reflection in the mirror before she left, then quickly shut the door as she muttered to herself, "What was that about?"

Heading in the direction of the boys' villa, she spotted Tae-Hyun sprawled on a wicker chair on the porch, a large turquoise mug of coffee steaming in his hand.

"Hey, Tae-Hyun!"

Shielding his eyes from the intense morning sun, the contestant's face broke into a broad smile at the sight of her. "Christina! What's up?"

"Well," she began, as she plopped into the chair across from him, "you know, we've been filming for a month now. You're such a great guy," she said, pausing as her stomach did a little unexpected somersault, "and we really want you to find someone here. So, I was thinking," she continued, fixing her eyes on his, oblivious to the gorgeous view of the sea, "that maybe you and Karina could go on a little mini-date?"

"No way," he replied, shaking his head so hard his fine jet-black hair flopped from side to side. "That chick scares me."

"Karina is actually very nice once you get to know her," she chastised him with mock seriousness. "She just has a bit of an…intense exterior. Plus, she told me yesterday that she's interested in you." Christina ignored the little twinge of guilt in her stomach at telling two half-truths in a row.

Tae-Hyun eyed her suspiciously. "Yeah, only because I'm a doctor. She wants someone with a 'successful' career like her. But does she even know what kind of doctor I am? I'm a pediatrician with two hundred thousand dollars of med school debt. Not exactly what she's looking for," he said, raising a sarcastic eyebrow. "And I don't want to sit through an interrogation of why I chose pediatrics and a lecture on lifetime earning potential and investment strategies. I hear enough of that 'why didn't you become a surgeon' crap from my parents," he added grumpily.

Christina pivoted, latching on to this new direction. "Okay, yes, I get it. I have Korean parents too, who are not exactly thrilled with my life choices either, you know? But," she continued, pausing for dramatic effect. "Other than careers, what else matters most to Korean parents?" When Tae-Hyun didn't respond, she leaned in closer, wriggling her fingers in excitement. "Marriage and grandbabies!"

He looked at her for a moment, considering what she'd said. "They would be very pleasantly surprised if I came out of this thing with a serious relationship," he admitted. "My *halmoni* is coming to visit from Busan next month and it would be great to not have her bugging me about finding a girlfriend the whole time."

"Exactly!" Christina responded with an enthusiastic clap, collapsing back into the white wicker chair with relief and a little internal flicker of pride.

Damn, I am good at this job. She smiled to herself, but excitement was quickly dampened by a small pang of disappointment that she couldn't quite place. Regaining steam, she swept her hair up into a messy bun, her characteristic style for when she was ready to get down to business.

"So, I have a plan all laid out for you. Karina's all-time favorite food is *arepas*, and luckily the cook's wife is Venezuelan so he knows how to make them. But you know she eats like super healthy all the time." She glanced at Tae-Hyun, not letting his side-eye deter her as she continued, "That is, unless she's had a few drinks. So, what we're going to do this afternoon is lay out a cute little picnic blanket for you guys on that cliff next to the spa, complete with some fruit and vodka sodas with lime. Her preferred drink," she added with a look that dared Tae-Hyun to comment. "Then, once she's feeling nice and tipsy, you tell her you have a surprise waiting for her at the restaurant. When you guys get there, we'll have a table set with roses and a big pile of *arepas*. What do you think?" she finished, smiling in encouragement.

Tae-Hyun sighed, not seeming at all convinced that this plan was going to work, or that he even wanted it to. "Sounds great," he said with a big false smile and cheesy thumbs up.

Christina leaned forward, reaching across the small, rustic table to put her hands on his broad shoulders. "Trust me, I know what I'm doing. This is going to be great." She studied his face, and felt his muscles relax beneath her fingers.

"Okay," he conceded. "I trust you."

"Wonderful," she replied with a grin, as she stood from the chair. "I'll go down to the kitchen and get everything organized for later."

Stepping off the porch with a slight bounce, she waited until Tae-Hyun's lanky frame was blocked by a large bush sage plant before she did a little excited wiggle of her hips. *Nailed it,* she congratulated herself as she strode happily down the path toward the restaurant. Next, she just had to get the last couple, Marcus and Rachel, to make moves. Given how painfully shy they both were, and Rachel's anti-abortion tirade, it was taking a monumental effort, but she felt like she was making steady progress.

In any case, Ava would be so pumped when she saw the footage of Tae-Hyun and Karina's mini-date that she would forget all about Marcus and Rachel for a while. If Christina wanted to get a kiss on screen, she'd probably have to ply Tae-Hyun with drinks, too—not because he wasn't physically attracted to Karina, but because he was a total gentleman who would likely hold back. His beverage of choice was usually a Corona with lime, but that wasn't going to be heavy hitting enough to get the job done. She made a mental note to ask the bartender if he'd ordered anything harder, so that they could have it ready at the picnic setup for him as well.

Lost in her thoughts, Christina absently approached the door of the kitchen to look for the chef, Jesús—or as most of the resort staff and production crew had come to affectionately call the rotund, light-hearted man, Osito. She didn't see him in the kitchen, where she gave a wave to the couple of dishwashers cleaning up after breakfast. She made her way to the employee break room, where Osito could often be found between mealtimes watching his favorite Mexican sketch comedy show, his rich laughter filling up the tiny space.

Pushing open the door to the small room, the corners of her lips turned up in anticipation of Osito's cheerful greeting. However, the smile froze on her face as she realized the room was not occupied by the jovial chef, but rather by two other people. Her brain scrambled to catch up as she processed what she saw.

It was the back of a man's head, his tall frame enveloping a more petite, feminine one. As he jerked away from the embrace, the woman's face was exposed and Christina felt a jolt of emotion at recognizing the waitress Maria's tear-streaked face. The producer opened her mouth to apologize for intruding on what was obviously a very personal moment, when the man suddenly turned toward her. Christina's heart dropped as her eyes met Andrew's brilliant green gaze.

Christina's stomach twisted, the chilaquiles from this morning's breakfast churning in her gut. Her cheeks burned and she leaned against the doorframe to steady herself. Seeing the helplessness in Maria's eyes, she felt like she was looking in the mirror again the morning after her assault at the fraternity. And worse, this time it *was* her fault. She was the one who had brought Andrew here, knowing who he was. *What* he was. She had knowingly put other women in danger in her own quest for revenge, and now Maria was paying the price.

Crossing the room in a few steps, Christina shoved Andrew hard, forcing her body between him and the waitress. "What the FUCK are you doing?" she growled, anger coursing through her.

"It's not what it looks like." Andrew's expression was calm and soft, and that enraged her further. How dare he act like this wasn't a big deal? Like Maria was another disposable item, just like Christina?

"I think it's exactly what it looks like," Christina spat. "Get the hell away from her. Get out of here!" She gestured wildly toward the door.

Andrew put his hands up in surrender. "Okay, I'm leaving. Can we please talk about this later?" he pleaded.

Christina didn't dignify his question with a response, just continued glaring at him until he retreated from the break room. When she heard the swinging door of the kitchen exit, she released a breath she hadn't realized she was holding.

Turning toward Maria, she launched into an apology, the guilt bubbling up inside her. "I am so sorry. What did he do to you? No, wait, you don't have to tell me if you don't want to. Just let me know how I can help." She paused, expecting the waitress to continue crying, but was surprised to see her chin lift in defiance.

"No, Señor Andrew did not hurt me," she said, shaking her head vehemently.

"What?" Christina asked.

"He did not hurt me. He nice man," Maria insisted, her eyes wide.

What is going on here? Christina wondered. *Maybe she's afraid of losing her job if she rats him out? Or maybe he even threatened her if she told anyone.*

"Are you sure?" Christina prodded. "He didn't try to force himself on you? You know, kiss you or…something else? You can talk to me, you won't be in trouble."

"Yes, I'm sure. Everything is fine, Señorita Christina."

Christina wanted to believe Maria, but a hint of fear and worry lingered in the woman's eyes, leaving Christina with a feeling of unease. After studying the waitress's face for a few more moments, she relented. "Okay. If you want to tell me anything later, please come find me, or call my room any time. Day or night."

Maria's head bobbed up and down, indicating her readiness for this conversation to be over.

Christina walked out, letting the kitchen door swing shut on its loose hinges as she raced toward the storage unit, the closest place she could think of where she could have some space to process what had just happened. A flurry of thoughts raced through her head, flittering like birds trying to escape a golden cage. Given what she knew of Andrew's past, of course the first conclusion she had drawn was that he was assaulting Maria.

But even as she leaned against the door of the storage unit, debating her next move, a flicker of doubt crossed her mind. She recalled Maria's insistence that he hadn't done anything wrong. Would he really try something so brazen on set? And in a foreign country where the police would do God knows what with a *gringo* like him? Unconscious girls at a frat party were apparently an easy target for him, but Christina reluctantly admitted to herself that he was probably too smart to outright coerce Maria.

Perhaps Andrew had been messing around with Maria on the side and leading her on, while he developed his supposedly fairytale romance with Thalia. *That's totally the kind of scumbag move he would make,* Christina thought to herself. Maybe today he had realized it was too risky and broken things off with the waitress, not realizing she had become emotionally attached. It would be easy for him to charm her into falling for him in a matter of weeks—a rich, handsome American who knew Spanish and feigned genuine interest in her. Had she witnessed him breaking Maria's heart?

Regardless of what had happened, she was sure that Andrew was at fault, and she felt a tiny thrill at having finally caught him red-handed being the asshole she had always known he was.

Her satisfaction was muted, though. Because as she considered various explanations for what she had just seen, one image seemed burned into her mind's eye: Maria's desolate face, tears streaking her flushed cheeks as her eyes pleaded silently for rescue.

Chapter 23: Blake - Now

Blake caught a glimpse of himself in the window as he approached Ava's room, the afternoon sun reflecting merrily off the glass, at odds with the unease swirling in his gut. The stress of the last twenty-four hours was evidenced by the bags under his eyes and wrinkles lining his mouth. He was used to looking like shit when he was hungover, but he hadn't had a sip of anything since the news of Andrew's death. The last thing he needed was for Ava to catch him drunk; that would be the death knell of his career.

Smoothing his hair down, he knocked on the heavy wooden door. As Sol swung it open, he tipped his head to Ava and Christina, who were already seated inside, serious expressions on their faces.

"Sorry I'm late," he said as he flopped into the armchair. "Lunch took forever. The waitress who is normally there was MIA today, and that other kid with the floppy hair doesn't know what the heck he's doing." Ava and Christina exchanged knowing glances. "What?" he asked in confusion.

"Actually," Ava began, "that's part of what we talked to Chief Martinez about."

Blake was confused. "You talked to her about...the waitress?" he asked, fixing a blank expression on his face to cover up the clueless one that threatened to poke through. He couldn't seem like he didn't know what was going on, not now, when Ava was working so damn hard to exclude him.

"Maria is her name," Christina retorted in an icy tone, and her little sidekick Sol shot him a glare. "And yes, we spoke about her. Because the detectives were trying to understand who else might have a motive for hurting Andrew, and I had walked in on..." she hesitated. "Something happening with them the day before he died."

"Like…they were hooking up?" Blake raised a sarcastic eyebrow. Honestly, he would have banged the waitress too, but he was still surprised. Andrew had really fooled him with that falling for Thalia stuff.

"Not really. I mean. I don't know exactly," Christina said, color rising in her cheeks as her eyes flitted between him, Ava, and Sol. "I only saw them hugging and Maria crying. I wasn't going to even say anything, but now that Andrew's death is officially a murder investigation…I don't know. I felt like I had to share it as a potential motive." Her eyes were downcast and Blake could tell she had struggled with whether to tell the police.

Wow, she must really not have liked the guy, to hold back info about his death, Blake thought.

He nodded to show Christina he understood why this created suspicion around Maria. "I see. So, you're thinking like, hell hath no fury like a woman scorned, am I right?" Without waiting for Christina's response, he added, "Men like Andrew who are really attractive and charming have it tough. Women fall for them all the time and then sometimes feel like the guys were leading them on. I can empathize."

A look of disgust flooded Christina's face, her eyes darkening. "Well, Blake," she spat out. "As *tough* as it must have been for Andrew to be a handsome straight white male, I'm not sure that's what was going on. But in any case," she continued, taking a breath and steadying her tone, "she didn't show up for work today. So that obviously adds to the suspicion. Chief Martinez and her team are going to investigate further."

Blake studied her with a dubious expression. "I don't know. It seems a little far-fetched, right? She seems like a pretty normal chick. Do you really think she would kill Andrew?" He shrugged. "Maybe you're reading too much into this."

"Reading too much?" she echoed indignantly. "Maybe I would be doing less if you would do your job—"

"Hey!" Ava interrupted. "That's enough. We need to stay focused. There has to be something that we're missing here." Glancing around the table, her eyes settled on Sol. "You've been quiet, Sol. What do you think?"

The PA had indeed been silent, her gaze focused away from them. As she snapped her attention back to the group, she said in a small voice, "I think maybe we missed something on the tapes. I kind of remember umm…well, I didn't really think anything of it because it's Maria right? But I think maybe I remember seeing her near the boys' villa that night."

Ava shot her a penetrating gaze, and Blake could see the corners of her mouth tightening as if to control what she really wanted to say.

"Go look back through the tapes, please," she said with restraint. "Now."

Sol nodded and grabbed her computer off of the desk, beginning to frantically click away.

Resting her chin on her fingertips, Ava appeared to be in deep thought and didn't move for what felt like forever. Blake glanced across the room at Christina for some indication of what to do or say, but the junior producer also sat motionless, her eyes fixed on Ava. As the silence grew, becoming almost unbearable for him, it was interrupted by a gasp from Sol, who sat tucked in the corner. Her face had gone pale, her tanned arms clasping the thin silver laptop against her black V-neck shirt.

"I found it," she said breathlessly, scooting into the center of the bed so they could crowd around her.

Christina plopped onto the firm mattress, while Ava leaned to see what the PA was pulling up on the screen. Blake rose from the desk chair and stood behind the group of women, his view partially obscured by Christina's mop of hair.

Fingers trembling, Sol clicked the mousepad to pull up a video and hit play. In the small rectangle of the video editing software, grainy footage appeared, the time stamp in the bottom left corner indicating the video was from approximately one a.m. the night Andrew died. The image displayed the view from the resort's security camera thirteen, which had been positioned outside the boys' villa. The night vision showed the palm trees near the two-story structure swaying in the gentle midnight breeze, the soothing picture oddly disjointed with Blake's feeling that they were about to see something sinister.

"One second," Sol said as she clicked ahead. Blake glanced over at the faces of his colleagues—Christina looking as if she might be sick, and Ava staring intently at the screen with her mouth set into a firm line—and his heart began to race, wondering what the PA had discovered.

Suddenly, the calm image was disrupted by a figure hurrying toward the boys' villa, their arms held not at their sides, but bent in an L shape, carrying something held carefully out in front of them. The tight pants and shoulder-length hair suggested it was a woman, but from the camera angle, it was impossible to see her face.

As if sensing the group's frustration as not being able to determine the woman's identity, Sol whispered, "Wait."

The video continued with the woman approaching the door to the villa, and shifting what she was carrying to one hand as she reached into her pocket with another. A moment later, the door swung open. "She had a key," Christina whispered in awe. "Not even all the crew have keys to the villa. So that means…" her voice trailed off, as if unwilling to verbalize the conclusion she was drawing.

Just as the woman on screen began to enter the doorway, something fluttered down toward the ground. As if the footage were in slow motion, Blake watched her shoulders swing around to pick it up, revealing that what she was holding was a tray with a carafe and mug. She stooped down to retrieve what he could now see was a paper napkin that had been carried away by the breeze. Her shoulders lifting, she placed the errant napkin back on the tray, then used that hand to sweep the hair out of her face, revealing the pretty features of their once-beloved waitress, Maria.

Chapter 24: Thalia - The Night Of

"Shhh!" Thalia whispered as Andrew did a little whoop. They had escaped the camera crews again, and were back in their favorite hiding spot behind the restaurant, out of sight of the security cameras.

This time Andrew had enlisted Nick to help distract the crew, whispering his request to his buddy during dinner, after Thalia had told him she needed to talk to him privately tonight. When they'd all gathered around the pool for drinks after eating, Nick had executed the plan masterfully, faking an accidental fall into the pool when he stood up to get another beer. He had splashed the crew and left Ashley in a fit of giggles, knowing exactly what her partner was up to.

"You have to admit, the guy is nothing if not committed," Andrew said with a laugh. "Who else do you know who would jump fully clothed into a pool to help his buddy get some alone time with his girlfriend?"

"Very true," Thalia agreed, grateful for Nick's actions but pained to hear that word on Andrew's lips. The elation of their escape was quickly counteracted by the weight of what she needed to do during this time with him, pulling her down as if she might sink into the earth.

"So, why the special need for privacy tonight? I hope you're not trying to get fresh with me," he teased with a little wiggle of his eyebrow.

Rather than laughing along with his joke, Thalia felt her smile fade. "I actually had something I've been thinking about for the last couple of days, since we watched the CNN report."

She saw the uneasy surprise on his face, but he prompted her to continue. "Okay..."

"Well, you know how important the bill passing is to me. It's everything to me. Almost everything," she added gently, her heart feeling as if it were in a tug of war match. "I need to make my plan work. I have to gain a big enough social following to get this bill to pass. But just being a fan favorite couple on the show…I don't think it's going to cut it."

"What do you mean?" he asked, his eyebrows knit in confusion.

"I think we need to do something more drastic. After I got cast on the show, I was listening to the *Love's a Pod* podcast, kind of like a crash course in the franchise, and they talked about Blake's history on the show. Do you know how he became so popular?"

Andrew nodded, and she could see the gears turning in his mind as he wondered where she was going with this. "The woman he was about to propose to rejected him during the finale. He was devastated, and women across America couldn't help loving this wounded soul. I remember my mom talking about this before. Listening to her, you would think this man walked on water or something." He paused, his expression lined with sadness, though whether it was for missing his mom or because he finally knew what Thalia was going to suggest, she wasn't sure.

Her heart broke knowing she was causing him pain, but she had to prioritize the bill—it was too important for her to let her own emotions jeopardize everything. Her eyes locked on Andrew, she said, "I think we should pretend to break up."

Holding her breath in anticipation of his protest, she let out a sharp exhale when he nodded and said, "Yes."

"Really? You'll do it?"

"It's the only way," he agreed, his voice sad but resolute. "I care too much about you to let you miss out on this dream. I know that is the whole reason you're on this show."

"That *was* the whole reason," she conceded. "But that's not the whole reason anymore. I don't want to be away from you, but I can't give up on this. It's killing me to think about being apart because…the truth is, I've fallen in love with you."

His features relaxed, the soft skin around his eyes crinkling as his lips stretched into a genuine smile. "I've fallen in love with you, too. And that's why we need to do this. I want what's best for you, Thals. I want to do this for you. For us," he whispered, squeezing her with the arm he'd draped over her shoulder.

Studying his handsome face, his eyes full of love and his strong jaw set in determination, Thalia felt relief flooding over her.

This is going to work, she reassured herself.

"Okay. Let's do it. But as soon as the bill passes, I'm flying my ass to LA to come jump your bones."

Andrew threw his head back and gave an endearing chortle. "That sounds like a deal. An excellent deal," he added with a wide grin.

"I love you," Thalia said, more confidently this time.

"I love you too," he replied, extending his arms to embrace her. After a few moments of holding her close, he bent his wrist toward his face, looking at his watch. "Oh crap, it's almost ten. Let me walk you back."

"Why, do you have a confessional you're supposed to film?" Thalia asked. The producers typically tried to schedule the female cast members' interviews in the morning, when their makeup was fresh, and slotted in the men for the evening. But still, they usually wrapped up well before now.

Andrew looked uncomfortable for a moment, then glanced at the staff's back entrance to the kitchen, which led right out to their hiding spot, ensuring no one was coming out.

"Okay listen, I wasn't going to tell you this, because it's not really my story to tell. But I trust you completely, and I don't want to keep anything from you. Please promise me you won't tell this to *anyone?*"

Her heart swelling at the confidence he was placing in her, Thalia answered fervently, "Of course."

"Okay, so you know how I'm always chatting with Maria in Spanish?"

She nodded, recalling their easy conversations and the pangs of jealousy she'd felt early on, before she'd realized Andrew was serious about their relationship. The way he made the waitress feel comfortable wasn't anything special between them—it was simply his way of being with everyone.

"Well, as we've been talking more, I started to notice she seemed kind of stressed and distracted sometimes. One day last week, I was sitting down here for a while after breakfast, sipping my coffee and writing a letter to my brother. I saw her looking at the clock a bunch of times, and didn't think too much of it. I figured maybe she was leaving early or something, maybe she had plans that day. But then she sort of zoned out while she was refilling my cup, and spilled coffee all over the place. She snapped out of it and apologized a bunch, but even then, it was like she was overcompensating, like she was nervous about something."

Thalia listened to Andrew's story, both admiring his empathy and feeling concerned for Maria.

Andrew continued, "I asked her what was wrong and at first she said everything was fine. The other waiter was on his break, Osito was in the kitchen busy prepping for lunch, and the rest of the cast had already left for the beach. Since there was no one around, I pressed her on it. I was worried about her, you know?"

Thalia nodded, her stomach clenching in anticipation of what he was about to reveal about Maria.

Running one hand through his floppy hair, he wrapped the other around Thalia's bare shoulder, sending goosebumps down her arm. "She broke down and started talking to me about her family. She is really close with her little brother, but he's gotten mixed up in some bad stuff."

"What kind of bad stuff?" Thalia asked hesitantly.

"Well, you know that the cartel violence has been really bad here?"

She nodded. "Yeah, my sister was worried about me coming because of it. I had to show her that security briefing package that Christina put together, to convince her it was safe."

"Yeah, same with my family," he agreed. "So, I guess her brother, Antonio, had gotten involved with one of them, the Rodriguez cartel. They're huge, super powerful. They even have a presence in LA—there was a shooting just last month that was supposedly related to them. And for these young men who don't have other economic options, it's a really attractive gig. A chance for them to make money for their families, and earn some respect in the town."

Thalia frowned. "That sounds really tough. Has he stayed safe?"

"He was for a while," Andrew said, his words foreshadowing the danger to come. "But then, he wanted out. They were making him do all these violent things, and he couldn't deal with it anymore. He told Maria it was 'painting his soul black.' " They were both silent for a moment, letting the phrase wash over them.

"So did he leave?" Thalia prompted.

"That's the thing," Andrew replied. "He tried to. But these cartels are not easy to leave. Since he tried to get out, they've been constantly threatening Maria's family, leaving dead animals in front of their home, mailing them notes threatening to rape and murder her."

Thalia shuddered despite the warm evening air. "That is awful."

Andrew nodded solemnly. "They finally agreed last week that he could be free if he paid them two hundred thousand pesos."

She gasped. "That's like…ten thousand US dollars, right?"

"Yup. And for her family, that's totally unattainable. I think she makes the equivalent of two dollars an hour at this job, and she's helping to support their entire family."

Throwing her head back in realization, Thalia said, "Ah, and the cartel knew that. So it was like this fake, unattainable offer."

"I think so, too."

Thalia thought for a moment. "Can she go to the police? Can't they help her?"

"It's a good idea," Andrew acknowledged. "I asked her about it too. But she said it would only make things worse."

"So, what is her family going to do?" Thalia asked sadly.

Glancing away from her, he ran his hand through his hair again. "Well, I have done pretty well for myself with my career. And, of course, it helped that my family paid for college. I recognize that I'm really lucky for that, because I know student loans can be crushing." He cleared his throat, clearly uncomfortable at this discussion of money.

He probably guessed I don't make a killing working at a nonprofit, Thalia realized, appreciating his sweet attempt to tactfully broach it, even when there was a much larger subject at hand.

Andrew rubbed her shoulder again. "The point is, I can comfortably afford to help Maria with this. I thought about it the last few days, and she seems like such a genuine person, I just really want to help her however I can. And this is one way I can. So, I managed to speak to her privately today and told her that I would give her the money."

"Oh, Andrew," Thalia breathed. She was at a loss for words, struck by his kindness. "That is so generous. I don't even…" she trailed off. "Here I was thinking I was Mother Teresa for buying the unhoused man on my block a sandwich last month, and you're out here saving an entire family's lives."

His cheeks flushed with embarrassment, clearly not wanting to be recognized as some sort of hero, and that endeared him to her even more. "This from the woman who is about to save the entire planet?" he said with a gentle nudge to her side, pulling her head in to place a tender kiss on her forehead.

"So anyways, I'm supposed to meet her at ten tonight so she can give me the details on where to send the money. I'm still trying to figure out if there's a way to contact my family to ask them to do it for me while I'm here. I don't want her family to have to wait another month until we get home from filming for me to send it."

Glancing at his watch again, he stood up, dusting off his khaki shorts and reaching for her hands to pull her up. "Do you want to wait here while I talk to Maria, then I can walk you back to the girls' villa? It should only take me a few minutes to get the info from her."

"That would be great," Thalia said with a smile as she rose to meet him, the muscles in his arms taut as he effortlessly lifted her off of the ground.

"Thank you for trusting me with this," she whispered into his ear as he enveloped her in a loving embrace.

Pulling away to look into her eyes, he responded earnestly, "I would trust you with my life."

Chapter 25: Christina - Now

Since Sol had discovered the footage of Maria going to the boys' villa around the time of Andrew's death, it felt to Christina that things were happening in slow motion. Christina had been in shock, and Sol and Blake appeared equally shaken. Only Ava looked unsurprised, her composure as collected as ever.

Ava had immediately asked them to step outside, so she could have a private conversation with the CEO and board president about the next steps. The trio of ousted crew members—Blake, Christina, and Sol—waited in the garden area outside of Ava's room, the trickling of a small pond seeming to mark the passage of time as ten, then twenty, and finally thirty minutes slipped by.

In typical Blake fashion, he'd seemed unperturbed by the situation, and flopped down on a bench and immediately pulled out his laptop. "Gonna shoot out some emails," he said, but Christina was ninety percent sure he was on Instagram, probably DMing some girls who wanted a chance to audition for the show.

Sol paced nervously, chattering away while Christina tried to focus, staring at the tropical fish swimming round and round the pond.

I feel like one of those fish, she thought. *Trying so hard to swim in the right direction, but I keep bumping helplessly up against a wall.*

There was a niggling guilt in the back of her mind that kept replaying the image of Maria's tear-streaked face in that dingy break room. How could she have thrown a potential victim under the bus? Especially without even really knowing what had happened between Maria and Andrew?

Just as Sol interrupted her thoughts with yet another question, Ava emerged from the room, her face stoic as she waved them back inside.

"So," she said, swinging the door shut, "Robert and the board president believe we should share the footage with the Mexican police. They're reviewing this with the CBC lawyers, and now that it's officially a murder investigation, they've decided that the legal team should take over all communication with the officials. Sol, can you please send me the footage, both a short clip of the relevant section, as well as the full unedited footage for that twenty-four-hour period?"

The PA nodded and grabbed her laptop.

Turning to Christina and Blake, Ava continued, "While we can no longer communicate with the police, we can work internally with our cast, crew, and resort staff to confirm any additional information they might have about Maria. I think we should have as much info as possible in our arsenal in case this gets ugly. But we need to do it quietly."

"Blake," Ava said, eyeing the showrunner warily, as if unsure it was wise to trust him with any job, "I want you to start interviewing the crew members, especially those closest to Maria—the logistics support staff, the junior staff, et cetera. And are there any resort staff you could ask some questions to as well? They would all know her, right?"

Christina could see Blake wracking his brains. She wasn't sure if he could remember a single staff member's name, or if they were all jumbled together in one big unimportant ball in his mind.

"Umm, yeah. The head of security, Alejandro," Blake said.

"That's perfect."

Christina's heart skipped a beat as Ava's eyes landed on her next.

"For you, Christina, I want to leverage your strong relationship with the cast members. Talk to all of them about Andrew's interactions with Maria, and especially Thalia. I know she's hurting," she added, her features softening for a moment, "but she may share something valuable. Something she may not have thought was important before now. You can tell her about the tox screen if you need to. That might help earn her confidence."

Christina was pleased her mentor trusted her and valued the trust she'd also built with the cast. "I'm on it," she assured Ava.

* * *

As she approached the girls' villa, Christina's feet grew heavier with each step. The sun had begun to set, casting long shadows over the grounds that mirrored those on her heart. She knew Thalia had developed real feelings for Andrew, and she wasn't sure that finding out how he died was going to make Thalia feel better—especially given Christina's suspicions there had been something going on between him and Maria, whether consensual or forced. Neither of those scenarios was something you wanted to hear about your boyfriend, though in Christina's view one was infinitely worse, and much more likely.

When she reached the whitewashed door, Christina gave a light knock and entered slowly. Ashley was strutting across the living room, her expression sultry and hair tousled, while Rachel sat on the cream couch, a beige macrame throw pillow hugged tightly on her lap and her eyes wide as she watched her fellow castmate's performance. With a little swing of her hips, Ashley turned around and jumped when she saw Christina, then collapsed into a fit of giggles next to Rachel.

"Umm…" Christina began, unsure what she had just walked in on.

Covering her eyes, Ashley gasped, "Oh Lord, I'm sorry you had to see that, Christina! I was giving our sweet girl Rachel here a little lesson in how to seduce Marcus." She straightened up where she sat, giving a nudge to Rachel, who turned beet red. "Sorry, just trying to provide a bit of comedic relief," Ashley added sheepishly. "It's been a rough couple of days."

Under different circumstances, Christina would've been thrilled to hear Rachel was plotting to win over Marcus, but this evening, her focus was completely on the conversation she needed to have with Thalia.

Seeing the look on Christina's face, Ashley's own expression grew serious and she asked with genuine concern, "Are you okay?"

"Yes," she replied, forcing a small smile. "I just need to talk to Thalia. Is she up in your room?"

"Yup. Doing her journaling. Poor sweet thing. She didn't eat lunch again today."

Christina nodded, her stomach constricting with nerves. "Thanks," she said, as she moved toward the stairs, climbing each one as if she were underwater.

When she reached Thalia and Ashley's room, she found the door open. Thalia's long, lean figure sprawled face down on the bed, her toes grazing the soft sheets as her fingers absently twirled a pen. Her journal was spread out in front of her, but her gaze was fixed out the window, the words seemingly out of her reach tonight.

"Thalia?" Christina called softly.

The cast member sat up abruptly, her hands snapping the cover of her journal shut.

"Hey, Christina," she replied. "What's up?"

"Can I sit down?" Christina asked, motioning to Ashley's bed opposite hers.

"Yeah, of course," Thalia said with a pained smile.

Christina eased the door closed, ignoring Thalia's questioning look. She propped herself on the edge of the bed, her foot anxiously flicking the heel of her worn black flip-flops.

"Well," she began, "there is some information we haven't been totally truthful with you about Andrew's m—" she caught the word before it escaped her lips, realizing she should provide more context before throwing out homicide accusations. "Andrew's death," she corrected herself, gaining confidence as she saw Thalia's expression spark with interest. "The CBC lawyers hired a doctor to do an independent review of the medical examiner's report. And when they did, they had a somewhat…different conclusion than what the Mexican police told us earlier."

Thalia's pretty face wrinkled into a frown. "What do you mean?"

"As you know, initially, the police thought that Andrew overdosed. But based on the review by CBC's doctors, the truth is that Andrew was likely murdered." She paused, watching as Thalia's brown eyes widened in shock.

"Murdered?" Thalia echoed, her voice sounding far away.

"Yes, that's what they think," Christina confirmed. Forging ahead, she added, "And there's more. Based on some footage and…" she paused, hesitant to reveal her role in the investigation, "…additional information about potential motives, there has been a suspect identified."

"Oh, my God," Thalia exhaled, as if making space in her body to process the information coming next. "Who is it?" Looking into her eyes, Christina saw a hunger for answers, but also a spark of fear. Perhaps bringing closure to the case would only make the loss feel more real for Thalia.

"I mean, obviously, nothing is proven yet and the police are only very early in their investigation. But they have reason to suspect Maria." Christina felt the woman's name heavy on her tongue.

"No," Thalia replied, her eyes wide with shock.

"I'm afraid it's true," Christina said, shaking her head sadly.

"I mean, *no*," Thalia repeated with more vigor, "there's no way she did this. Why do they even think she would do this?"

The moment Christina feared had come, where she had to take all of Thalia's beautiful, shining memories of her late boyfriend and smash them into a thousand sharp pieces on the ground.

"Thalia," she began, choosing her words carefully, "Andrew was not…who you think he was."

"Of course, he was," she said, eyes flashing. "You're the one who doesn't know anything about him. He was trying to *help* Maria. She had zero reason to hurt him."

"What do you mean he was trying to help her?"

Christina saw a flicker of hesitation pass across Thalia's face, her eyes darkening and her lips mashed together, as if to physically contain some bit of information she didn't want to divulge. Her eyes widened anxiously, before she lifted her chin in determination. "I'm going to tell you something, but you *cannot* tell anyone. Do you promise you won't?"

Looking into Thalia's eyes, pleading for a confidant, a friend, Christina felt something in her shift. This was bigger than her doing a good job for Ava, or getting a promotion. Thalia had really and truly been in love with Andrew, and she was fighting her way through a riptide of grief right now.

She couldn't leave her alone. Despite herself, Christina felt her head nodding almost involuntarily, her mouth forming a promise.

She then listened in silence as Thalia told her about one of her final conversations with Andrew—how Maria's brother was in trouble, and how Andrew planned to give her money so her family could be safe. Christina sat in stunned disbelief.

As Thalia recounted the story, Christina felt doubt creeping in. She *knew* Andrew was a bad person. A rapist. He had ruined her life. Why would he try so hard to help save another woman's?

Lost in her thoughts, she was jolted back into the conversation by Thalia's insistent voice. "Christina? What do you think we should do now?"

Staring at the contestant blankly, Christina's heart hardened, enveloped by her rage at Andrew. She narrowed her eyes. "I don't know, Thalia. It sounds pretty unbelievable. Are you sure he wasn't making this up?"

Thalia's face contorted into a dumbfounded expression. "Making this up? Why the hell would he make up this story about a nice woman?"

Christina shrugged. "I don't know. Maybe to impress you? Show off how much money he has?"

"I don't care about his money!" Thalia exclaimed.

"Oh, you might when you find out who his daddy is," Christina sneered. "Let me tell you a little secret, Thalia. Guys like Andrew, who come from rich families, always have some kind of weird power trip. They think they can walk all over everyone that comes into their orbit. Me, and you, and certainly a random waitress, are completely disposable to them. I can guarantee you that he would think nothing of taking what he wanted from Maria, and making up some bullshit story to tell you to cover his tracks, so that he could keep getting what he wanted from you." Christina's chest heaved, her eyes brimming with tears as years of anger rushed out of her.

Thalia looked at her in silence, and Christina thought she saw a flash of something like compassion in her eyes before she glanced at the floor. Twisting the tassel of her knit sweater, Thalia whispered, "You're wrong about him."

Christina opened her mouth in protest, but Thalia's eyes met hers again and she held up a finger to silence her. "I don't know what your story is. I don't know who hurt you. But I knew Andrew, and he was not like that." She paused, studying the smooth tile of the floor.

Without lifting her gaze, Thalia continued in a soft voice, "A week or so after we met, we were asking each other a bunch of deep questions. Biggest fear, biggest dream, you know. 'Early days of a serious relationship' type questions." A sad reminiscing smile played across her lips. "I asked him what his biggest regret was, and he got really emotional. He told me that in his senior year at UCLA, he was at a frat party one night."

Christina's breath lodged in her throat, and her vision began to swim at the corners. Despite the cool ocean breeze flowing through the night into Thalia's open window, a prickly heat climbed up her neck and down inside of her, making her stomach churn. Over the years, she'd longed for a confession, an apology, but now that she was being confronted with it, she wasn't sure she could handle hearing the details of her assault recounted from her attacker's point of view. She tried to quell her oncoming panic, recounting the soothing words her counselor Linette had uttered as she'd coached her through her frequent panic attacks in the early days after the assault.

Give me three good deep breaths. In...out. In...out. In...out. That's my girl. Now I want you to picture that you're on your cozy red couch, petting Rosie's fuzzy ears. Let's focus on that bright red couch and those soft, velvety ears.

Feeling her breathing ease and the knot in her throat loosen, Christina tried to refocus on Thalia. The cast member was still looking at the ground as she spoke, and hadn't noticed the producer's wave of emotion.

As if through a fog, Christina heard her saying, "...he sent the guys out of the room and got the girl dressed, and into an Uber. Then he—"

"Wait," Christina interrupted, her senses snapping back into place. "What guys?"

Thalia lifted her head, then tilted it slightly, her eyebrows furrowed in confusion. "The guys who were assaulting this poor girl."

"But Andrew..." Christina trailed off, at a loss for words.

"Yeah, like I said, he walked in on two of his frat brothers forcing themselves on a woman who was passed out on the bed, and he stopped them. Weren't you listening?"

Christina shuddered as the memories poked at her, like broken shards of glass she was trying so desperately to put together. Yes, the scent of cedar and orange, Andrew's signature aftershave—the one that had wounded her with its pointed familiarity during the audition, and haunted her every time she'd gotten near him during filming—was there. The careless laughter of entitled men was there. But there was also something new emerging from the fragments. An angry male voice. Angry at her? No, angry at them. The guys.

What the hell are you guys doing? Get off of her!

The casual responses, *Chill, Andrew, we're just having a good time, and so is she.*

The first voice growing more enraged, *I said get OFF of her*, and a sudden freedom to breathe as a weight that had been pinning her down was removed. *Get the fuck out of my sight.* And then the same voice, this time soothing. *Hey, are you okay?*

"Are you okay?"

Thalia's gentle voice pulled her out of the dizzying realization. Sweat beaded on Christina's forehead as Thalia stared at her with concern.

"No," Christina whispered, then shook her head. "I mean, yes." She swallowed hard, needing to hear the rest of the truth. "So, what happened next? Did he say?"

Thalia studied her, as if unsure she was really fine, but hesitantly continued, "Yeah, I mean, he tried to follow up the next day and see if she was okay, but for the Uber she'd given him the name of a huge dorm, so he had no way to track her down. And he was pretty drunk too, so he barely remembered what she looked like. Only that she was Asian American. He said he still thinks about her all the time," she finished sadly.

Christina sat motionless, the shattered image now finally taking its true form, after years of distortion in her mind. "And that was his biggest regret? Not being able to make sure she was okay?"

She was surprised when Thalia shook her head. "No. I mean yes, that part sucks, but he did as much as he could for her. His biggest regret was not doing what *was* in his control. He told the president of their frat, and those assholes got kicked out. But the president didn't want to report it up any further, because he was afraid the university might shut down the whole frat. He forbade Andrew from telling anyone in the UCLA administration or the police. Andrew said he felt guilty every day that he listened to the president and didn't report the assault."

Christina sat in silence as this new knowledge crashed over her like a powerful wave. After a long moment, she said, "I'm so sorry for your loss." She looked across the room at Thalia, watching the cast member's eyes brim with tears. Rising from Ashley's bed, Christina plopped next to her and pulled her into a tight hug.

Blinking back tears, Thalia looked up at her with a small sniffle. "Now you know why I say there's no way he would have assaulted Maria. Or even been unfaithful to me with her."

Christina nodded in earnest agreement, her mind still swimming.

Thalia's expression was fiercely protective. "I *know* he was really trying to help her."

"And he does have the means for it," Christina acknowledged.

"Exactly. So why would she want to hurt him? Maria makes zero sense as a suspect."

Suddenly, Christina's phone buzzed in her pocket. Pulling it out, she scanned the text message that had come in from Ava. Her heart dropped.

"I agree," Christina said, holding her phone out to Thalia. "But she's just been arrested for Andrew's murder."

Chapter 26: Blake - The Night Of

Blake released a sigh, letting the day's tensions ease away as the first shot of liquor coursed through him. Sometimes Señor Tequila played folksy Mexican crap, but tonight was Thursday and his boy Eduardo was DJing. He was bumping reggaeton over the bar's tinny speaker system, which had probably been here since the nineties, and Blake was gearing up for a great night.

"*¡Hola*, Eddie! My man," he said, bumping fists with the part-time bartender, part-time Daddy Yankee wannabe. "What's going on?"

"Not much," Eduardo replied with a wide smile, his English heavily accented. "How are you?"

"I'm alright, man. Rough day of work, you know? People think working in TV is all glamour, but it's actually tough fucking work."

Eduardo nodded. "Yes, but you meet many celebrities, no? Like Scarlett Johansson? I love her," he yelled over the coursing bass.

Blake chuckled, always enjoying an opportunity to name drop. "Oh yeah, I met her last year at a party," he confirmed. "And this year at the Emmys, Mila Kunis was at my table."

His eyes lighting up, the DJ exclaimed, "Wow, I love her too! Beautiful ladies. You are lucky man, Blake."

"Yeah, I guess it's not all bad," Blake agreed with a boyish grin.

"What about music celebrities?" Eduardo pressed on. "Do you know them? Because I think maybe you can give my tape to them, what do you think?"

As Blake was about to respond with some bullshit promise, the profile of a man entering the bar caught his eye. A long, slender nose extended from a face partially covered by shaggy dark hair. Blake cursed to himself as he recognized Manuel.

In the twenty-four hours since they last met in the storage unit, the cartel member had been texting him constantly, asking if he'd figured out who had overheard them talking about smuggling the drugs. So far, Blake had ignored him and tried to avoid the issue, not wanting to get anyone else involved in his mess—especially not Andrew. He winced again now, thinking of the black leather bracelet and the undeniable clue it held.

"Sorry Eddie, I gotta go," he said, clapping the DJ on the back.

Heading toward the bathroom, Blake wondered if he could somehow make an exit out the back door. He had never tried to leave that way, preferring to make plenty of social stops on his way out the main door once he was ready to call it a night, but he figured it likely led to the alley behind the bar. The only issue was he needed time for Alejandro to come pick him up. He didn't want to run out the door then be stuck waiting for the security guard to circle back on his motorcycle. And the first time he'd met Manuel in an alley had not exactly ended well for him.

Blake ducked into the bathroom, figuring he could call Alejandro and hide out there until he arrived. Standing in front of the grimy mirror, he pulled his phone out of his pocket and peered at the screen through a haze of tequila and coke.

Suddenly, the bathroom door flew open, its rusted handle smacking the wall behind it. Manuel's face appeared behind Blake's in the mirror, shadowed with anger.

The cartel member sneered. "There you are."

Turning to face him, Blake did his best to play it cool. "Hey, what's up?"

"Don't pretend like nothing's going on," Manuel said, closing the space between them as he stomped across the small bathroom with clenched fists. His beet red face now inches from Blake's, he demanded, "You don't know how to answer your fucking phone?"

"Oh yeah," Blake replied in what he hoped was a casual tone. He waved his phone in front of him, as if he'd just remembered the texts and was prepared to respond to them now. "Sorry, work has been crazy. My boss has been riding my ass and—"

With a swift movement of his hand, Manuel smacked the phone out of his grip and it fell, the slap of the screen against the dirty cement floor echoing in Blake's shocked silence.

"Stop giving me bullshit excuses!" he shouted. "I want to know who saw us in the storage unit. Now."

Blake's mind scrambled. He couldn't give them Andrew's name. He'd have to pretend that he didn't know.

"Hey, man," Blake said, raising his hands in a show of transparency. "I tried looking at the security footage, but there's no camera there." That part at least was true, and Blake thought his tone sounded convincing. Gathering confidence, he continued, slipping into lies, "I checked out some other cameras, even asked around with the kitchen staff, but nobody saw anyone near there. I tried my best but there's no way for me to know who—"

In a flash, Manuel rammed his shoulder into Blake, slamming him against the wall with surprising force, given his wiry frame. He pinned Blake to the wall, pushing his forearm across his neck, until Blake was gasping for breath. Manuel silently held him in position for what felt like an eternity. *This is it. I'm going to die,* Blake thought wildly.

When Manuel finally spoke, his voice was as smooth and deadly as the edge of the knife jutting out of his belt. "I've told you before and I'm only going to tell you once more. This is the Rodriguez cartel. Do. Not. Fuck. With. Us." Manuel shoved his shoulder harder into Blake's chest with each word. "Or we will slit your throat. Is that clear?"

Blake nodded.

"Good." Manuel eased the pressure on Blake's neck. "Now I'll give you one last chance to answer my question. Who saw us in the storage unit? I have almost ten million dollars' worth of product stashed there, and I'm not about to lose it because of some nosy asshole from your dumb show."

Blake exhaled, contemplating his options. He'd tried so hard to avoid this moment, but he was out of time. In his mind, he saw Andrew's handsome face, and his easy smile, and his gut wrenched knowing he had to sacrifice the contestant in order to save himself.

The name caught in Blake's mouth, as if every fiber of his body was resisting condemning his protégé to an awful fate. But he swallowed the lump in his throat and whispered, "Andrew. It was a cast member named Andrew."

Studying him carefully, as if to determine whether he was lying, Manuel leaned even closer, so that his long, crooked nose was almost touching Blake's own.

Seemingly satisfied, the cartel member took a step back, letting Blake slump against the wall, and nodded. "Good, that's good. You did the right thing, my man."

Blake highly doubted that, but didn't contradict him.

As Manuel turned to exit the bathroom door, he added, "Remember, not a fucking word." Without waiting for a response, he slammed the door shut.

Once his adrenaline dissipated, Blake's knees grew weak, and he leaned against the chipped sink. Frantic thoughts began scurrying through his mind. What had he done? What were they going to do to shut Andrew up? Should he warn him somehow?

He picked up his phone from the floor, hanging his head in defeat as he saw a long crack across the black screen. Now he didn't even have a way to call Alejandro to pick him up and bring him back to the resort. He could brave a taxi, but given the situation he was in and the hold the Rodriguez cartel had on this town, getting into a car with a stranger seemed like a terrible idea.

He tried to reason with himself. There was no way they'd hurt Andrew. Firstly, they didn't even have proof he'd seen them, or if he had, that he planned to tell anyone about it. Secondly, it would raise huge alarm bells if an American were found shot or beheaded at a fancy resort. The cartel wouldn't want the US agencies intervening on their turf, right?

Gradually, Blake's pulse slowed as he managed to convince himself that nothing was going to happen to Andrew—at least not right away. Since he didn't have a way back to the resort anyways, he figured he might as well just stay here and party until Alejandro circled back looking for him. He always tipped the security head well, so he felt confident Alejandro would come for him. Plus, getting obliterated and forgetting this awful night seemed like the best possible plan to Blake right now.

Exiting the bathroom, Blake strode over to the bar, avoiding eye contact with his usual pals, in case someone had noticed how long he'd been gone or who had followed him into the men's room. Puerto Engaño was a small town, and it wouldn't surprise him if many of the bar's patrons knew who Manuel was. Blake certainly didn't need anyone associating him with the cartel if he could avoid it.

"*¡Hola*, Francisco!" he called, waving a 500 peso note in the air. "Another round, *¡por favor!*" As the bartender poured out several shots of tequila, Blake carried two over toward Eduardo, who was focused on transitioning to his next song, another reggaeton classic.

Blake whooped as the bass kicked in. "Let's do it!"

The pair clinked shot glasses and threw back the liquor, the DJ waving his empty glass in the air.

Blake wasn't sure exactly how much time or how many shots had passed, but eventually he found himself on the dance floor, bumping to Eduardo's beats. Looking across the room, he spotted a woman he'd never seen at Señor Tequila before. Her tall, thin frame leaned against a high wooden table, the angle displaying her plentiful cleavage beneath a tight black tank top, which was tucked into jeans that tapered at the ankle of her long legs. Blake glanced around, assuming she came with someone, or at the very least had men already flocking to her. But she stood alone, her expression content as she sipped what appeared to be an old fashioned. Her long finger twirled the delicate orange peel around and around in the glass. He had never seen Francisco mix a proper cocktail like that.

After pausing for another moment to ensure no one was else joining the mystery woman, Blake sauntered over to her. *"Hola. Me llamo Blake."* These two phrases had pretty much exhausted his knowledge of Spanish, and usually at this point after meeting a local woman at Señor Tequila, he let his looks and dance moves speak for themselves. There wasn't much need for vocabulary in any language after that.

However, his new companion surprised him, responding in perfect English, "Wow, you must have worked really hard on learning that." Her tone was deadpan, but Blake caught a sparkle in her eyes that let him know she was flirting. His suspicions were cemented when she extended a beer to him.

Game on, he thought to himself.

"Clearly, your English is way better than my Spanish," he conceded with an exaggerated bow. "A woman who is beautiful and smart? I'll toast to that." He raised his bottle to meet her glass before taking a long draught of the cheap local beer.

She took a slow sip, her intense eyes never leaving his. Licking the whiskey off of her lips, she leaned in closer to him, so he could smell its bitter scent on her warm breath. "And what brings you to Puerto Engaño, Blake?"

Smiling inwardly at this chance to impress her, he kept his tone nonchalant as he said, "I'm the head of an American TV show called *Love's a Beach*. We film here every summer. Have you heard of it?"

She nodded, smiling. "Yes, I know a little about it. My coworkers talk about it all the time."

"Hah, I love it," Blake replied with an endearing chuckle. "Glad to hear we have some international fans." Taking another swig of his tequila, he felt things start to go fuzzy around the edges. "So, what do you do?"

"I have a boring government job," she replied with a laugh. "Definitely not as exciting as being on a TV show! But I do have a small business on the side. What do you Americans call it?" She paused for a moment, searching for the term, then snapped as she recalled it. "Side hustle!" she exclaimed with a little shimmy of her graceful shoulders.

"Now I'm really impressed," Blake said, edging his way closer so their faces were just inches apart. "You're smart, make your own money, and gorgeous." Reaching up to brush a strand of hair from her luminescent eyes, he let his fingers graze her cheek for a moment, then eased his way into a kiss. His lips pressed against hers gently at first, then more hungrily as she responded in turn, her curvaceous figure pressing into his chest and against his hips.

She pulled her mouth away from his, her sultry voice shooting straight down his spine as she whispered in his ear, "Should we take this back to your place?"

Some tiny voice in the back of Blake's mind made him hesitate for a moment, as if his subconscious were trying to steer him away from trouble. But glancing up and down the woman's body, and meeting her big, expectant eyes, he cast his doubts aside.

"Hell, yes." He shot her a roguish grin, his hands traveling down her back. "Do you have a car? I got a ride here."

"No car," she said, shaking her head, and his heart dropped in disappointment, before she flashed a mischievous smile, adding, "But I've got a motorcycle with room for two."

With a loud laugh of relief, he exclaimed, "Okay, that seals the deal. You're officially the sexiest woman alive."

She giggled as he grabbed her hand and steered her toward the door. He tried waving goodbye to Francisco and Eduardo, certain he'd get a little thumbs up from his boys, but they were both preoccupied and didn't catch his glance before he exited.

The evening air was warm and sticky, creating an odd sensation on his skin that mirrored the dewiness of his brain. He probably had hit the tequila a little too hard.

Oh well, he thought to himself, *we'll deal with that in the morning.*

Grasping his hand firmly, the woman led him across the parking lot to a shiny red motorcycle. Situating himself on the seat behind her, Blake took a moment to admire the curve of her ass before placing his hands possessively on her hips. "What's your name, by the way?" he asked, leaning in close to her ear.

She turned to face him, and with her full lips curved into a tiny, secretive smile, answered, "Rosa." Then she slid her dark motorcycle helmet over the top of her head, a set of thin, gold bracelets tinkling on her wrist, and they rode off into the dark night toward Paraiso Maya.

Chapter 27: Blake - Now

Blake left Ava's suite and headed directly for the south building where most of the crew were being housed. For a group of people used to working sixteen-hour days during the season, they weren't sure what to do with themselves when filming ground to a sudden halt after Andrew's death.

Without their phones, the last few days of doing nothing but waiting for further instructions had left his staff in complete and utter boredom. Blake ran a pretty tight crew for a show of their size, and other than the few junior producers like Christina, the crew was mostly made of technical staff like camera and audio guys who tended to be more introverted. Even before he began talking to his staff, he suspected they weren't going to have anything meaningful to divulge. He couldn't picture any of them chatting up a pretty waitress like Maria.

His hunch proved right, and over the next three hours he spoke to over thirty staff members, none of whom told him anything he didn't already know about Andrew or Maria. In the midst of one particularly boring interview with a sound technician who kept going on about how Thalia's voice sounded like wind chimes, he glanced at his watch and saw it was almost eight p.m., which meant Alejandro would be arriving for his shift. Using this as the perfect excuse to exit this conversation, Blake cleared his throat loudly and thanked the guy for his time before hurrying toward the security office near the front gate.

He knew Alejandro, unlike the crew, would have some good info for him. As the head of security, Alejandro not only directly oversaw a staff of six security guards who rotated shifts for guarding the front gate and perimeter of the resort, but also had a good rapport with the rest of the staff. Given his role, he seemed like the perfect person to not only give him intel on Maria, but also on anything else unusual going on around the hotel.

As dusk settled over the grounds, the light posts began to illuminate, casting a warm glow over the stone path as he made his way to the guard house. When he reached the small building, he knocked on the open door, calling out, "¡*Hola*, Alejandro! How are you?"

The man's back was to Blake, facing the computer monitor perched upon the worn but sturdy wooden desk. As Alejandro swiveled toward him, Blake was surprised to see the guard's normally cheerful face drawn with worry, the lines creasing between his eyebrows and the corners of his mouth.

His eyes unfocused, Alejandro greeted him with a weak smile. "Oh hi, Blake. I'm okay. How are you?"

Blake's face screwed into a dubious expression. "You don't look okay, my man."

"Yes, well, I…" Alejandro paused, frowning. "You know Maria?"

"Yeah," Blake said, relieved that he didn't have to broach the topic out of nowhere. "That's actually why I came, to talk to you about her."

"It's so sad the police arrest her!" Alejandro cried suddenly, as if releasing a dam of emotion he had been holding back.

Confused, Blake responded slowly, in case there had been some misunderstanding. "Well, it's looking like she killed Andrew. So, isn't it a good thing that they arrested her?"

"No, no," the man insisted, shaking his bald, wrinkled head. "Maria is good girl. She do not hurt anybody. Three years she's working here. She's very hard worker, very friendly to everybody."

"I know. I thought she seemed like a nice person too. But there is some evidence that makes a pretty clear case that she did it."

"What evidence?" he demanded, slipping into the mode of a protective father. "I don't believe it." His eyes hardened as shook his head.

Blake hesitated, unsure how much to reveal to Alejandro, who had an obvious loyalty to Maria. It was only natural that he would side with his fellow staff members and prioritize their wellbeing.

"Well," he began cautiously, "we think that Andrew may have hurt her, either by leading her on, or maybe even assaulting her."

Alejandro gasped, an angry gleam in his eyes. "You mean…" he pointed to his crotch, either because he didn't know the word in English, or because he couldn't bring himself to speak of someone violating Maria in that way.

Blake held his hands up. "We don't know yet. Let's not jump to conclusions. But the point is, she likely had a motive. And then even more important," he continued, deciding there was no point in holding back information that Alejandro could easily find on his own security tapes, "we found some camera footage of Maria entering the boys' villa right around the time that Andrew died."

Blake paused dramatically, expecting shock to sweep across the security guard's face. However, he was disappointed when the man only nodded placidly.

"Yes, Maria bring the coffee and food to the villas many nights."

Blake's excitement deflated at this anticlimactic response to his trump card. "Yes," he said, scrambling to recover, "that makes sense. But the timing is weird, don't you agree? Pretty big coincidence?"

"Maybe somebody call her to ask for coffee," Alejandro shrugged.

"Maybe," Blake responded, now getting exasperated at the hypothetical scenarios of the waitress's innocence. "But there's no way to prove that."

"*Sí, señor,*" Alejandro replied. "I can check the phone calls."

"What do you mean?"

The guard swiveled the worn office chair back toward the computer, and began to poke at the keyboard. "Look, I check the date, seventeen of June, okay?" A long list of room numbers and time stamps had appeared on the monitor. Pointing one stubby, gnarled finger at the screen, Alejandro traced it down the list.

He parsed through the call log for a minute or so, then leaned back away from the computer and tapped his fingers on the desk a few times. "*Muy raro. Qué extraño,*" he muttered to himself, before slowly pulling his gaze up toward Blake's face.

"What?" Blake asked impatiently. "What did you find?"

"Only one call between midnight and three a.m.," Alejandro confirmed. "Someone call the restaurant at twelve forty-two a.m."

"Wow," Blake exhaled. "So, someone in the boys' villa *did* ask Maria to bring up the coffee?"

"No, *señor*. The call not coming from that villa." He paused, his eyes narrowing as his stare bored into Blake. "The call from Presidential Suite. Your room."

Blake's heart jumped into his throat as Alejandro's words echoed in his head. *Your room.* His mind spun in a thousand directions, whipping like a hurricane. He scrambled to remember the events of that fateful evening, but still came up completely blank after greeting the bartender and DJ at Señor Tequila.

"No way. I didn't call the restaurant," he insisted, willing himself to believe it, though he couldn't be certain.

Alejandro nodded, as if considering whether this may in fact be true.

Blake held his breath. *Please believe me.*

His prayer seemingly answered, the security guard agreed, "Maybe you not the one who call. Maybe the woman you bring back that night call from your room."

His mouth gaping, Blake struggled to compose himself. There was no way he had brought a woman back here. Sure, he had his share of dance floor make-outs with women at Señor Tequila, and had even brought women back to the resort during prior seasons, but this year it was out of the question. Between the increased security measures, the risks he was taking with the cartel's bullshit, Ava breathing down his neck as his new boss, and Christina's freakish ability to spot anything he did wrong and be as judgmental as humanly possible…there was no chance in hell he would have brought someone back here.

"I…no, that's impossible," he sputtered. "You must be confused."

"No, I remember." Alejandro's tone was firm. "Because you very generous," he continued, rubbing his fingers together to indicate that Blake had given him a sizable tip to allow the woman onto the grounds. Blake had to admit that didn't sound particularly out of character for him. "Next day eighteen of June is my wife's birthday. I buy her very pretty necklace, thanks to you."

With the specificity of the security guard's memory, Blake began to doubt himself. After all, he didn't remember anything from that night, so it was technically possible, even if he'd sworn to himself he wouldn't bring anyone home this season.

His mind racing, Blake asked Alejandro, "Do you remember what she looked like? Or anything about her?"

"*Sí*, she drive a red motorcycle. I can't see her face because her helmet. But she look very nice," Alejandro said with a coy smile, his hands gliding through the air as if caressing an hourglass figure. "Oh, and you said her name! I think was…Rosa? You say, 'Alejandro, please let my friend Rosa come in!' Do you want me to find security video?"

"No," Blake answered quickly. "Thanks for your help." He turned and headed toward his room.

At the sound of the name Rosa, a dam had broken inside him and memories of that night flooded back to his consciousness. In fragments, still, but they were there. Manuel's long profile appearing behind him in the bathroom mirror. Blake's ribs aching as the cartel member pinned him against the wall. Andrew's name escaping his lips almost involuntarily. A pretty woman leaning eagerly toward him. The taste of whiskey and orange on her breath. A strange fog taking over his mind. His limbs feeling heavy. The vibration of the motorcycle under him as they sped back toward Paraiso Maya. And then the endless softness of his bed embracing him as it all faded into nothing.

Chapter 28: Christina - Now

Christina stared again at the text message from Ava, informing her of Maria's arrest. Her body felt physically exhausted from being tugged into so many different emotions in the whirlwind that had been today: relief at sharing what she'd seen with Andrew and Maria, shock at discovering she had been wrong about Andrew's role in her assault, and an overwhelming guilt for her role in what she now knew to be an unjust arrest of the waitress.

Looking back up at Thalia's dismayed expression, she felt a gravitational pull to set things right. Her brow set in determination, she squared her shoulders toward the cast member. "We're going to set Maria free and find Andrew's real killer."

Thalia nodded, but her eyes revealed some hidden hesitation. "I want to get closure for him, of course. I'm just…nervous."

Christina paused for a moment, wanting to be transparent. "That's fair. I also need to warn you: the CBC executives may not be happy with us. They've told us to let the CBC Legal team handle things, and for us to stay out of it going forward. So, if you're part of some unofficial operation with us, they could retaliate by giving you a bad edit. I won't be able to control the narrative around you. I know how important it is to you to get the public support you need for your bill. If you want to keep your distance and let the network give you a sympathetic edit as the grieving girlfriend, I'll totally understand. And I'll happily do that for you."

An expression of trepidation washed over Thalia's face, and Christina could see how conflicted she was. Christina was offering her a chance to achieve her life's dream and make peace with her parents' memory.

Thalia exhaled slowly. "I really appreciate that, Christina. I do. And it makes perfect sense."

Christina held her breath, trying to hide her disappointment.

"But," Thalia countered, "I know Andrew wouldn't want any innocent person sitting in jail, and especially not Maria. So, if the only way to free her is to find the real killer, then I'm in. Let's do the damn thing."

Christina's chest flooded with relief at having a partner in her quest for justice. Breaking into a grin, she beckoned for Thalia to follow her. "We need to go update Ava. I realize you don't know her well yet, but we can trust her. She is a total boss and she will know what to do."

As the pair walked down the stairs, they saw the rest of the female cast members huddled on the couch—even Raina, who notoriously never left her room to socialize with the other women. Upon seeing Thalia and Christina, Ashley jumped up from her seat, her long blonde ponytail bobbing as she bounded over to them.

"Thals, is everything okay?" Ashley glanced back at the other women, then admitted, "When Christina came to talk to you, we figured something was up."

Christina glanced at Thalia expecting her to respond anxiously, but a strange expression of resolute calm spread across her face.

Thalia lifted her chin. "Everything isn't okay right now. But I have a feeling it will be. We need to go take care of some things."

Ashley nodded, her eyes soft with understanding. "Okay. We'll be here if you need us."

"Thanks, Ash." Thalia's voice cracked with emotion as she pulled her into a quick hug. Turning to Christina, she gave a quick nod to indicate she was ready to go.

The producer turned to her cast, whom she'd carefully chosen and supported throughout the season. "I'll send Sol back to update you all as soon as we can share something." She paused, expecting the women to demand to know what was happening—at least Karina, who never shied away from asking tough questions—but was met with only somber silence. With that she turned and walked out the door, Thalia trailing behind her.

They walked without speaking for a few moments, each lost in their own thoughts. As they drew closer to Ava's room, Christina still didn't know how she was going to tell Ava about the new direction of the investigation. Maria's arrest had moved it toward closure, and now they'd be starting over. Christina was afraid that shaking things up would risk the good favor she'd earned with Ava, and thereby her career, but she felt a deep responsibility to make things right for Maria and Andrew.

Approaching Ava's door, she took a deep breath and knocked firmly, Thalia hanging slightly behind her. The humid evening air hummed with the local insects and a pulsing energy that Christina couldn't quite define. As the door swung open, the blast of air conditioning from within the room washed over her, as cool as Ava's gaze once she registered Thalia standing there.

"Christina, what's going on?" Ava demanded.

"I know, I know we said to keep things within our small group," she replied, stumbling to explain herself. "But when I was talking to Thalia, I became more and more confident that Maria didn't do this. And then when you told me she's been arrested, I just thought…" she threw her hands up, exasperated. "We have to do something!"

Ava studied Christina. "You're sure about this?"

Glancing back at Thalia whose brown eyes were wide and earnest, Christina returned her focus to her boss and nodded. "We're positive."

With a look of restrained acceptance, Ava responded, "I trust your judgment," and waved them both into the room.

Christina's heart swelled with pride. As they entered the small room, she spotted Sol still perched on the bed, her head bent low over the laptop screen, and her hair pulled into a messy bun. Christina smiled seeing this little mark she'd made on the young PA.

"Hey," Sol said, barely glancing up from the screen.

"So," said Ava as she sunk down into the desk chair, crossing her legs and smoothing out her pants, "what makes you so confident that Maria is innocent?"

With Christina's prompting, Thalia explained what Andrew had shared with her about Maria's brother being indebted to the cartel, and his plan to give her the money so that her family could live peacefully. Ava listened to the account without interrupting, the tips of her long, manicured fingers pressed together in front of her chest as she processed this new information.

"Interesting," she said when Thalia concluded her story. Turning her attention to Christina, Ava said, realization spreading across her face, "So when you saw them in the kitchen…"

A flush of shame rising to her cheeks, Christina swallowed then admitted, "It seems I misread that situation."

Thalia jumped in tactfully. "Andrew said she was really emotional when he offered her the money. She was crying and hugging him and super relieved."

"I see," Ava replied, turning back at Christina. "And you mistook those as distressed tears."

"Yes," she said, deflating at the thought that this admission could completely invalidate the compliment Ava had just paid her. She glanced down at her lap, tears welling in her eyes as she awaited an admonishment from the executive.

Instead, Ava said gently, "It happens to the best of us."

Christina snapped her head up in surprise, then nodded in gratitude, her jaw set against the coming tears. She hadn't known how much she'd needed to hear that. She could only hope that once this was all over, Maria would feel the same way.

Eager to change the subject, she glanced over at Sol, who was still clicking furiously away at her keyboard, and muttering to herself in the corner. "What's she doing?" Christina asked Ava.

"She's been reviewing more of the tapes. We originally were looking to see what time Maria exited the boys' villa, so that we could understand how long she was inside, thinking that might be a good clue as to what she did in there. We started watching from the moment she entered, but then we never saw her come out."

"What?" exclaimed Thalia.

Christina's eyes narrowed. "How is that possible?"

Finally breaking her focus, Sol looked up at them, her eyes flashing with the victory of a major breakthrough. "Maria enters the villa at twelve fifty-seven a.m. The next person we see coming in or out of the villa is Nick, time stamped at two thirty-seven a.m., which lines up with when he and Ashley told us they said good night. But then we watched the tape back more carefully. You know that black and white cat that is always hanging around the restaurant?"

Christina nodded, waving her hand in a circle to hurry Sol along.

"Well, I saw it come up and sit on the porch of the villa once, but then I saw it a second time, and then a third. That's when I realized that from about one a.m. until one forty-five a.m., the tape is on a loop. Someone has altered it."

"What!" Thalia gasped. "Like someone from the crew? One of the camera guys?"

Her mind spinning, Christina shook her head. "Not necessarily. This is one of the resort's security cameras. As part of our contract with them and the security plan, we have access to all their footage, in case we want to use it for the show. But they have access to it too, so it could have been one of the hotel staff as well."

"But why would they?" Sol interjected, frowning. "I mean, if it was a staff member, their most likely motivation would be protecting Maria. But they left that part in. Why not delete the part with her *entering* the boys' villa?"

Christina looked to Ava. The executive remained in the desk chair, her elbows resting on the curved mahogany arms. Looking at Ava's furrowed brow, she could almost see the wheels turning in her brilliant mind.

Ava stared at the wall, speaking slowly. "I don't think it's one of our crew members. And I don't think it's one of the resort staff." Gathering momentum, she looked around the room at the group of talented women before her. "One thing that I've learned in my career is that when I approach a problem, I need to think about it in terms of power."

"Power?" Christina asked.

"Yes. Power," Ava repeated with an emphatic nod. "In this case, who had the power to make this happen and avoid any repercussions with the law? And even more importantly," she continued, her voice dropping in volume but ratcheting up in intensity, "who had power to gain from Andrew's death?"

Her question hung in the room, weighing on each of them as they considered it. "Because I'll tell you this," she said, leaning back in her chair and crossing her legs, "for some people, power is like a drug. It gives them a high, a euphoria, being on top—having control over other people. And once they've had a taste, they'll do almost anything to get more. On this show, you ladies have experience in dealing with love. And it's true that love can make people do crazy things. But the longer I've been in this business, the more I've realized that power trumps love every time."

Ava's dark words settled over them like the damp chill creeping into the night air. Christina shivered, pondering her questions. *Who had the power to make this happen without repercussions, and who had power to gain from Andrew's death?*

A series of sharp knocks on the door startled them all out of their thoughts.

"I'll get it," Christina said, jumping up and crossing the room. She swung open the heavy wooden door and came face to face with Blake, looking unlike she had ever seen him. In contrast to his usually smooth composure and jaunty smile, Blake's complexion looked ashen, his eyes wild with some emotion Christina couldn't quite place.

"Hi, Blake," she said, pulling the door open wider as she struggled to hide her surprise at his appearance. "Come in."

Christina watched her boss stride into the room, his gait jerky as he approached the desk where Ava sat, then abruptly circled back toward the bed, before turning back again toward the desk. The rest of the women looked as confused as she felt.

After a few moments of his erratic pacing, Christina ventured, "Umm, Blake…everything okay?"

He spun to look at her, as if she had appeared out of nowhere. "Oh. Yeah. Well, kind of. I mean, I'm not sure." The showrunner looked around the room at the four faces studying him with a mixture of confusion and concern. "The thing is…I think I fucked up."

Christina raised an eyebrow; she was accustomed to Blake's fuckups, but an admission of those fuckups was a new development. "How so?"

"Well, I just talked to Alejandro. The resort's head of security. And uh…it seems like there may have been someone who wasn't part of the staff or crew who was on the grounds that night."

Christina itched to demand more information, but reading the expression on Ava's face, she forced herself to be patient and let Blake unravel the details in his own way.

Glancing nervously around the room at their expectant faces, he sighed heavily. "Well, I don't know exactly who it was. But I went off site that night to a local bar and brought a woman back here."

Christina wanted to scream. She had suspected Blake was sneaking off at night, a blatant violation of their security plan, but she'd held her tongue over the last month. Even she hadn't thought he was dumb enough to bring someone back to the resort.

She looked at Ava, but rather than seeing her own anger reflected, she saw the executive's composed face studying Blake with the vaguest hint of disdain. "And you think that this woman may have had something to do with Andrew's death?" Ava asked him.

"No, I wouldn't say that. I mean…not necessarily." Blake stumbled over his words, and Christina could tell he was holding back something bigger, his usual charisma shadowed by some dark secret.

Her dark eyes piercing into the showrunner, Ava asked coolly, "Why would a woman you picked up at a bar want to hurt Andrew?"

"Well, the thing is…" Blake stopped, tousled his fingers through his wavy blond hair, then collapsed into a velvet armchair in the corner of the room, apparently giving up. "I got into some trouble a few months ago," he mumbled.

Watching his internal struggle, after years of his smug grin putting her in her place, Christina wanted to gloat. But against her own wishes, she found herself feeling bad for him.

When he didn't resume his story, she gathered all of her restraint and forced herself to ask gently, "What kind of trouble?"

"It all started when I got pulled over for a DUI. And, unfortunately, when they searched me they found some illegal substances," he admitted, staring at the ground and refusing to make eye contact with his boss.

Not surprising, Christina thought to herself.

"My lawyer got the police to drop the charges in exchange for giving them my dealer's name. Which would have been fine, except it turns out that my dealer was pretty high up in a cartel."

"Like…a drug cartel?" Sol asked, wide-eyed.

"Yes. The Rodriguez cartel."

"Holy shit," Christina whispered, the revelation knocking the air from her lungs. After they'd spent countless hours planning how to avoid problems with the cartel in Puerto Engaño, Blake had somehow managed to get himself entangled with them back in LA? Literally only Blake could create this level of mess. She looked at Ava, trying to gauge her reaction, but the executive continued to display the ultimate poker face.

"Okay," Christina prompted him. "So, that must have made them mad, right? Did they threaten you or something?"

"Yes. And they told me the only way they wouldn't kill me was if I helped them."

"Helped them how?" Christina frowned.

"Some of their old routes have gotten cut off, apparently there was some kind of big FBI crackdown. They were looking for a new way to get drugs into the US. And they knew that the show was chartering a private plane from here back to LA."

Christina's hand flew to her mouth. "Blake, no you fucking didn't."

"I did," he confessed, his voice hollow. "I agreed to smuggle drugs back on the plane. All summer they've been bringing shipments and keeping them in the storage unit with our equipment."

Christina replayed their conversations back in LA when they discussed the cartel violence. "Blake, is that why you kept shooting down my ideas about moving the filming location? You had already told the cartel we'd be here?"

His eyes looked desperate. "I didn't have a choice. What would they have done to me if we'd moved filming to another country? I had to keep us here, and I had to help smuggle the drugs."

Christina cringed at his cowardice. However, something still wasn't making sense. "Blake, this is obviously a huge…fuckup, to use your words. But I'm still confused about what this has to do with Andrew."

Blake finally stilled his pacing around the room, bringing his gaze to meet hers. For perhaps the first time in their relationship, Christina saw something that looked like genuine remorse haunting his brilliant blue eyes. When the showrunner spoke again, his voice was barely audible.

"One night, someone saw us bringing the drugs into the storage unit, and overheard us talking about it. I realized later that person was—"

"Andrew," Thalia whispered suddenly, startling them all. Her voice emanated from the corner where she sat curled in a tight ball, speaking for the first time since Blake's arrival.

Blake's silence confirmed her guess.

Thalia tilted her head back, staring up at the stucco ceiling in disbelief. "He told me that he had seen something weird the night before he died, but we got distracted with my problems and him telling me about helping Maria, and he never got around to telling me what it was."

The pieces were starting to fall into place in Christina's mind. *Who had power to gain from Andrew's death?* It seemed clear now that the answer was someone in the Rodriguez cartel.

"So," Christina said slowly, "the cartel decided they needed to take care of whoever had seen you, to make sure they didn't risk blowing up your whole secret operation. But how did they know who it was? Did you…" she hesitated, not wanting to believe that even this guy who she thought was a useless human being would stoop so low as to put an innocent man in harm's way to save his own ass. "Did you tell them it was Andrew?"

Blake's blue eyes bored into hers, clouded with emotion as his face twisted in regret. "I had to," he said, his voice pleading. "They were demanding a name from me. They were going to kill me. I had no choice."

Christina's stomach writhed in disgust at Blake's level of utter selfishness.

"One of the cartel guys came to the resort that night?" she demanded, her voice hardening. "And then what? Snuck into his room and murdered him?"

"I don't know," Blake responded, his hands coming up to grip his head in desperation. "I was at a bar, and I blacked out. But when I spoke to

Alejandro, he said that when I came back that night, I was with a woman. So, it could have been her that did it. He said when we saw him at the security gate, I called her Rosa."

Rosa. The name jarred something in Christina's mind, a tiny pinpoint scratching insistently against her brain. "Who had the power to make this happen, without repercussions from the law," she muttered to herself, echoing Ava's question. Her eyes widened as everything snapped into place.

Jerking her head toward the desk where Ava sat, Christina spotted the piece of paper she was looking for, laid neatly on the corner of the smooth mahogany surface. She crossed the room and reached over Ava without a word, picking up the business card they had been handed two days ago.

The blood froze in Christina's veins as she read in clear, bold print: ***Daniela Rosa Castillo Martinez - Jefe de Policía, Estado de Oaxaca.***

"What is it?" Sol asked.

Christina looked around the room and swallowed. "Rosa is Chief Martinez. She killed Andrew."

Chapter 29: Blake - Now

Blake's heart dropped. "Wait, that police officer you've been working with? No way."

"What do you mean, 'no way'?" Christina replied angrily. "You gave the cartel Andrew's name for a hit order, then led the hitwoman straight to him, dumbass!"

Ava cut in sternly, "Calm down, Christina. Everyone needs to keep it together. We need to figure this out. I agree it's entirely possible that Chief Martinez could have pulled this off. But why? Why would she want to help the cartel?"

"I think…" Christina started, then trailed off, her eyes screwed closed with focus. "I remember when I was researching the cartels and preparing our security plan, there was this mini-documentary I found on YouTube. A British journalist who was trying to uncover the inner workings of the Rodriguez cartel. He was trying to figure out who the leader is, because no one knows. He was interviewing a local policeman about it and the officer said *la jefa*. Feminine. As in, the cartel boss was a woman. The officer got all flustered and said he'd misspoken, that he meant *el jefe*. The journalist tried to press him on it, but he shut down and said the interview was over. Then the journalist went down this rabbit hole of trying to dig in deeper with his other sources, but no one else would talk to him."

Blake's brain throbbed against his skull as he tried to process all of this information. "So, you think the head of the Rodriguez cartel is…this police officer?" He glanced at Ava to gauge her reaction to this theory, but her expression was impossible to read.

"Not just any police officer," Christina retorted. "She's the chief of the state police department."

"I don't know," he said. How could any woman who was not only a police chief, but also a drug lord, have captured his attention at a bar? He hadn't met Chief Martinez when she'd been at the resort, as he'd been preoccupied dealing with the CBC execs that first morning, and then handling the crew each time she'd come again. But from Christina's updates, he had imagined someone more…stodgy.

"It would make sense, right?" Thalia's voice interrupted his thoughts. "The stuff about the tox screens getting all messed up? What if it was her trying to cover up that he was murdered? She was so adamant at first that it was an overdose. And then when it started to look like a murder, she tried to question me and my relationship with Andrew."

Christina chewed on her lip. "When I brought up the potential motive for Maria, Daniela practically jumped on that idea. How lucky for her, she needed a suspect, and I served her one on a silver platter." Her face falling, she turned to Ava, who remained calmly seated. "And Maria may actually have known who she was. Remember how Maria was all jumpy when she brought the police coffee? And then she was MIA when we had a meeting with Daniela at the restaurant? She was probably terrified of her because of this thing with her brother."

Blake frowned at this new piece of information. "What thing with her brother?"

Christina exchanged a glance with Thalia. The cast member explained, "Andrew told me that Maria's brother was in the cartel and was trying to leave. They were threatening her family and demanding money in exchange for his freedom. Andrew was going to help her with the money."

Maybe the woman you bring back that night call from your room, he heard Alejandro's voice in his head. "What if…" he said slowly, the horrifying thought forming in his mind. "What if Chief Martinez didn't get *lucky* that you introduced Maria as a suspect? What if she framed her?"

Christina frowned. "How would she do that?"

Blake hesitated, not wanting to reveal any more details of his idiotic decision to bring "Rosa" to the resort. But guilt gnawed at his stomach, driving him to do better by Andrew posthumously than he had while he was alive.

"Alejandro checked the call logs. Someone called from my room to the kitchen that night." Blake studied the floor, not daring to look in Ava's direction. "She could have asked Maria to bring coffee to the boys' villa. That would explain why Maria went there. And Daniela must have known that Maria would be caught on camera delivering the coffee. Then, after Maria leaves, Daniela sneaks in and kills Andrew. But why didn't we see Daniela on the footage?"

"Sol found a loop on the tape. It cuts out right after Maria left. Daniela must have found a way to edit it," Christina said. "She's like an evil genius."

"It was a master plan, right?" Thalia agreed. "Get rid of the guy who could blow her whole smuggling operation, and at the same time frame Maria for his murder. It's the perfect leverage over her brother—you come back to the cartel, or I keep your sister locked up for a crime she didn't commit. Two birds with one stone." Turning to Ava, she concluded, "You wanted an explanation about power. Here it is."

Ava nodded thoughtfully, the creases in her ebony skin hardly shifting in reaction to this revelation. "It sure checks that box."

After a long silence, Christina spoke. "So, Ava. How do we catch someone like this? Someone driven by power?"

Ava rose gracefully from the modern teak desk chair, and Blake could sense a shift in her energy. They had found answers, and now it was time for action—or maybe even vengeance. Perhaps she was eager to crush the woman who had tried to make a mockery of Ava on her own set. The glint in her eyes as she began pacing the room hinted to Blake that it was the latter.

"Daniela has played all of this exactly right," Ava began. "She kept her operation a secret, and she did it in a way that showed Maria's family who was the boss. You mess with the cartel, we mess with your family." She turned back toward the desk, picking up the police officer's business card and turning it absently in her fingers. "With the video footage of Maria entering the boys' villa right around the time of Andrew's death, she obviously had enough to justify charging her with the murder. She runs the police, who are responsible for charging criminals. But," she said, the gleam of opportunity shining in her deep brown eyes, "she may not have the judges in her pocket. And if she wants to make absolutely sure Maria gets convicted, she'll need more evidence. Physical evidence linking her to the crime."

Blake scrunched his nose, confused. "But aren't we all in agreement that Maria didn't do it? So, there won't be any physical evidence, right?"

A *gotcha* expression crept across Ava's face. "There won't be any *real* evidence. But I would bet my Malibu house that she will go to any lengths to *pretend* there's evidence."

Christina's eyebrows up in understanding. "Oooh. So, we give her a chance to plant some fake evidence?"

Ava smiled and nodded.

"How is that going to help?" Blake asked. "Won't that make things worse for Maria?"

"Not if we catch her in the act," Ava said, her lips curved into a smug smile.

"Exactly!" Christina rubbed her hands together in excitement. "Sol, pull up the security plan we worked on. Let's see where our network cameras are and how we can make this work."

* * *

Over the next two hours, the group pored over the location of each and every camera on the hotel grounds, debating fiercely over the best location to discreetly capture footage of Daniela fabricating evidence against Maria. They considered setting up a new camera, but were wary that any of the staff who saw them doing so might tip off Daniela. They had no idea who may be working with her given how well she knew Maria's schedule and how easily Manuel had been able to move about the grounds.

Considering all of this, they decided that using one of the existing cameras, already well-hidden to capture contestants more naturally, was their best bet. Ava immediately dismissed any camera owned by the resort, since the chief had already proven capable of manipulating that footage.

With their scope of focus narrowed, Christina pressed forward with her proposed plan. "Okay so, we have camera twelve, which has a perfect view of the restaurant, and beyond it, the door to the kitchen. Now, we know that the kitchen staff's lockers are right behind that swinging door. That would be the *perfect* place for Chief Martinez to try to plant evidence. Think about it. If you were Maria and you really had committed this crime, it would make total sense. You hide the drugs in your locker, you wait for one night when he asks you to bring something up to his room, and then you mix the drugs into his drink in the kitchen before walking it over."

"Excellent plan, Christina. Really great." Blake's voice oozed with sarcasm. "Except one small detail: the solid metal door between the camera and the lockers."

"Yes," she responded, her voice determined. "But, do you remember when the hinge broke a few weeks ago and the door got stuck open? Osito was complaining about the flies getting into his kitchen, and Raina was complaining that the smell of fried food wafting out was making her sick?"

Blake nodded, remembering the nearly twenty minutes he'd spent coaxing Raina back to the restaurant so they could get a group scene of the women discussing Ashley's blossoming relationship with Nick.

Of course, he'd cooed at her, *I can tell you never eat fried food. That's obvious looking at you. But could you try to come sit there for a few minutes? For me?* The combination of flattery and his boyish grin had eventually won her over, and they'd gotten a cut of juicy girl talk that Ava had praised during the next day's check-in.

"Okay, yes, I remember the door being stuck open for a while," he confirmed to Christina.

"Right." She nodded curtly, forging ahead. "Sol, show us the footage from that day." As the production assistant pivoted the laptop toward them, the group looked in excitement past the tables in the foreground and the heavy swinging door wedged open with a hastily scribbled sign proclaiming *"Rota"* taped to the doorframe. There, in clear view in the background, stood the ten shiny, black employee lockers, printed with each employee's name.

Reading from left to right, Blake scanned the names: Osito, Juan (*oh, I guess that's the awkward pimply teenager's name,* he mused absently), and then there, right in the middle on the top row, in neat, looped handwriting, was Maria's name.

"It's a perfect shot," he admitted. He was relieved a plan was moving forward to make up for his mistakes, but still somewhat resentful Christina had come up with the idea instead of him. "So, how do we get the door to stay open? Won't this Daniela lady be a little suspicious if we ask her to leave it open while she tries to slip some drugs into the locker?"

Ava shook her head. "No, we don't need to ask her to leave it open. We can ensure it's 'broken' again before she arrives."

Christina nodded eagerly. "Yes! But we should do it now and check the camera view before we suggest that Daniela comes to search the locker. If we can't get her planting the evidence on camera, then our whole plan is for nothing."

Blake balked, glancing at his vintage silver watch. "It's a little after ten p.m. The evening staff will be at the restaurant until one. If we go down and do it now, we'll attract attention for sure, and we don't know who we can trust. What if they tip her off?"

"We'll need to make it look like an accident," Ava conceded.

A sly smile slid across Christina's face. "I have an idea. What if *one of us,*" she paused dramatically, with a pointed look in Blake's direction, and his stomach clenched in anticipation, "pretends to be stumbling drunk and slams into the door?"

His face screwed up in disgust, he retorted, "Oh, so you think I'm the drunk one?" Christina gave a quick side eye to Thalia, who pressed her lips together in an apparent attempt to suppress a giggle.

"Blake," Ava added calmly, though he thought he saw a glimmer of amusement in her eyes, "you are the biggest and strongest of us, so you're the most likely to be able to pull it off."

Blake shook his head in resignation, knowing the argument was lost once Ava had latched onto the idea. "Fine, I'll go down there acting like I'm looking for a drunken snack. But I really am going to eat some tamales while I'm there!" he added with a pout.

"Thank you for doing your part to help catch this murderer," Ava responded with forced gravity, and this time he was sure he caught a smirk on her lips.

Chapter 30: Thalia - Now

Thalia tried to focus as Blake ran through the plan with them one last time in Ava's room, but kept finding herself pulled back down into her own whirlpool of emotions. Despite her attempt to barricade her heart from love, keeping it locked into the fortress of pain and guilt over her parents' death, Andrew had somehow broken through. He'd brought waves of joy crashing upon her in the few weeks they'd known each other. It was easily the happiest she'd been since losing her parents, elevating her to the highest high, but also sinking her to the lowest low when she'd seen his stiff, sprawled figure that fateful morning.

Of course, she'd felt heartbreak over the last few days, processing the loss of him, but it was only tonight when Christina had presented her with a choice—the environmental bill or finding Andrew's killer—that she had truly allowed herself to acknowledge how deeply she'd fallen in love with him. She knew that was true because it hadn't even felt like a choice. It was what her soul was calling her to do.

Now, as Blake prepared to go to the kitchen, resigned to playing the role of the drunken mess, he pulled her out of her thoughts. "Hey, Thalia." Glancing up at him, she saw a new flash of emotion cross his face: a mix of inspiration and muted pride.

"What's up?" she asked him hesitantly.

"I have an idea. What's your Insta handle?"

"Blake…" Ava began with a warning tone.

"No, no change to the plan, I promise," he assured her. "Think of this as…a backup. An insurance policy." Seeing his boss's eyebrow raised dubiously, he added gently, almost pleading, "Please. Let me do this one small thing to try to make this right."

Thalia glanced at Ava, waiting for her reaction. As Ava studied Blake, her lips pursed, the executive finally gave an almost imperceptible nod.

Looking back toward him, Thalia answered his question. "It's *thali-aearthyoga.*"

"Perfect, that's all I need."

Blake strode over to the minibar and grabbed a tiny bottle of whiskey. Thalia cocked her head. *What is this fool doing now?*

"Blake!" Christina exclaimed.

"Oh, don't get your panties in a bunch," Blake replied as he screwed off the cap. "I'm not going to drink it. It's for effect!" He threw his head back and swished the alcohol around in his mouth, before moving to the bathroom sink and spitting it out. Tilting the bottle, he dribbled the last few amber drops directly onto his shirt. "And that's why I'm a star producer," he concluded with a playful grin.

Thalia's face remained impassive. The whole thing would have been endearing if not for the fact that Blake was a huge part of the reason they were in this situation.

Undeterred, Blake walked toward the door, turning to the group and giving a mock salute as he opened it. "Wish me luck!"

Left alone again, the group of women watched in anxious silence, huddled around the laptop as Sol panned between various live camera views, allowing them to trace Blake's footsteps in real time as he approached the restaurant. Thalia observed each of the crew members in turn: Ava's serious but steady countenance, Christina's worried eyes behind a thin veil of forced poise, and Sol's anxious expression. The silence was punctuated by the intermittent tapping of Christina's sandal against the cool marble floor.

They watched Blake's tall figure pass down the path, swaying a bit as he approached the restaurant. His gait was punctuated by an occasional stumble, his loafers pattering unevenly down the stone-lined way. While there was no audio available for these stationary cameras, they could get the gist of the conversation as he greeted the waiter, Juan, with enthusiasm, the young man laughing as Blake extended his fist for a bump. After a few moments of the producer speaking, the waiter motioned for him to take a seat at a table. Blake shook his head, pointing insistently at the kitchen door. Juan met him with hands upheld, attempting to corral his drunken guest into sitting and waiting for his snack—but Blake slapped him on the back in mock revelry, and pushed his way past him toward the swinging door.

Thalia could almost feel the air escape the room as all the women held their breath. Blake ambled toward the kitchen entrance, then staged a perfect theatrical fall, his muscular frame slamming with full force into the door. It swung back violently, and Thalia saw the metal hinge at the top hyperextend, then snap.

Juan's hands flew to his head in dismay before he rushed forward to assist Blake. The producer acted briefly dazed, then began laughing hysterically, wiping his eyes so convincingly that Thalia wondered for a moment if he might actually be crying tears of relief that this plan had worked. Once he recovered, he began speaking to the server, clapping him on the back again, as if in apology. The waiter disappeared into the kitchen, then quickly reemerged with a takeaway box, which he handed to Blake, eager to get rid of his destructive, tipsy guest. Pointing at him with both hands in the shape of guns, the producer wriggled his eyebrows as if to say, *You're the best!* and flashed him a winning smile before stumbling away.

After he departed, the women watched anxiously as Juan entered the kitchen again, and came back out with Osito, the loveable chef. The two staff members examined the door, trying in vain to cajole it back into its resting position. Thalia grimaced each time Osito's rotund torso slammed into the metal surface, but try as he might, the broken hinge would not allow the door to close. When he finally shrugged and Juan hung his head in defeat, the air rushed back into her lungs.

"YES!" Christina shouted next to her, jumping up and punching the air.

Ava beamed and threw her head back in laughter, her blindingly white teeth shining as her lips pulled into a smile. Sol simply sat in disbelief, either that the plan had worked or that she had been a part of it.

When Blake knocked on the door a few minutes later, Christina ushered him in with a smile and they cheered as he crossed the threshold.

"You nailed it," Christina said with genuine warmth, something Thalia had never heard her direct at Blake.

The showrunner raised his shoulders, as if it weren't a big deal. "It was the right call having me do it," he conceded. "Good idea."

"Well, this is touching," Ava cut in drily, "but we still have work to do. This was only step one."

"Right," Christina responded. "Are you going to call Daniela now?"

Ava nodded, grabbing the business card from the desk and inhaling. "All right," she said. "Let's see if she bites." She dialed the chief's cell phone number, then put the call on speaker.

"*Hola*?" a melodious voice answered the call. Thalia glanced quickly at Blake, whose tightlipped expression confirmed he recognized the sound.

"Chief Martinez? It's Ava Taylor-Washington from CBC."

"Ava, so good to hear from you," Daniela replied, her tone buttery. "Is everything alright?"

"Yes, yes," Ava responded. "I'm sorry for calling so late. I've been on calls all evening with the executives from the network, and they really want to ensure that this gets closed out quickly and thoroughly. How is everything going with charging Maria?"

Thalia sensed the briefest hesitation on the line, as if the chief were debating how much information to share with Ava. From what Christina had told her, the two women's interactions had been fraught with tension, which made sense now that they knew Daniela was responsible for Andrew's murder. She'd clearly been trying to mislead the investigation all along.

Daniela responded, "It's fine, very good. The video footage was very helpful, thank you. She's being interrogated as we speak."

Thalia shuddered, imagining the discomfort or even pain Maria might be subjected to as she was being held by Daniela's cronies in the police force.

"Good, I'm glad to hear that." Ava nodded encouragingly, though the chief couldn't see her. "So, Christina just remembered seeing Maria doing something a bit suspicious at her employee locker a couple days before Andrew's death. Did your officers search her locker?"

"Oh," Daniela responded eagerly. "That is very useful information. No, no we haven't conducted a search yet, but I'm sure we can get permission from the resort manager within a few hours."

Thalia could practically hear the cogs turning in the cartel boss's brain, devising a plan to put the final nail in Maria's coffin.

"I will be there tomorrow morning," Daniela confirmed.

"That's wonderful." Ava's smooth voice remained even, despite the excitement dancing in her eyes and the smirk playing at the corners of her lips. "My CEO and board president will be so relieved to have the charges formalized and to put this whole nightmare to bed. Thank you *so much*, Chief Martinez." Her tone oozed with flattery.

"The pleasure is all mine," Daniela replied with equal sweetness. The artificial tone made Thalia's stomach churn as she realized this woman had probably taken some twisted pleasure in murdering Andrew.

Once the call had disconnected, Ava let out a whoop. "We got her!"

"Well played," Christina gushed, gazing at Ava with admiration. "You were *perfect*." She held up her hand to her mouth in a chef's kiss gesture.

Thalia hid a smile at Christina's fangirling, but had to admit Ava was pretty legit. When she started at GlobeAction, she'd felt the same awe at Veronica's experience and connections in climate activism. As Thalia thought about these similarities, she wondered if she and Christina would have been friends if they'd met in different circumstances, meeting up for happy hours to praise their mentors and bitch about other coworkers.

Who knows, Thalia thought to herself, *maybe we still will be friends once this is all over.*

"Thalia?" Christina's insistent voice startled her. Heat rose to her cheeks, as if the producer had been able to read her thoughts.

"Umm, yeah, what's up?" she responded, brushing a stray curl from her face.

"I just wanted to make sure you're all set for tomorrow. Feeling good?"

Thalia thought for a moment, her stomach knotting in anticipation of their plan, everything that could go wrong, and how incredible it would feel if it all went right. "Yes, I think so." She paused, a sudden wave of longing washing over her. "Actually, could I talk to my sister? I think it would really help get me in the right headspace." She yearned to hear Sasha's voice, her heart aching to connect with her best friend. She knew that despite everything going on, Sasha's love would ground her.

Christina glanced at Ava, deferring to her judgment. Without hesitation, the executive nodded. "Of course. We'll get an iPad for you. I hope you understand why we can't give you access to your phone." Her face clouded with a serious expression. "We absolutely cannot let the network get a whiff of our plans. They will shut this whole thing down. One accusation of CBC meddling in the investigation could cause a shitstorm of political drama. So, don't give her any details about Daniela or the plan, please."

Thalia nodded, feeling something in her chest loosen knowing she'd be speaking with Sasha momentarily. "I get it. Thank you. It means a lot."

Ava bobbed her head in acknowledgment. "Alright. Christina, I'll let you take Thalia to make her phone call. See you all tomorrow morning."

Thalia glanced at the bedside clock, startled to see that it was almost eleven here, so one a.m. in New York. Her call would wake Sasha up, but she knew her sister wouldn't mind.

As the group filed out of Ava's hotel room, the weight of tomorrow's mission weighing on their shoulders, Christina jerked her head, indicating Thalia should follow her to the spa, where the confessionals and iPads were set up. The pair walked in silence down the path, the anxiety about tomorrow weighing on them.

When they reached the spa, Christina held open the door and grabbed one of the tablets from the cabinet, punching in a code only a few producers had access to. She scrolled down the screen until 'Thalia – Sasha' appeared in the contact list, then handed the tablet over to the contestant.

"Let's make it quick, yeah? We have a big day tomorrow, and you need your beauty sleep." Christina smiled ruefully. "Well, maybe you don't, but I do."

Thalia laughed. "I'll be quick."

As the high-pitched ringing began, Christina plopped down on a comfortable chair in the waiting area of the spa, pointing to the closest treatment room. Thalia flashed a grateful smile at Christina, her heart swelling in appreciation of the trust the producer had placed in her.

On the sixth ring, Thalia began to worry that maybe Sasha wouldn't wake up after all, but then relief washed over her as her sister's dimly lit face appeared on the screen, her usually energetic voice entangled in a blanket of grogginess.

"Hello?" she muttered.

"Sash. It's me."

A light snapped on, flooding her sister's smooth skin, her hair concealed under her favorite lime green silk bonnet. "Thalia? Oh, my God! What's going on there? How are you doing?"

Thalia's throat constricted with emotion over her sister's love and concern, the tightness stopping everything that happened from spilling out.

Swallowing the tension, she said carefully, "I can't tell you a lot. But I can tell you that Andrew's death was not an accident. Or a suicide." She paused, waiting for her sister's sleepy brain to process what she was saying.

Sasha's eyes widened, the whites gleaming in the dim lighting of her bedroom, and her lips popped into a perfect *o*. "You mean he was like… murdered?"

Hearing that word on Sasha's lips took Thalia's breath away. She closed her eyes for a moment, then responded, "Yes. And we think we know who did it."

"Y'all found the guy who did it? Did you report him to the Mexican police?"

If not for the gravity of the situation, Thalia might have found some humor in how far off track both of these questions were. "It's a little complicated. But a few of the producers looped me in on a plan to catch the killer. And I—"

"Oh no, girl," Sasha interjected. "Why do you need to get involved in this mess? This happened under CBC's watch. Let them clean up their own shit."

"It's not that easy," Thalia said. "The police have the wrong person in custody, and she's the sweetest woman. And I know that's the last thing Andrew would want. I have to do this—for him."

Sasha gazed at her through the screen, her expression strained. "I get it," she replied softly. "You know I'll support you no matter what, right?"

"I know," Thalia said, trying to summon the courage for what she really wanted to ask Sasha.

Immediately sensing her trepidation, her sister asked, "What's up?"

"The producer told me that being involved in this might piss off the CBC execs. They might edit me to be a villain, which would risk me getting support for the bill. But I told her that I wanted to do it anyway. Do you think…" she paused, hardly able to choke out the question. "Do you think," she started again, her gaze fixed on Sasha, "Mom and Dad would be disappointed in me? That I chose Andrew over the bill?"

"Thalia." Sasha's voice ached with compassion. "This whole thing about needing to pass the legislation…you put that on yourself. Mom and Dad wouldn't need you to accomplish this monumental task for them to be proud of you. All they ever wanted was for you to be happy, and to find someone who loves you as much as they loved each other, and as much as they loved us. Even if they weren't always the best at showing it," she admitted with a sad smile.

Tears streamed down Thalia's face as she realized her little sister was right. She gathered up the last five years of pain and let the first layer of it melt away as she let out a giant exhale.

"Thank you, Sasha. I didn't know how much I needed to hear that."

"Damn, I wish I could give you a big hug right now!" Sasha exclaimed, wiping her own eyes. "You got this, Thals. Just be careful, okay? I love you too much to let some Mexican serial killer get you."

"I will," Thalia promised in return. "I'll come home to you very soon."

Chapter 31: Christina - Now

All night, Christina tossed and turned, her sleep punctuated with dreams that floated between being stranded at sea, alone on a yacht, and a recurring image of Daniela's beautiful face mocking her, a silver gun gripped in her long, slender hand. When her alarm went off at 6:30 a.m., the anxiety transferred from her dreams to a growing pit in her stomach.

She threw off the fine white sheets and jumped out of bed, her nerves too high for her usual habit of snoozing. Immediately she checked her laptop, which she had left open streaming the view from the camera in the restaurant. Her shoulders relaxed when she saw the kitchen door still open, the shiny lockers still clearly visible. They knew the maintenance guy didn't start until nine, but had worried some other staff member might manage to fix the door before his arrival. Luckily, Blake's handiwork had survived the night. Now they only needed it to last for another hour or two, until Daniela arrived.

As Christina brushed her teeth, she spotted the Korean skin care product from her mother sitting on the countertop, and an intense wave of emotion washed over her. For the first time she could remember in a long while, she ached for her mother's embrace, to feel her fingers calmly stroke her hair.

From the moment she'd met Andrew on casting day, she'd been obsessed with the idea of revenge, thinking that somehow if she made her rapist suffer, she would finally move forward in a way that she hadn't been able to for the last five years, despite the endless group therapy sessions. But reflecting on Thalia's revelation about Andrew's frat brothers, she realized that chasing revenge was not going to magically make things better. She needed to open up to the people who cared about her, and let them love and support her in the way she desperately needed—starting with her parents.

Impulsively, she grabbed her phone and texted her mom, *I miss you guys. Let's have dinner when I get back to LA.* She watched the screen for a moment, then felt a pang of disappointment when there was no immediate response.

Brushing away her feelings, she stared at her reflection and tried to pump herself up for today. "You are strong," she said to herself out loud. "You are strong," she repeated, letting the affirmation take hold as she had practiced so many times in group therapy.

A few minutes later, she was dressed in her most comfortable black outfit and favorite worn flip-flops, pulling her hair up as she walked out of the hotel room. The morning was overcast, and a mist had rolled in from the water overnight, leaving a damp chill in the air. Across the horizon, dark clouds loomed, threatening to close in.

When she reached the restaurant shortly before their agreed meeting time of 7:15, she found Ava seated at a table near the entrance. In her crisp white pantsuit, serenely sipping a large mug of coffee and responding to emails on her computer, Ava was the epitome of grace under pressure.

"Hi," Christina called out, her voice wracked with nerves. Her eyes flitted from Ava to camera twelve, which was subtly positioned behind a large hanging basket of bougainvillea in one corner of the restaurant. Its vivid pink flowers spilled down toward the ground and obscured the tiny blinking red light above it.

Ava glanced up at her, smiling as she closed the laptop. "Hello, there," she replied. "You ready?"

"As ready as I can be," Christina confirmed, wanting to put on a brave face, despite her roiling insides. Just looking at the pile of scrambled egg whites sprawled on Ava's bright turquoise plate was enough to make her stomach lurch.

"Well, have a seat," Ava said, pointing to the wicker chair across the table from her, "and let's get you some coffee." Lifting the ceramic carafe in the center of the table, she flipped over a mug and filled it to the brim.

Christina clung to it, letting the rich aroma and heat of the mug calm her nerves.

The pair sat in silence for a few minutes until the young waiter, Juan, emerged, looking bleary eyed after working late then opening early. He mumbled his way through taking Christina's order, but looked embarrassed when the sounds of Osito singing in the kitchen flitted through the open door.

"I sorry, door is broken," he said haltingly, having stepped outside the realm of his English vocabulary, which basically consisted of the Paraiso Maya menu. "Your friend last night he come, he," the waiter glanced around searching for the word, then settled on miming taking a shot. "I sorry, I try again to fix the door, okay?"

"No!" Christina said, and heard Ava's voice proclaim the syllable in unison with her. Juan looked between them, startled by their adamant response.

Ava recovered first, her voice calm and authoritative. "What we mean is, you have enough on your plate today, especially with Maria being gone. Don't worry about the door."

"Okay. Thank you, miss," Juan said, then headed back through the open door to put in Christina's breakfast order.

Once he was gone, Ava lowered her voice and launched into reviewing the plan one more time with Christina. Thalia would arrive down for breakfast soon and pretend to be writing in her journal, so that she could act as an extra pair of eyes. When Daniela arrived around eight, they would greet her and then leave the restaurant, letting the chief believe she had free rein to plant the evidence. Blake and Sol would be watching the security camera from the spa, which was the closest building to the restaurant, and in case of any issues, Sol would come down and cause a distraction, since they didn't want to let Daniela see Blake and realize he'd put two and two together. Once they had the clear footage of the cartel leader planting the evidence, they would immediately send it to CBC's legal team and ask them to liaise with the Mexican federal police—the Policia Ministerial Federal, or PMF. The important thing was to keep their cool and not let Daniela know they were on to her, otherwise she might disappear before the federal officers could arrest her.

Christina nodded along, forcing herself to eat some of her breakfast burrito when Juan brought it out. She managed a few bites, and deserted the rest on her plate.

"Anything else we need to remember?" Ava asked in conclusion.

Christina shook her head absently, then forced a tight smile. "All good." Glancing at her phone, she saw it was 7:45. Thalia should be arriving shortly.

As Christina took another long swig of coffee, she saw her approaching, emerging from the fog that had rolled in even more heavily over the last hour, enshrouding the entire resort. Thalia's curls bounced as she moved toward them, her wide-legged pants, crop top, and oversized cream knit sweater giving her an air of casual elegance that masked the gravity of the day. Last night they'd discussed keeping up their usual appearance of separation between cast and crew, so Christina gave her a brief wave before turning back to Ava.

Thalia sat a few tables away from them, positioning herself with a partial view into the kitchen, and spreading her journal in front of her. A few minutes later, Juan appeared with a steaming carafe of coffee for her, and she bowed her head over the notebook, pretending to be in deep concentration.

Putting on a perfect display of nonchalance, Ava shared industry news that had come out overnight and reminded Christina to submit the invoice for the offsite date they'd held at a zip-lining center before Andrew's death. Christina tried to focus on the forced conversation, but couldn't help checking her phone as the minutes crept by: 7:49. 7:52. 7:53. 7:56.

Just when she couldn't bear the suspense any longer, a figure approached them from the direction of the front desk. Christina recognized Daniela's tall, lean frame, clad in fitted black pants and a tan trench coat thrown over a draped black silk blouse. She carried a large bolt-cutter, its sharp jaws menacing, ready to break open Maria's locker. A black leather messenger bag with the Oaxaca Police emblem emblazoned across it was slung on her shoulder. Christina's heart leapt as she realized the bag likely contained the drugs she intended to plant as evidence against the waitress.

"Good morning," Daniela said with a wave, reaching for Ava's hand as the executive stood to greet her.

Christina stared at Daniela's beautiful features, amazed at how well they had hidden her true nature for so long. It must have taken years to build her empire.

"Good morning, Chief Martinez," Ava replied. "Thank you so much for coming."

"I'm happy to be of service," Daniela replied, her tone brighter than usual. "We all want to ensure that the person who did this pays for it."

"That's exactly right," Ava said, and if she felt even a fraction of the rage that flushed in Christina's belly, her voice didn't betray it.

"Now, I'll have to ask that you give me some space to work," Daniela continued, pointing toward the kitchen.

"Yes, of course," Ava said with a nod. "Christina and I actually have to go join a board meeting virtually. The president and CEO want an update, and I'm sure they will be thrilled to hear you're back today searching for more evidence."

"Perfect," Daniela replied, her eyes lighting up. "I'll keep you informed."

"Thank you," Ava said. "We'll see you soon." With that, she and Christina turned and headed up the hill to join Blake and Sol in the spa, where they would watch the events unfold via the camera feeds. Christina could practically feel the excitement radiating in the air.

Once they were safely out of earshot, she said quietly, "Do you think it'll work?"

Ava's face grew somber. "We've done all we can. Now we have to watch and see."

Chapter 32: Thalia - Now

As she watched Christina and Ava disappear in her peripheral vision, Thalia remained seated at the table, her head bowed over her journal. She glanced up as Daniela passed on her way into the kitchen, giving a slight wave of feigned disinterest before retraining her eyes on the pages before her.

Daniela moved through the open doorway. Given the angle of her table, and the way the chief was positioned in front of the locker, Thalia couldn't really see what was happening, but she didn't dare adjust her chair and draw attention to herself. Her frustration rose, and she said a silent prayer that the camera, which was mounted high on the wall, would be able to capture a better viewpoint.

In a flurry of movement, Thalia saw Daniela shrug her shoulder, letting the messenger bag slide down onto the floor before she bent to unzip it. Next, she saw a glint of metal under the fluorescent lights, and a sharp snap cracked through the quiet, indicating the lock had been cut.

This is it, Thalia thought to herself, the pen sliding in her grip as her palms began to sweat in anticipation.

Suddenly, cheerful whistling burst through the still morning air. Both Thalia and Daniela spun around, spotting the maintenance man approaching the restaurant. Thalia's heart leapt in her throat. He wasn't scheduled to start work until nine a.m., and he often showed up late, according to Christina. She'd previously had to stalk him one morning to fix the refrigerator at the pool bar after a night of complaints from the cast about drinking lukewarm beers.

Of course, he would choose today to show up early. Thalia tried to maintain an uninterested expression while her inner voice screamed in frustration.

Juan scuttled out of the kitchen, momentarily breaking Daniela's concentration as he greeted the maintenance worker in rapid Spanish, gesturing toward the broken door and mimicking Blake's false drunken stumble from the prior evening. The handyman turned to the chief, his hands clasped in apology as Thalia heard him say something about *rápido*. Annoyance flashed in Daniela's hazel eyes, but she hid it behind a professional smile and nodded agreeably. She walked over to the closest table and sat down, ready to wait until the maintenance man had finished repairing the door before completing her "search" of the locker.

As Thalia's phone was still being held by production, she had no means of communicating this derailment to the team, and had to pray they were watching the cameras and could read the body language to figure out what was happening. She continued pretending to write in her journal, sneaking a glance upwards as often as she dared to see the chief still seated at the table, and the handyman working away at the door, pulling various tools and parts from a rusted red tool kit. The minutes seemed to stretch on for hours, and still none of her co-conspirators had appeared to help salvage their plan. Thalia frantically searched her brain for anything she could do.

Suddenly, a high-pitched creak interrupted her thoughts. Looking up, her heart dropped. The door swung merrily on its hinges before coming to a rest, fully closed.

"*Todo está bien,*" the maintenance man called out to Daniela, as he began packing up his tool kit.

"*Muchas gracias,*" the chief replied, a satisfied smile creeping onto her face. As the maintenance worker straightened and walked away, she strode back toward the kitchen and disappeared through the door, its metal mass wavering until it closed, blocking the view of anything going on inside. Their plan was officially ruined.

Before she could pause to think, or motion to the camera, or do anything else, Thalia found herself on her feet, moving toward the kitchen. As if watching from outside of her body, she saw her long fingers and their soft pink polish pressed against the shiny metal of the kitchen door. When she swung it open, Daniela looked up in shock, startled by her sudden arrival.

Taking in the scene, she knew Ava and the team had been right all along: Daniela could not resist the opportunity to pin Andrew's death on Maria. The leather bag sat open on the floor, and Daniela held a plastic bag in her white latex gloved hand. Her arm was reaching over the threshold of the waitress's open locker. When she saw Thalia, she withdrew it, placing the item back into the messenger bag.

"I know what you're doing," Thalia heard herself say, as if from a distance. "And I know what you've done."

A flash of uncertainty crossed Daniela's face, before her lovely features twisted cruelly, a wild animal cornered and ready to defend itself by any means necessary.

"You know nothing," she sniped at Thalia. "Now, please step aside and let the professionals handle this investigation." She pushed past her and out the door before Thalia could react.

Rushing out after Daniela, Thalia's heart beat wildly, realizing she had confronted a dangerous criminal without any kind of plan, driven solely by her rage on Andrew's behalf. Now she watched helplessly as the chief walked calmly back toward the storage unit, whether to retrieve her illicit goods now that the jig was up, or to take the back route out to the resort reception area where she had likely parked, Thalia wasn't sure. She only knew that with each step Daniela took, her chances to avenge Andrew grew more and more faint, like the chief's figure disappearing into the fog.

Just as desolation began to set in, she heard a *click clack click clack* on the stone path behind her, and turned to see Christina running down the path at full speed. Daniela must have heard it too, because she stopped next to the door of the storage unit and turned to face them, sneering.

"Stop," Christina huffed as she reached Thalia's side. Christina grasped her hand, and a wave of calm washed over Thalia, feeling her reassuring grip. "Daniela, it's too late. CBC has already told the PFM everything," she said. "The Mexican federal agents are on their way here right now."

Thalia was impressed by Christina's ability to pull off the bluff without a trace of betrayal in her voice.

A deep-throated chuckle escaped from Daniela's full lips, her long hair whipping in the strengthening wind as her head tilted back. "You may be a good TV producer, Christina, but you're not a good liar. The PFM has been trying to bring down my cartel for years. If you'd given them so much as a hint of how to do so, they would already be here with a full sting operation, ready to strike. Not letting some useless American girls try to confront the most powerful cartel boss in the country."

Though in her grip Thalia could feel Christina's pulse racing as quickly as her own, the producer didn't hesitate before she retorted, "You may be a powerful cartel boss, Daniela, but you're not a very smart one." The detective's eyes narrowed in annoyance at Christina's mimicry. "We now have proof. And when we tell the PMF that you murdered someone in cold blood on the set of one of the biggest American TV networks, there will be hell to pay."

"Proof?" Daniela laughed dismissively. "What proof? You have nothing."

"I saw you with my own eyes," Thalia said. Emboldened by Christina's bravery, she added fiercely, "And I will gladly testify to that."

Daniela's gaze hardened into stone, and when she spoke again her voice was tight with anger, containing the quiet, coiled intensity of a viper poised to strike. "As you told me yourself during your interview, Thalia, this is the only spot in the whole resort without any cameras. So, I can take care of this *proof*, right here, right now, and no one will ever know."

Thalia gasped, realizing she was right. Before she could even blink, Daniela had slipped her gun from her holster to her hand, its barrel pointed directly at Thalia. Her heart stopped, and along with it, seemingly everything around her. Daniela's eyes were locked on hers. The officer's lips continued moving, probably instructing Thalia to do something, but her brain refused to process the sound, and a dull throbbing filled her ears instead, as if she were swimming underwater.

Suddenly something pulled the cartel leader's gaze away from her, and it was as if the break in eye contact allowed Thalia to resurface.

As the sound came rushing back to her ears, Blake's voice rang out, "I wouldn't do that if I were you, Daniela. Or should I call you Rosa?"

Thalia turned to see him standing up from where he'd hidden behind the thick bushes lining the path to the restaurant. In his hand he held up a phone, pointing it at the chief.

"Blake." Daniela smiled smugly. "So nice to see you again. Not sure I'll be taking input from someone who allows himself to be drugged and seduced, but thanks for your opinion." She pointed to the phone in his hand. "Give me that."

Blake shook his head, and before he could even speak, Daniela closed the distance between Thalia and herself. The chief's slender arm was shockingly strong as she grabbed Thalia's shoulder and roughly spun her to face the producers. As Daniela's forearm encircled her throat, Thalia felt the shock of cold metal against her temple. She tried to take a deep breath, but the air entered her body in small fits, struggling against the constriction of Daniela's grip. Looking up, she met Christina's wide, fearful eyes.

The cartel leader spoke again, her voice searing like acid in Thalia's ear. "I said, Give. Me. The. Phone."

"Whoah, whoah," Blake cut in nervously. "Fine, you can have the phone."

Through the tiny black dots swimming in her vision, Thalia saw the showrunner approaching Daniela and extending the phone forward, while he raised his other hand next to his head, as if to indicate he wasn't going to try any tricks. Christina glanced anxiously between Thalia and Blake and the phone as he drew closer.

Suddenly Thalia realized she couldn't let Blake hand over the video—that was the only hard evidence they had. She wasn't going to let Daniela get away with Andrew's murder. She would make her pay, no matter the cost.

"No," Thalia croaked, arms swinging wildly as she tried to stop Blake. "Don't give," she gasped, her eyes pleading, "it to her."

"Trust me," Blake murmured, his blue eyes locked intently on Thalia's as he inched closer to her and Daniela.

As soon as he was within arm's length, the chief snatched the phone away, at the same time releasing her hold on Thalia and shoving her back toward the producers. Spinning to face Daniela, Thalia caught a familiar glimpse of gold flowers on the phone case. She felt a jolt of recognition, then confusion.

That was *her* phone. Why had Blake given it to Daniela?

"There," Blake said with relief. "Now you have the phone." He paused, a little twitch at the corner of his lips hinting at what he would say next. "Of course, it's not going to help you much to destroy that phone."

"And why not?" Daniela demanded, swinging the barrel of her gun toward him.

"Because I was live-streaming that whole thing on Thalia's Instagram. Where—thanks to Reality Pete getting an 'anonymous' tip that Thalia is heartbroken over the fishy circumstances of her boyfriend's death—she now has over a hundred and ten thousand followers. Or at least, that was the count when I last checked this morning. I'm sure it's much more now that this crazy, dirty-cop-cartel-boss video is probably going viral," he said with a wicked grin.

Thalia's jaw dropped. *Over one hundred thousand followers? And they are all watching this unfold in real time?* She wondered for a fleeting moment if Sasha was watching and freaking out.

Focusing back on Daniela, Thalia saw a flash of fear cross the woman's face for the first time since she'd met her. The chief looked down at the screen, cursing wildly in Spanish when she realized they were in fact being live-streamed. As if it were a venomous spider, she dropped the phone to the ground and mashed her boot into it, violently cracking the device.

Daniela spun on her heel and strode toward the front gate, without so much as another glance at the *Love's a Beach* team, as if unable to face them after they'd defeated her.

"We can't let her get away!" Thalia cried, starting after the chief.

"No," Christina said, grabbing Thalia's arm before she could follow. "Ava really did call the Mexican federal agents, as soon as the maintenance guy showed up to fix the kitchen door. Well, actually she called her best friend who is a senator, and told her to get the FBI on the phone so they could call the PFM. They should be here any minute."

Thalia's knees gave out beneath her, and she sagged against Christina's small frame. "So, it's really over? We did it?"

"Yes," Christina whispered, pulling Thalia into a tight embrace, "we did it."

Chapter 33: Blake - Now

The next day, Blake sat at a table in the resort restaurant, enjoying his breakfast tamales. Osito had insisted that breakfast tamales were not a real thing when Blake tried to order them, but he loved the chef's tamales so much he insisted Osito throw some scrambled eggs on the plate and *voila*, breakfast tamales. How hard was that? Blake wished he'd figured this out before their last day at the resort.

It was a stunningly beautiful morning, the sun banishing the fog that had enveloped the grounds yesterday. Within fifteen minutes after Daniela had stormed away, Ava had come down to the restaurant where Blake, Christina, and Thalia sat recovering from the confrontation, her arms waving triumphantly as she shouted over the approaching police sirens. "They got her! Daniela has been arrested!" The PFM had found the chief trying to flee on the highway, and after a high-speed chase had finally surrounded her and taken her in.

Now, Blake sat enjoying his tamales and listening to the subdued chatter of the full cast, minus Thalia, at the next table over. He'd awoken this morning with the tension of the last few days gone from his shoulders. While some niggling guilt over Andrew's death remained, Blake was ready to forget this all happened.

He looked up the hill and saw Ava and Christina walking close together in deep conversation. As they approached his table, they wrapped up their discussion, and he saw a wide smile spread across the younger woman's face.

"Morning, Blake," Ava said, taking a seat across from him, while Christina sat herself next to the executive. "Have you recovered?"

"I think so. Still trying to process the news about Alejandro, though…"

The security guard had called Blake yesterday evening with a confession: he had been helping the cartel all summer. "I'm sorry," he said, his voice cracking with guilt. "Manuel come and offer me a lot of money to let him bring some things into the resort. I not ask him any questions, because my family need the money. He give me more every time he come. I cannot say no."

He also admitted that Daniela had bribed him to edit and loop the security footage when she left the resort the night of Andrew's murder. At the time, Alejandro hadn't known what she'd done, so it didn't seem like a big deal. Only later did he learn what had happened, and realize his part in covering it up. "I feel so bad, Señor Blake. I cannot tell you what happened or the cartel hurt me. But after they arrest Maria, I cannot keep quiet. I try to give you a hint. That's why I tell you about the woman you bring back that night."

Christina sighed heavily, setting down her coffee mug. "I know. I was shocked when you told us, too. But I can imagine the Rodriguez cartel was not easy for people around here to say no to. And the police said since Alejandro's confession will be such critical evidence for Daniela's trial, they were willing to offer him immunity."

"That's a relief," Blake said, his jaw relaxing a bit. "I think he's a good man. He didn't mean for anyone to get hurt."

He glanced at his watch. "Now, I just need to prepare for the McKennas to arrive." He grimaced, not looking forward to speaking with the grief-stricken family. He hoped they would understand the impossible situation the cartel had put him in.

After Daniela's arrest yesterday, the PFM officers had told them they would expedite some additional tests on Andrew's body overnight so he could be repatriated to the United States today. When Blake had called to inform Andrew's parents that the killer had been arrested and that his body was coming home, Mrs. McKenna had broken down into sobs.

His voice strained, Mr. McKenna had asked, "Can we come down there and get him? I want to bring my boy home."

The PFM liaison had advised against it, stating that because Daniela had been arrested, the Rodriguez cartel would likely experience a chaotic power vacuum, and the violence may escalate in the region before it got any better. But Blake had insisted on the family's behalf, and the liaison ultimately gave in. CBC had arranged a charter flight for Andrew's parents and their other son, Michael, and they would be arriving any minute to the resort, with a full police escort from the PFM.

"Blake, these people raised a wonderful young man. I'm sure they will find the strength to get through this," Ava said resolutely.

"Thank you," he replied, not convinced it was true, but still grateful for her efforts to console him.

"It's going to be tough for us to see Andrew's family, but what about for Thalia?" Christina said. "That's got to be even harder."

Ava nodded sadly. "But she's pretty strong, herself."

"Hey, speak of the devil!" Christina exclaimed, spotting Thalia coming toward them.

The cast member paused at their table, then held up her finger indicating for them to give her a minute. As she walked to the table where the rest of the cast was eating breakfast, Nick and Ashley rose from the bench where they'd been cozied up next to each other, and embraced her in a group hug.

"How're you doing, sweet pea?" Ashley twanged, her eyes full of concern.

"Better," Thalia replied with a muted smile.

"Good," her roommate said, then cleared her throat. "There are a few cast members who wanted to say something to you." Blake watched curiously as she tossed a pointed glance around the table.

"I'll start," Raina said, tossing her dark hair over her shoulder. "I'm sorry if I haven't been nice to you, or to Andrew. I was bummed he wasn't interested in me. I'm not used to that, you know?"

Blake saw Thalia and Ashley exchange a secretive glance of humor, before Thalia nodded her acknowledgement.

Rachel spoke second, her voice meek. "I wanted to say I'm sorry for calling Andrew a murderer during our political…discussion."

Blake raised an eyebrow. *That's one word for it.*

"I've prayed a lot about it and I'm truly sorry for my unkind words," Rachel finished, and Thalia nodded in wordless thanks.

"I'll go next," Marcus piped up. "I admit I was talking shit about Andrew at first, too. I mean, he was kind of a finance bro, and his private equity fund messed up my job. But honestly, after getting to know him, I realized he was a pretty good guy."

"He was," Thalia agreed, her voice wistful as she turned her attention to Karina, who sat stoically, her back a ram rod as she fixed her gaze in the distance.

No way this ice queen is going to apologize, Blake thought to himself.

"Karina?" Ashley prompted with a heated glare.

Her chin lifted proudly, the Venezuelan cast member pursed her lips before finally speaking. "Okay, I also did not say nice things about Andrew. If you're going to make me admit it…fine, I was jealous he landed the private equity deal for his firm, instead of me." Blake's eyes widened in surprise.

Last to speak was Jake. "I was jealous too," he admitted quietly. "Of Raina's interest in him, of Blake's attention on him, everything. But he was a good dude."

Blake watched as Thalia's eyes glistened. She said softly, "Thank you all for this. It means so much to hear you recognize how wonderful Andrew was. And thank you, Ashley, Nick, and Tae-Hyun for being by his side all along. And mine," she added.

Seeing this impromptu memorial, Blake felt the guilt tugging at his heart again, but shoved it away. *I didn't have a choice,* he repeated to himself.

Across the table from Blake, Christina glanced at her watch, then jumped at the time. "Hey, gang," she called out to the cast members' table. "I need you all to get packing. Van to the airport leaves at five p.m." The contestants got to their feet, each giving Thalia a hug or pat on the back in turn as they filed out of the restaurant and toward their villas.

Turning her attention to the producers' table, Thalia greeted them as she sat down. "Hey team, what's up?"

"Not much, just waiting for the McKennas," Christina replied. "Are you ready for it?"

Blake looked at Thalia, unsure how she would react.

Thalia cocked her head, pondering the question. "You know? I am. Obviously I wish the circumstances of meeting Andrew's family were very different. I wish he were here, introducing us, maybe at a nice cookout, or gathering at Thanksgiving this year." She paused, longing clouding her face before she rearranged her features into the brave front Blake had gotten used to seeing over the last few days. "But no matter what, it will be a blessing to meet the people who raised someone as incredible as Andrew."

A lump raised in Blake's throat, and was saved from responding by a joyful voice calling out, "*Hola*! Señorita Christina! Señorita Thalia!" He turned to see Maria bounding toward them. As she approached their table, Christina and Thalia rose to meet her.

"Maria, you're free!" Christina exclaimed.

"*Sí*, they let me go last night!" the server replied with a relieved smile. "I go home to my family. They so happy to see me! Then Osito call me, he say you leaving today. So, I have to come and say thank you and goodbye!"

"Maria, you don't need to thank us." Thalia shook her head. "We couldn't have let you stay in jail for something you didn't do. And I'm so glad the PFM caught Daniela."

"Me too. The local police, they all liars!" Maria said, her eyes fiery.

Christina looked startled at her outburst, then a dawn of recognition crossed her face. "Maria," she asked tepidly, "did you post on Twitter about the murder?"

The waitress's cheeks flushed in embarrassment. "Yes," she admitted, her gaze cast down. "I too scared to tell you anything. But I really want them to know who did it. Because Señor Andrew really nice man." Maria looked up at them, her large brown eyes glistening with emotion. "I think he told you about my brother, Antonio?"

Thalia and Christina nodded.

"Andrew was going to give a lot of money to help my family. And I never even ask him. Now my brother okay, because the bad woman is gone. She is the one who said he must pay the money. But I never forget how kind Andrew is to me."

"He certainly was kind," Thalia agreed, the same small, aching smile forming on her lips once more. "I loved him very much."

The waitress extended her arms, embracing the cast member. "He love you too. He tell me he want to marry you. He say, 'Maria, maybe we have our wedding at Paraiso Maya, you come as guest, not waitress. As guest.' "

"Thank you," Thalia whispered, dabbing a tear from her long lashes and composing herself. "Now, Osito and the rest of the staff are probably so excited to see you, I'll let you go say hi to them!"

"Okay, bye!" Maria pulled them each into a quick hug before bouncing away to the kitchen.

Blake heard a crackle from the radio in his pocket, then Sol's voice announced that the McKennas' car was almost here.

"Shall we go up and meet them?" he asked the group.

"Christina and Thalia, you go ahead. Blake, before you and I go, there's something we need to discuss," Ava said. The two younger women exchanged glances, then nodded and said they'd see them in the lobby.

Blake watched in confusion as they walked away, unsure why Ava would need to speak to him in private. "What did you want to talk about?" he asked, his voice hesitant.

The executive removed the linen napkin from her lap, smoothing it on the table and studying him intensely for a few moments before she began speaking. "Blake, I appreciate your help catching Daniela yesterday. Your backup plan with the live-streaming saved our skins, and leaking Thalia's info to Reality Pete in advance was, I'll admit, a stroke of genius."

Blake grinned, hardly able to believe what he was hearing. After almost a year of her dismissing him and nearly every idea he had, he had finally won over Ava. He wondered whether she was going to offer him a bonus, or perhaps even a job as showrunner for a bigger show. There was talk of a celebrity dating show being produced at CBC—could that be it?

"But," Ava continued, and as quickly as his hopes had elevated, they sunk back down into a pit in his stomach, and he knew that whatever she was about to say next was not good. "Your actions leading up to yesterday, and your role in this tragedy, are simply unacceptable. I wanted you gone after your arrest this spring, and Robert insisted we give you a second chance—"

"Wait, you knew about my DUI?" Blake asked, dumbfounded.

Looking at him as if explaining something to a small child, Ava said, "Of course. It's my job to know what my people are up to, on and off set."

Blake let this revelation sink in, realizing that if he'd simply been upfront about his mistake and not gone to such incredible lengths to hide it, perhaps this all could have been avoided—getting involved with the cartel, Andrew seeing something he shouldn't have, and the young man paying the ultimate price for Blake's stupidity.

As he tried to process this, Ava said, "I told Robert I would be down here myself to monitor you and the show, so I came down when filming started, and had been staying at a nearby hotel."

Blake looked at her in shock, suddenly understanding how she'd managed to arrive here so quickly after Andrew's death, and why she'd had so many suitcases in her room.

Ava continued, "Though I have to say, despite knowing you had made a mistake with the DUI, I couldn't have imagined the complete and utter stupidity of everything you've done since then. And despite my personal dislike from the moment I met your selfish, entitled ass, I couldn't have even fathomed you would turn over an innocent young man to his death at the hands of the cartel." Disgust twisted her features, unleashed after months of maintaining a professional demeanor towards Blake.

Her words felt like a slap across the face. "I'm so sorry, Ava. I fucked up, I know I did." Hanging his head, he muttered, "So, I guess this means I don't have a job at CBC anymore?"

"A job?" she said with a dismissive laugh. "Blake, you are going to be arrested. The PMF and the FBI have already agreed on an extradition process. You're lucky you'll be charged and serve time in the US, rather than rotting in a Mexican prison. The PFM will be here any minute to take you into custody and transport you back to LA."

As if on cue, two Mexican federal agents appeared striding down the hill toward the restaurant, one of them pointing in Blake's direction.

Stomach churning, bile in his throat, Blake sputtered, "Jail? But I didn't hurt Andrew! Daniela did that! And the drugs…the cartel made me do it! You have to help me, Ava," he pleaded.

"What you have done is not only wildly illegal, Blake. It's also unconscionable. So, there is no way on God's green earth that I would help you, even if I could. Fortunately for you, I hear that you have a pretty good lawyer."

"But Ava, please," he insisted. "I—"

She held a hand up to stop him. "I'm done here. I have much more important things to do—I need to go see the McKennas," she said, rising to her feet.

"Ava," he called to her, as she turned to walk away. Even knowing that he was facing criminal charges, the humiliation of losing his career and status in the production world was almost harder to swallow. "Who will you get to replace me?"

"Oh," she said, the corners of her lips curving upwards. "Don't worry, I have someone very good in mind. Goodbye, Blake."

Chapter 34: Thalia - Now

"What do you think they're talking about?" Thalia whispered to Christina as they began their ascent to the hotel lobby.

"You'll know very soon," the producer hinted with a sly smile.

When they arrived, greeted by the lush foliage decorating the sleek interior, they sat in silence on a carved stone bench and waited until Ava arrived a few minutes later, a satisfied look on her face.

Shortly after, they saw the flashing lights of the federal police cars, which flanked a black SUV that pulled up in front of them. Thalia's heart was pounding, knowing she was moments away from meeting Andrew's family.

One by one, the McKennas emerged from the car: first Mr. McKenna, whose light blue golf shirt matched his kind eyes, and quickly following him, a petite blonde woman wearing a simple black shift dress and large designer sunglasses. She grabbed her husband's outstretched hand as she climbed out of the large vehicle. From the other side of the car exited Michael, who wore his brother's same easygoing smile.

"Bill McKenna." Andrew's dad spoke first, outstretching his hand. "And this is my wife, Susan, and son, Michael." Thalia stood back from the producers, watching as he shook hands with Ava, then Christina, before his eyes finally landed on her. "And you must be Thalia."

"I am," she replied nervously. "Mr. McKenna, I—"

"Bill," he insisted, stepping forward and pulling her into a sudden, firm embrace. "It is truly an honor to meet you."

Bill McKenna, she thought to herself. Why did that name sound familiar?

Susan stepped forward to greet Thalia as well, her thin arms encircling her. "My sweet boy really cared about you," she whispered, and as she pulled away, she pushed up her sunglasses onto her head. Thalia's breath caught in her chest. Looking into Susan's piercing emerald eyes, it was as if she were looking at Andrew all over again.

"Okay, my turn," Michael said, engulfing her in a big, warm hug. "You are pretty, just like Andrew said in his letter," the brother said with a grin. "But he never replied when I asked if you have a sister!" His joke broke the tension of the moment, and Ava invited the group to head down to the pavilion, where the staff had prepared some refreshments. The plan was for them to speak privately before the McKennas headed to the medical examiner's office.

They made small talk on the walk to the pavilion, with Andrew's family commenting on the beautiful grounds, asking about the other cast members, and anything else they could speak about to delay the heavy topics ahead of them. When they reached the pavilion, the vast expanse of the turquoise sea stretched out before them. Mr. and Mrs. McKenna exchanged a look, then hugged each other tight. Thalia glanced between them, unsure of what had triggered the sudden wave of emotion.

"I'm sorry," Susan said with a sob. "Andrew loved the ocean. He took us for a seaside hike every time we came to visit him in LA. It makes me happy to know that he spent his last month seeing this marvelous view every day."

After the group got some coffee and plates of food, they settled into the soft couches. Ava began by giving the family a formal apology on behalf of CBC, for not having more thorough security, and for the poor judgment of one of their senior employees and his part in the situation. She assured them that he had since been fired and was facing criminal charges. Thalia shot a surprised look at Christina, who returned a knowing glance.

So that's what Ava needed to talk to Blake about, she realized.

Mr. McKenna expressed his gratitude to the group for finding Andrew's killer and ensuring she faced justice. Christina shared her regret at casting Andrew—without referencing why she had done so in the first place—and bringing him to where he had ultimately met his end. Mrs. McKenna insisted that Andrew had viewed this as another grand adventure, and she could tell from his letters how happy he had been, how in love. Only Michael said nothing.

Thalia listened in silence, absorbing the swirl of emotions around her. When she finally spoke, her voice was pensive, and she looked down at her lap, absently smoothing the pleat in her pants. "You know, I didn't come here intending to fall in love. I came here on a mission to pass a piece of environmental legislation by drumming up followers and public support for it. It was my way of honoring my parents, who passed away a few years ago. But when I met Andrew…something clicked. I tried to ignore it and stay focused on my goal, but there was this irresistible pull drawing us together. He made me feel safe, and happy, and supported. The night before he died, we told each other 'I love you,' and I meant it. I know some part of me will always love him. And I'll always be grateful to him for showing me that love is what I really want and deserve."

When she looked up, the McKennas were all crying. "I'm sorry," Thalia said quickly. "I didn't mean to—"

"No, don't be sorry," Susan insisted. "You loved our son, and that is all we could ever ask of you."

Mr. McKenna appeared deep in thought, his gaze directed out over the crashing waves. "Thalia, I don't know if Andrew ever told you what I do?"

She shook her head, confused. "Umm, he mentioned you were a corporate executive of some kind, but we didn't talk much about your job. More about your family time."

He looked over at her, and the frown lines around his eyes softened. "That sounds like my Andrew." He paused again, then continued, "I'm the CEO of Agracon."

Thalia's jaw dropped. *Of course,* she thought, her brain scrambling to catch up. *That's why I recognized his name.*

"Like…the biggest agricultural company in the country?" she confirmed. Agracon consistently appeared on GlobeAction's lists of biggest carbon emitters and polluters. Somehow, perhaps because Paraiso Maya felt like a different universe than New York, she'd never made the connection to Andrew's last name.

"Yes." Bill nodded. "I am aware that it is time for us to change the way we do business. I want to leave a better planet for my sons. Son," he corrected himself, his voice catching as he glanced lovingly at Michael, who remained silent. "I'm ashamed to say that until now, I haven't been brave enough to actually do something about it. But seeing Andrew's love for you, and the courage you showed in pursuing justice for him, I think the best way to honor his legacy would be to announce Agracon's support of this legislation, and lead the industry in making the change."

Thalia's head spun, unable to process what he was saying. She opened her mouth, then closed it again, completely at a loss.

As if he could tell that she was floundering, Bill held up his hands to indicate she could relax. "It's okay," he soothed. "We don't need to talk more about it right now. But please know that my team will be reaching out to GlobeAction to arrange a meeting."

"Mr. McKenna, I don't know what to say. Thank you," Thalia breathed. This was all she had dreamed of, coming onto the show, but at what cost? Everything felt a little bit emptier now, with the hole where Andrew's love had been gaping in her heart.

"Mom, Dad?" Michael spoke suddenly, breaking his silence. "These people are nice, but I miss Andrew. Can we go see him now?"

"Of course we can," Susan said, wrapping her arm around her son. "Let's go bring your brother home."

After some tearful goodbyes with the family, Sol came down to the pavilion to walk the McKennas back up to the hotel lobby. From there the police escort would take them to the medical examiner's office. Left alone under the bright afternoon sun, Ava, Christina, and Thalia sat for a moment without speaking, letting themselves recover from the emotional conversation.

Finally, Ava broke the silence. "Well, I need to start packing. Our charter flight leaves at seven p.m. sharp, and my wife has promised to have a giant glass of merlot waiting for me."

Christina giggled. "Somehow I don't think the plane is going to leave you behind."

"You either," Ava retorted. "Miss *showrunner*."

Thalia's heart leapt. "Oh, my God, what? Christina, is she serious?"

The new showrunner nodded happily. "Ava just told me this morning. The CEO approved me last night as Blake's successor."

"That is incredible!" Thalia said, leaning over to Christina's chair to give her a congratulatory hug. "I'm so proud of you. You deserve it, ten thousand percent."

"I couldn't agree more." Ava beamed.

"So, does this mean the board wasn't mad at us for interfering in the investigation?" Thalia asked with cautious optimism.

"When I first told the CEO, he freaked out," Ava admitted. "But once I explained the circumstances to the board, they realized that the case would never have gotten solved had we left it to the police."

"I'm relieved to hear that," Thalia replied.

"Our PR head immediately started pitching an idea for a documentary mini-series about how we tackled a cartel boss and saved an innocent woman from prison. I told her one step at a time," Ava said with a grin.

"Also," Christina added, "being showrunner means I have control over how you're edited on the show. America is going to be lapping up your environmental message by the time this season airs."

"I appreciate that so much," Thalia said sincerely.

"I had pretty good source material to work with," Christina teased.

Ava stood from the sofa. "Alright, ladies, we really should get packing."

"I'll start soon," Thalia said. "I just…need a minute alone."

"Of course." Ava's eyes softened with compassion. "We'll see you later."

As the two producers disappeared toward their rooms, Thalia walked down to the beach, making her way across the rocks to perch on a large one. She took a deep, calming breath, letting the cool air wash over her, its salty tang bringing her into herself.

It was hard to believe that in a few short hours, she'd be leaving this place, after the wildest month of her life. She'd gained and lost so much here, and her heart ached a bit to know she'd soon be away from the place where she'd met and fallen in love with Andrew. Once she set foot outside this resort, it would become another painful chapter in her life.

Reaching inside her shirt, she extracted the note Andrew had slipped to her the night he died. She had kept it safely tucked against her skin ever since. She was grateful Daniela hadn't ended up seizing it for evidence, or else she probably never would have seen it again. So far, she'd held off on reading it, not ready for the words he'd written with so much hope and love in his heart. But she knew she had to do this now, before she returned to New York, while his presence was still here with her. Slowly she unfolded it and began reading:

Dear Thalia,

I could write something cheesy about how this last month has been the happiest of my life, but I think that goes without saying. People always say that love is like a drug, but loving you has been like medicine for me. It has healed my soul and filled a part of me that I didn't even know was missing. Being apart from you for the next few months during our "break-up" is going to be so tough, but seeing your radiant smile when your bill passes will make all of the pain worth it. There are so many kinds of love in this world—romantic love like ours, friendship, and unconditional love for our families, which you know painfully well. But while we are apart, please don't forget the most important thing, which is to love yourself. You are truly the most radiant, magical woman I have ever met. Trust in yourself, knowing that I'll be next to you in spirit every step of the way.

Love always,

Andrew

Epilogue: Christina - 6 Months Later

"Hey, girl!" Christina exclaimed, storming into the Thai restaurant. "I'm sorry I'm late!"

Thalia jumped up to greet her. "No worries! It's so good to see you!"

As the women settled down at the cozy table, Christina removed her jacket. "Yes, I'm so happy work brought me to New York!"

"Work?" Thalia asked with a sly wiggle of her eyebrows. "Or was it…a certain somebody?"

"OMG, stop," Christina said, rolling her eyes. "Tae-Hyun and I are just *talking*. We're taking things slow. I finally told him all about my history, and he's been really sweet and understanding."

"That's amazing to hear," Thalia said seriously, before a mischievous smile tugged at her lips. "Sounds like Dr. Tae-Hyun is operating on your heart, huh?"

"You're the worst." Christina laughed at the corny joke despite herself, feigning swatting Thalia with the menu. "Okay, enough about my love life, how are you? How is work going? Has it been even more hectic since the bill passed?"

Her face lighting up, Thalia put her hands face down on the table, as if willing herself to remain calm. "You won't even believe this, but…I got invited to speak at the UN about climate change. The *United freaking Nations*!"

Christina gasped. "Oh. My. God. Thalia, that is incredible!"

Nodding her head in agreement, her curls bouncing this way and that, the activist said, "I know. I can't even believe it. It's like I'm living in a dream."

The women continued chatting, chowing down on their Panang curry and drunken noodles, discussing more about Thalia's work and the next phase of planning for how to leverage her huge and still-growing social media following in support of the cause.

"Anyways," Thalia concluded, "that's what we're thinking, and I'm so excited about it. We are making real change happen, and I just...I don't know. It's amazing. My parents would be so proud and excited to see it. And it all wouldn't have been possible without you casting me." She smiled in gratitude, but a sadness lingered behind it, and Christina knew the unspoken end to that sentence was, *and without Andrew dying*. The achievement of her goals at the expense of losing her love must be bittersweet for Thalia.

"What about your love life?" Christina prompted gently.

Thalia gave a subtle shake of her head. "It's still too soon for me. But I'll get there. I know now what is possible and what I want for my life."

Christina sat in silence, letting this reflection wash over them both.

"Anyways," Thalia said, a bit too brightly, "how is work for you? Is casting for next season starting soon?"

"Yes," Christina said, allowing the conversation to shift topics, but making a mental note to circle back and ask Thalia about her feelings later. "It's been awesome. I'm learning so much working with Ava, and after the huge ratings jump from your season, she is so supportive of all these changes I've wanted to make on the show for years. And," she continued, leaning in and lowering her voice. "There are talks that Robert is retiring soon, and Ava is in the running to replace him as CEO."

"Wow!" Thalia gasped. "That would be amazing. She would only be what, like the fifth Black female Fortune 500 CEO ever? What an absolute queen."

Glancing at her phone, Thalia exclaimed, "Crap! I'm late to meet Sasha. She wants to take me shopping for my UN speech outfit. My own personal stylist," she said with a laugh.

"Okay, yes, go!" Christina encouraged her. "But give me a hug first."

The women rose from their seats, then threw their arms around each other in a long, tight embrace.

"Thalia?" Christina whispered. "I'm so glad we became friends. And that I got to see you today. Spending time with you is like, I don't know...medicine for my soul."

Thalia's heart swelled, and she replied, "Me too. Love you, girl."

"Love you, too."

Acknowledgments

There are so many people to thank for making this book come to life, but two in particular without whom it would not have been possible.

First and foremost, to my incredible husband, Niiamah—thank you for your support. You made me go and write even when I was tired or didn't feel like it. You put our son to sleep and held our newborn daughter so I could get extra time to edit. You stepped in to help make my beautiful cover come to life. And, like always, you encouraged me to dream big dreams for my book.

Thank you also for your patience. I made you wait a whole year to read a word of my book, or even hear anything beyond the fact that it was a murder mystery set on a reality dating show. It was so important to me to have your honest feedback and see whether you could guess who did it, because I knew if I could fool you, I could fool anybody! Your feedback since being my first reader has been so appreciated.

Secondly, I must thank my dear friend, Laura Holtzclaw, who inspired me to begin writing. While I was on maternity leave with my first child, we met for coffee and she told me that she'd written a novel and been accepted to Pitch Wars. It was the first time I'd heard of someone close to me having written a whole book, and she made me believe that I could do it too.

Once I began writing, Laura introduced me to Save the Cat!, which was crucial for my plot development. She also spent hours talking through ideas and issues I was having with my multiple points of view and narrators with secrets. And when my first (very rough!) draft was ready, she was one of my first readers and shared her time and skills to write an invaluable edit letter for me.

Beyond Niiamah and Laura, I am so grateful for the several other beta readers who provided feedback to help produce the finished novel you see here:

- To my mother, Lisa Cronin—it meant the world to me to have you read and enjoy my work. Now that my book is published, I can let out a breath I didn't know I was holding.
- To my friend Ike Perkins—thank you for your enthusiasm and I'm sorry about Blake's fate.
- To Demi Schwartz—it was such a joy connecting with another writer. Thank you for saving my readers from death by adverbs.
- To Kathleen Jerome—I appreciated having an avid mystery reader's perspective, and I thank you for helping to bring Thalia more to life.
- To Natasha de Silva—you have a gift for making words simple and powerful, and I am so grateful to you for sharing that gift with me.

In addition, this book wouldn't have become what it is without the help of very talented professionals. I'm so glad that I found my editor, Michelle Krueger. In addition to her incredibly detailed line edits, she also provided feedback that helped strengthen the characters, increase suspicion and red herrings, and heighten the tension in key scenes. I'm also very grateful for Andrea and Rockwell Pantig from Sillable Digital for creating the perfect cover for my novel.

Last, but certainly not least, thank you to every friend and family member who has given me your support and enthusiasm over the last two years. You have kept me motivated and inspired, and I sincerely hope you enjoyed the finished product!

About the Author

Nicole lives in San Diego with her husband and two kids, and works in enterprise sales for a financial technology company. She has a passion for exploring the world, and spent four years of her career living in Singapore and traveling all over Asia. After her first child, she wanted a creative outlet to carve out space for herself. Thus, her debut novel, *Love's a Beach*, was born.

You can connect with me on:
- https://nicoleashong.com
- https://twitter.com/novelist_nicole
- https://www.instagram.com/novelist_nicole